# SEA OF DEATH

## JORGE AMADO

Translated from the Portuguese by
Gregory Rabassa

 A BARD BOOK/PUBLISHED BY AVON BOOKS

SEA OF DEATH is an original publication of Avon Books. This work has never before appeared in book form in English. This work is a novel. Any similarity to actual persons or events is purely coincidental.

AVON BOOKS
A division of
The Hearst Corporation
1790 Broadway
New York, New York 10019

Copyright © 1984 by Jorge Amado
Translation Copyright © 1984 by Gregory Rabassa
Published by arrangement with the author
Library of Congress Catalog Card Number: 84-91140
ISBN: 0-380-88559-X

First Bard Printing, October, 1984

BARD TRADEMARK REG. U.S. PAT. OFF. AND IN OTHER COUN-TRIES, MARCA REGISTRADA, HECHO EN U.S.A.

Printed in the U.S.A.

OPB 10 9 8 7 6 5 4 3 2

For

Raquel de Queiroz
Érico Veríssimo

and

Álvaro Moreyra

*** Now I should like to tell the dockside tales of Bahia. Old sailors who mend sails, pilots of sloops, tattooed blacks, rogues, all know these stories and these songs. I would hear them on moonlight nights on the Market wharf, in fairs, in small ports around the bay, next to huge Swedish ships at the piers in Ilhéus. Iemanjá's people have much to tell.

Come listen to these stories and these songs. Come hear the story of Guma and Lívia, which is the story of life and love on the sea. And if you don't find it beautiful, the fault won't lie with the rough men who tell it, but because you're hearing it from the mouth of a man of the land, and only with great difficulty can a man of the land understand the heart of sailors. Even when that man loves these stories and these songs and attends the rites of Dona Janaína, even then he doesn't know all the secrets of the sea. For the sea is a mystery that even old sailors don't understand.

# SEA OF DEATH

# IEMANJÁ, MISTRESS OF SEAS AND SLOOPS

# STORM

Night was running ahead of itself. People weren't expecting it at all when it fell upon the city with heavy clouds. The lights on the docks hadn't been turned on yet; in the Beacon of the Stars sad bulbs illuminated the glasses of cane liquor; many sloops were still cutting the waters of the sea when the wind brought on a night of black clouds.

The men looked at each other as if asking a question. They gazed at the blue of the ocean, asking where that night that was ahead of time had come from. It still wasn't time. But it came on loaded with clouds, preceded by a cold twilight wind, obscuring the sun as in some fearsome miracle.

Night arrived on that day with no music to greet it. The bells of the end of afternoon didn't echo through the city. No black man with a guitar had appeared on the sands by the dock yet. No concertina greeted the night from the bow of a sloop. Nor did the monotonous drumbeat of *candomblés* and *macumbas* come rolling down the hillside. Why, then, had night come so soon without waiting for the music, without waiting for the signal of the bells, the cadence of the guitars and concertinas, the mysterious pounding of the religious instruments? Why had it come like that, before its time, out of time?

It was a different night, a night of anguish. Yes, because the men had a look of uneasiness and the sailor drinking by himself in the Beacon of the Stars ran to his ship as if going to rescue it from an inevitable disaster. And the woman who was waiting on the small dock by the market for the sloop on which her love was coming began to shiver, more from a coldness coming out of her lover's heart as it filled with evil omens of the night that was suddenly spreading itself out.

For they, the sailor and the dark woman, were familiar with the sea and they knew very well that if night arrived before its time many men would die at sea, ships wouldn't reach port, widows would weep over the heads of little children. Because—they knew—it wasn't the real night, the night of moon and stars, of music and love, that had come. That night only came at its proper time, when bells rang and a black man sang to his guitar on the docks, a song of longing. The night that had come loaded with clouds, carried by the wind, was a storm that capsized ships and killed men. A storm is a false night.

The rain came down with fury and washed the docks, kneaded the sand, rocked the tied-up boats, raised up the elements, chased off all those waiting for the arrival of the ocean liner. A stevedore had told his companion that a storm was coming. Like a strange monster, a hoist moved through the wind and rain, carrying crates. The rain lashed the black men in the hold pitilessly. The wind went through rapidly, whistling, knocking things over, frightening women. The rain obscured everything, it even closed men's eyes. Only the hoists moved in their own blackness. A sloop overturned in the sea and two men fell into the water. One was young and strong. Maybe he'd murmured a name in that final moment. It wasn't a curse, certainly, for it sounded soft in the storm.

The wind tore the sail off the sloop and carried it to the docks like a tragic message. The swelling waters rose up, the waves beat on the stones by the docks. The canoes by the firewood pier were bouncing, and the canoemen resolved not to return to the small towns around the bay that night. The sail of the shipwrecked sloop fell onto the breakwater and then the lights went out on all the sloops, women said the prayer for the dead, the eyes of the men looked out to sea.

Over his glass of cane liquor black Rufino wasn't smiling

anymore. With a storm like that, Esmeralda wouldn't be coming.

The lights went on. But they were weak and wavering. The men waiting for the ocean liner couldn't see anything. They'd gone into the warehouses and could barely make out the shape of the hoists and the stevedores, who, bent over, were crossing through the rain. But they didn't see the ship they were expecting, aboard which friends, parents, brothers and sisters, maybe sweethearts were arriving. They didn't see the man weeping in third class. The face of a man arriving by sea in the third class of a lugger that had made port in twenty different places, where the rain mingled with tears, where the memory of the lights of his village mingled with the hazy lights of the city in the storm.

Master Manuel, the sailor who knew those waters best, resolved not to go out with his sloop that night. Lovemaking is good on stormy nights and Maria Clara's flesh has the taste of the sea.

The lights in the old fort had gone out. The lanterns on the sloops too. That was when the power in the city went off. Even the hoists stopped, and the stevedores came into the warehouse. Guma, from his sloop the *Valiant*, saw the lights go out and was afraid. He was going along with his hand on the tiller, the ship heeling to one side. Those waiting for the liner had gone off in automobiles to places where there was more activity. Only one man remained to shake the hand of another as he came off the liner:

"Everything all right?"

"Everything." The other one smiled.

The one waiting called for a car and the two went off in silence. Their companions would already be expecting them.

The man who had arrived in third class stood looking at that city with different customs, a different language. He clutched the almost empty briefcase against his chest and with his suitcase plunged into the first uphill street he found. The dock emptied of people.

Only Lívia, frail, with thin hair strung against her face by the rain, remained by the sloop dock looking out to sea. She heard Maria Clara's moans of love. But her thoughts and her eyes were on the sea. The wind shook her as if she were a reed, the rain lashed her face, legs, and hands. But she stood motionless, her body leaning forward, her eyes on the darkness waiting to see the *Valiant*'s red lantern crossing through the storm, lighting the starless night, announcing the arrival of Guma.

# SONGBOOK OF THE DOCKS

Suddenly, as rapidly as it had come, the storm went off to other seas, off to wreck other ships. Lívia could now hear Maria Clara's moans. They weren't long but were sharp shouts of pleasure and pain, the cries of a wounded animal coming through the storm with an air of challenge. Now that true night was spreading through the city, along the docks, over the sea, the night of love and music, of stars and moon, the lovemaking on board Master Manuel's sloop was sweet and restful. Maria Clara's moans were like sobs of joy, almost muted, almost a song. Lívia took her eyes off the calm sea for a moment and listened to those moans. Guma would arrive soon, the *Valiant* would cross the bay, and she would hold him in her dark arms and they would moan with love. The storm had ceased now, she was no longer afraid. She wouldn't be long in catching sight of the sloop's red light shining through the sea night. Little waves were breaking on the rocks by the docks and the sloops were softly swaying. In the distance the lights gleamed on the wet pavement of the city. Groups of men who were no longer in any hurry or had any fear were walking toward the tall elevator. Lívia turned toward the sea. She hadn't seen Guma for a week. She'd stayed in the little old house near the docks. She hadn't gone with him this time on an always different adventure of a trip across the bay and up the calm river. If she had been on the sloop when the storm broke it would have been better. He would have been afraid for the life of his companion, but, on the other hand, Lívia wouldn't have been afraid at all because she would have been with him, and he knew

7

every path in the sea, his eyes were like searchlights and his hands were firm on the tiller. He wouldn't be long in coming. He would arrive soaked from the storm, telling stories, muscular and smiling, with Lívia's name and an arrow tattooed on his arm. She smiled. Her long dark body turned completely in the direction of Maria Clara's moans. It was dark on the docks, here and there a lantern glowed among the sloops, but she could make out Master Manuel's perfectly, that was where the moans were coming from. There it was, moored to the dock, rocking in the waves. There a man and a woman were making love and their moans reached Lívia. Later on, a short time from now, she would be the one in the bow of a sloop hugging Guma's strong body to hers, kissing his dark hair, catching the taste of the sea on his body, or the taste of death that would still be in his eyes that had just come out of the storm. And her moans of love would be much softer than Maria Clara's because they would be filled with the long wait and the fear that had come over her. Maria Clara would stop making love to listen to the music of sobs and laughter that would be coming from her lips while Guma held her tight, clasped her in his arms that were wet from the sea.

A sloop master passes and says good evening to Lívia. A group farther off is examining the sloop sail that had blown in. It's very white, torn, near the dock. Men had already gone out in a sloop to look for the bodies. But Lívia is thinking about Guma who's coming soon and the love that awaits her. She'll be happier than Maria Clara, who didn't wait, wasn't afraid.

"Do you know who died, Lívia?"

She's frightened. But that sail isn't from the *Valiant*. The one on his sloop is much larger and wouldn't be torn like that. Lívia turns and asks Rufino:

"Who was it?"

"Raimundo and his son. They capsized quite close to the city... The storm was rough."

That night—Lívia thinks—Judith won't have any love in her little house, or on her husband's sloop. Jacques, Raimundo's son, had died. She'd stop by later. After Guma arrives and they see each other again, make love. Rufino looks at the moon coming out:

"People have already gone out to look for the bodies."

"Does Judith know yet?"

"I'm going over to tell her..."

Lívia looks at the black man. He's huge and smells of cane liquor. He was drinking, most likely at the Beacon of the Stars. Why must it be? she thinks, as he looks at the full moon rising over the middle of the sea and lighting everything with a silvery beam. Maria Clara is still sobbing with love. Judith won't have any love tonight. Lívia will make love when Guma arrives all wet from the storm, with a taste of sea. How beautiful the sea is as the moon turns everything white! Rufino is standing there. Music is coming from the old fort. They're playing the concertina and singing:

> "Night is made for love..."

The powerful voice of a black man. Rufino is looking at the moon. Maybe he too is thinking that Judith won't have any love tonight. Or ever again... Her man died in the sea.

> "Come, let's love in the waters
> That shine in the moonlight..."

Lívia asks Rufino:

"Is Judith still living with her mother?"

"No. The old lady sailed off to Cachoeira..."

He said that listlessly, glancing at the moon. A black man is singing in the old fort, but his song won't console Judith. Rufino holds out his hand:

"I'm taking off..."

"I'll stop by later..."

Rufino takes a few steps. Stops:

"It's a sad thing... Awful to have to say... Say that he died..."

He scratches his head. Lívia is sad. Judith will never make love again. Never again will she come to make love in the sea at a time when the moon is shining bright. For her night won't be made for love anymore, it will be made for tears. Rufino throws his hands out in front of him:

"Come with me, Lívia. You know what to say…"

But love is waiting for her, Guma will soon be in on the *Valiant*, the red lantern won't be long in appearing, the time when their bodies come close together won't be long off. He won't be long in passing over the band of light that the moon has stretched out over the sea. Love is waiting for her, Lívia can't go. On that day, after her fear, after the vision of Guma drowning, she wants love, she wants happiness, moans of possession. She can't go and weep with Judith who will never love again.

"I'm looking for Guma, Rufino."

Will the black man think she's awful? But Guma won't be long. She speaks:

"I'll stop by later…"

Rufino throws up his hands:

"Good night, then."

"So long…"

Rufino takes a few more steps, listlessly. He looks at the moon, hears the man singing:

> *"Come, let's love in the waters*
> *That shine in the moonlight…"*

He turns around to Lívia:

"Did you know she was pregnant?"

"Judith?"

"Yes…"

He walks off. Still looking at the moon. From the fort they sing:

> *"Night is made for love…"*

Maria Clara sobs and laughs in the arms of her man. Lívia goes off almost at a run and shouts to Rufino, whose shadow can be seen in the distance:

"I'm coming with you..."

They walk off. She still stares at the sea. Who knows, that lantern burning in the distance might belong to the *Valiant*.

Judith is a mulatto, and her belly is already sticking out, altering the shape of her cotton dress. Everybody is silent. Black Rufino waves his hands, he hasn't any place to put them, he looks at the others, frightened. Lívia takes a full position of consolation, her hands sheltering Judith's head. Other people had already arrived. They paid their respects and there, around the room, they're waiting for the bodies that the men have gone for in the sea. Broken sobs come from where Judith is, and Lívia's hands are lifted in loving gestures. Then Master Manuel and Maria Clara come in, she with heavy eyes.

There is nothing to remind one of the storm anymore. Nor is Maria Clara sobbing from love anymore. Why is Judith weeping, then? Judith is a widow, the men are waiting for two bodies. How Rufino would like to leave, flee from there, go seek joy in the arms of Esmeralda. He bears the sadness of the house, Judith's sorrow, he has no place to put his hands, and he knows that he'll suffer even more when the body comes in and Judith has her last meeting with the man who loved her, who made a child in her, who possessed her body.

Lívia is the brave one. She's even more beautiful like that. Who wouldn't like to marry Lívia and be wept for by her when he died in the sea? She is like a sister to Judith at that moment.

Of course she too has an urge to flee, to go wait for Guma on the edge of the dock for a night under the stars. Judith's suffering hurts everyone, and Maria Clara thinks that perhaps one day Master Manuel will stay behind at sea on a stormy night and that Lívia will stop waiting for Guma and come give her the news. She squeezes the arm of Master Manuel, who asks:

"What is it?"

But she is weeping and Master Manuel falls silent. A bottle of cane liquor was brought in. Lívia takes Judith to her room. Maria Clara goes with them and now takes Lívia's place and weeps with the widow, weeps for herself.

Lívia returns to the parlor. The men are conversing now, commenting on the storm in low voices, talking about the father and son who had died that night. A black man says:

"The father was a good man... Enough courage for three people..."

Another begins to tell a story:

"Do you remember that squall in June? Well, Raimundo..."

Somebody opens the bottle of liquor. Lívia passes through the group and goes to the door... She hears the sound of the calm sea, a sound that's always the same, an everyday sound. Guma shouldn't be long, and he will doubtless come looking for her at Judith's. In the shadows of the docks she can make out the sails of the sloops. And, suddenly, she's attacked by the same foreboding that had attacked Maria Clara. What if one night they came to bring you the news that Guma was at the bottom of the sea and the *Valiant* was drifting, without a rudder, without anyone to guide it? Only then did she feel Judith's pain, feel completely her sister, Maria Clara's sister too, sister of all women of the sea, women with the same fate: waiting some stormy night for the news of the death of a man.

Judith's sobs are coming from the bedroom. She was left with a child in her belly. Maybe one day she'll weep yet again, for the death of that son in the sea. In the group in the parlor a man is speaking:

"Five were saved... It was a night like the end of the world... A lot of people saw the mother of waters that night. Raimundo..."

Judith is sobbing in the bedroom. It's the fate of all those women. The men from dockside only have one path in life: the path of the sea. They follow it, it's their fate. The sea owns all of them. From the sea comes all joy and all sadness because the sea is a mystery that not even the oldest sailors understand, not even those ancient masters of sloops who don't sail anymore and only mend sails and tell stories. Who has ever deciphered the mystery of the sea? From the sea comes music, love, death. And isn't it over the sea that the moon is the most beautiful? The sea is unstable. The life of the men of the sloops is like it. Who among them has ever had a fate to live like that of men of the land, who dandle grandchildren and gather families together for lunch and dinner? None of them walks with that firm step of a man of the land. Each one has something at the bottom of the sea: a son, a brother, an arm, a sloop that capsized, a sail that the windstorm tore apart. But, also, who among them doesn't know how to sing those songs of love on dockside nights? Who among them doesn't know how to make love with violence and softness? Because every time they sing and love it could well be the last. When they take leave of their wives they don't give her a quick kiss like men of the land going off to business. They make long goodbyes, hands that wave as if still calling.

Lívia looks at the men coming up the little hillside street. They're coming in two groups. Lanterns give a ghostly air to the funeral procession. As if sensing their arrival, Judith's sobs grow stronger in the bedroom. It's enough to see the men with their heads uncovered to know that they're bringing in the bodies. Father and son dead together in the storm. Without doubt one tried to save the other and they both perished in the sea. Behind it all, coming from the old fort, coming from the docks, from the sloops, from some distant and indefinable place, comforting music accompanies the bodies. It says that:

*"It's sweet to die in the sea..."*

Lívia sobs. She shelters Judith at her breast, but she sobs too, she's sobbing because of the certainty that her day will come, and Maria Clara's and every woman's. The music crosses over the docks to reach them:

*"It's sweet to die in the sea..."*

But at that moment not even the presence of Guma, who arrives with the cortège and was the one who found the bodies, can comfort Lívia's heart.

Only the music that comes from an indefinable place (maybe it does come from the old fort), saying that it's sweet to die in the sea, reminds them of the death of Judith's husband. The bodies are laid out in the parlor now, Judith weeping, kneeling beside her husband, the men standing, Maria Clara with the fear that someday Manuel will also be drowned.

But why think about that, why think about death and sadness, when love is waiting for her? Because they're in the bow of the *Valiant,* Lívia stretched out on the planks under the furled sail, peeping at her man, who is calmly smoking his pipe. Why think about death, about men struggling against the waves, when your man is there, safe and sound from the storm, smoking a pipe that must be the prettiest star of this sea? But Lívia is thinking. She's sad because he doesn't come to hold her in his tattooed arms. And she's waiting, her hands under her head, her breasts half-emerging under the dress that the night breeze, calm now, lifts and sways. The sloop sways softly too.

Lívia is waiting and she is beautiful in her waiting, she's the most beautiful woman dockside and among the sloops. No sloop master has a woman like Guma's. They all say that and they all smile at her. They would all like to hold her in their arms that have been made muscular by so many crossings. But she belongs only to Guma, he was the one she married in the church of Monte Serrat, where fishermen, canoemen, and sloop masters marry. Even sailors who sail to distant seas in great steam packets come to be married in the church of Monte Serrat, which is their church, perched on a height, dominating the sea. She was married there, to Guma, and since then on nights by the docks, in their sloop, in the rooms of the Beacon of the Stars, on the sand by the docks, they've made love, mingled their bodies over the sea and under the moon.

And today, when she waited so long in the storm, today, when she wanted to so much because she feared so much, he's smoking without thinking about her. That's why she remembers Judith, who will never have any more love, for whom night will always be a time for weeping. She remembers: She was lying beside her man. She was looking into his face, the face that didn't move anymore, that didn't smile anymore, a face that had already passed under the waves, eyes that had seen Iemanjá, the mother of waters.

Lívia thinks of Iemanjá with rage. She is the mother of waters, she is the mistress of the sea, and that's why all men who live above the waves fear her and love her. She punishes. She never shows herself to men unless they die in the sea. The ones who die in storms are her favorites. And those who die saving other men, those who go with her out to sea, just like a ship, touching all ports, sailing all seas. The bodies of these are never found, for they have gone with Iemanjá. In order to see the mother of waters many had already jumped into the sea smiling, never to reappear. Can it be that she sleeps with all of them in the depths of the waters? Lívia thinks about her with rage. At this moment she's probably with the father and son who died in the storm, and they might even be fighting over her, they who were such good friends all their lives. Dying, the father still tried to save his son. When Guma found the bodies the hand of the old man was clutching the shirt of the son. They had died friends and now, who knows, maybe because of Iemanjá, mistress of the sea, a woman whom only the dead see, they're fighting, Raimundo pulling out the knife the men didn't find in his belt because he'd taken it with him. They might be fighting in the depths of the waters to see who will travel through the sea with her to see cities on the other side of the world. Judith, who is weeping, Judith, who has a child in her belly, Judith, who will end up doing heavy work, Judith, who will never love a man anymore, has probably already been forgotten because the mother of waters is blond and has long hair and goes about naked under the waves, dressed only in the hair that people see when the moon passes over the sea.

Men of the land (what do men of the land know?) say that they're moonbeams on the sea. But the sailors, sloop masters, canoemen, laugh at the men of the land who don't know anything. They know full well that it's the hair of the mother of waters who's come to see the full moon. It's Iemanjá who's come to see the moon. That's why men stand looking at the silvery sea on moonlit nights. Because they know that the mother of waters is there. Black men play the guitar, the concertina, beat drums and sing. It's the offering they bring to the mistress of the sea. Others smoke a pipe to light the way, so Iemanjá can see better. They all love her and they even forget their wives when the hair of the mother of waters spreads out over the sea.

That's how Guma is as he looks at the silver swelling of the waters and hears the black man's song with its invitation to death. He says that it's sweet to die in the sea, because there you will meet the mother of waters who is the most beautiful woman in the whole world. Guma is staring at her hair, having forgotten that Lívia is there, her body stretched out, her breasts offered, Lívia who has waited so long for the moment of love, Lívia who saw the storm destroying everything, overturning sloops, killing men, Lívia who was so afraid. Even though Lívia would like to hold him in her arms, kiss his mouth and from it discover if he had been afraid when the lights went out, clutch his body to see if the sea had wet him. But now he's forgotten about Lívia, he's only thinking about Iemanjá, the mistress of the sea. Maybe he even envies the father and son who died in the storm and are perhaps now sailing through the world that only sailors on great ships know. Lívia has hatred in her heart, she feels like crying, she feels like getting away from the sea, going far away.

A sloop passes. Lívia gets up on one arm to see better. They shout to Guma:

"Ahoy, Guma..."

Guma waves his hand:

"Have a good trip..."

Lívia looks at him. Now that a cloud has covered the

moon and Iemanjá has gone away, he's put out the pipe and smiled. She huddles all up with pleasure now, already feeling his arms. Guma speaks:

"Where's that black man singing from?"

"How should I know... Maybe from the fort."

"Nice music..."

"Judith, poor thing..."

Guma looks at the sea:

"She really is... It's going to be hard for her. And with a baby in her belly..."

His face tightens and he glances at Lívia. She's beautiful like that, offering herself. She doesn't have the hands for hard work. If he stayed out at sea she'd have to belong to someone else in order to live. She doesn't have the hands for hard work. That thought brought on a dull rage. Lívia's breasts show beneath the dress. Everybody on the docks wants her. They'd all like to have her because she's the prettiest. And what if he went off with Iemanjá too? He has an urge to kill her right there so she'll never belong to anyone else.

"And what if one day I tipped over and became food for the fish?" His laugh is forced.

The black man's voice crosses the night again:

"*It's sweet to die in the sea...*"

"Would you have to do hard work too? Or would you go with somebody else?"

She's weeping, she's afraid. She, too, is afraid of that day when her man might stay at the bottom of the sea, when he would never come back, when he would go with Iemanjá, mistress of the sea, mother of waters, sailing off to other lands and seas. She rises up and puts her arms behind Guma's neck:

"I was afraid today. I waited for you at the end of the dock. It looked as though you were never coming back..."

He comes. Yes, he knows how much Lívia waited, how

much she was afraid. He comes for her arms, for her love. A man sings in the distance:

*"It's sweet to die in the sea..."*

And now in the moonlight, the hair of Iemanjá, mistress of the sea, no longer gleams. The black man's music is silenced by the sobs of love from Lívia, the woman from dockside that everybody desires, and who, in the bow of the *Valiant*, is loving her man very much because she was very much afraid for him and she's still afraid.

The winds of the storm are far away now. The waters from the clouds of the false night are falling on other ports. Iemanjá will travel with other bodies through other lands. Now the sea is serene and soft. The sea is the friend of the sloop masters. Because isn't the sea the path, the road, the home of all of them? Isn't it on the sea, in the bow of the sloops, that they love and make their children?

Yes, Guma loves the sea and Lívia loves it too. The sea is beautiful at night like that, blue, endless blue, a mirror of the stars, full of sloop lanterns, full of the lamps that are the embers of pipes, full of the sounds of love.

The sea is a friend, the sea is a sweet friend for all of those who live on it. And Lívia gets the taste of sea on Guma's flesh. The *Valiant* rocks like a hammock.

# LANDS OF THE ENDLESS WAY

A voice as full and deep as that chases off all other night sounds. It comes from the old fort and spreads out over the sea and the city. It's not good for what it says to strike the hearts of men. Its sweet and melancholy melody makes conversations grow softer. But the words to this old song say, "Unlucky is the woman who follows a man of the sea. Good luck isn't what she'll get, unlucky fate is hers. Her eyes will never cease to weep and they'll wither away early from peering out to sea so much, waiting for the coming of a sail." The voice of the black man covers the night.

Old Francisco knows that music and that vast world of stars reflected on the sea. If not, of what use were the forty years spent on board a sloop? And it's not just the stars he knows. He also knows all the sandbars, bends, and channels in the bay and the Paraguaçu River, all the harbors in the region, all the songs sung there. The people who live along that stretch of river and by the docks are his friends, and there are even those who say that once, on a night when he rescued the whole crew of a fishing boat, he saw the face of Iemanjá, who had shown herself to him as a reward. When there's talk of that (and every young sloop master asks old Francisco if it's true), he only smiles and says:

"They talk about a lot of things in this world, lad..."

So no one knows if it's true or not. It might well be. Iemanjá has her whims, and if anyone was worthy of seeing her and loving her it was old Francisco, who has been on the waterfront since no one knows when. Even better than all the sandbars, shifts, channels, however, was the fact that he

*19*

knows stories about those waters, about those festivals of Janaína, about shipwrecks and storms. Can there be a story that old Francisco doesn't know?

When night comes he leaves his small house and comes down to the docks. He crosses the mud that covers the cement, goes into the water, and pulls himself up onto the bow of a sloop. Then they ask him to tell stories, to tell about things that have happened. No one knows about such things better than he.

Today he lives by mending sails and from what his nephew Guma gives him. There was a time, however, when he had three sloops that the storm winds carried off. The one they couldn't get the better of was old Francisco. He always returned to port, and the names of his three sloops were tattooed on his right arm along with the name of his brother, who stayed behind in a storm too. Maybe he'll write Guma's name there someday if Iemanjá gets it into her head to love his nephew. The truth is that old Francisco laughs at all that. That's their lot: to capsize at sea. If he hadn't stayed behind too it was because Janaína didn't want it that way, she preferred that he see her alive and stay to talk to the lads, teach them cures, tell them stories. But what good had it been staying like that, mending sails, looking after his nephew, having become a useless thing never able to sail because his arms had grown weary now, his eyes could no longer see in the dark? It would have been better if he'd stayed under the water with the *Morning Star,* his fastest sloop, which had capsized on Saint John's night. Now he watches all the others leave and doesn't go with them. He stands watching Lívia, just like a woman, trembling during storms, helping bury those who die. It's been a long time since he crossed the bay, his hand on the tiller, his eyes piercing the darkness, feeling the wind on his face, running with his sloop to the sound of the distant music.

A black man is singing today too. He says that sea people's wives have a terrible lot. Old Francisco smiles. He buried his wife, the doctor said it was her heart. She died suddenly one night when he came back in a storm. She threw herself into his arms and he noticed that she wasn't throbbing anymore and she was dead. She'd died from the joy of seeing him come back, the doctor said it was her heart. The one who stayed behind that night was Frederico, Guma's father. A body no one found because he'd died to save Francisco, and that's why he went off with Iemanjá to other beautiful lands. It was his brother and his wife in one single night. Then he reared Guma on his own sloop, at sea, so he wouldn't be afraid. Guma's mother, no one knew who she was, appeared one day and asked for the boy:

"Are you Mr. Francisco, sir?"

"The very same, ma'am, at your service..."

"You don't know me..."

"I don't recall you, no..." He put his hand to his head, trying to remember people he had met in the past. "I don't know you, no, I'm sorry."

"But Frederico knew me well..."

"That's quite possible, because he sailed on those packets of the Baiana Line a lot. What parts did he meet you in?"

"Up there in Aracaju, Mr. Francisco. He put in there one day, the ship had a big hole in its side. It was a miracle it made port..."

"I remember now, it was the *Maraú*... It was a rough trip, Frederico told me about it. Was that where he met you?"

"The ship stayed for a month. He got all dolled up for me..."

"He was worse than a monkey when it came to chasing women..."

She smiled, showing her broken teeth:

"He told a lot of tales, that he'd bring me home, get a house for me, give me clothes and lots to eat. You know what he was like..."

Old Francisco made a gesture. They were at the edge of the docks and in the nearby market people were selling oranges and pineapples. They sat down on some crates. The woman went on:

"He did me dirty by saying he wasn't going to leave with

the ship. But when the bug came out of his hole he didn't hear a word, he climbed aboard and it was just goodbye..."

"I can't say he did the right thing, ma'am. He was my own flesh and blood, but—"

She interrupted him:

"I'm not saying he was awful. It was my luck and I went with him, even if I knew he'd be ungrateful. I was really crazy over him."

Old Francisco stood looking. He was wondering why she'd come after so many years. Maybe looking for money, and he was broke now, he had nothing to give. Frederico had always been a woman-chaser...

"He said he'd send for me. Did the gentleman send for me?" She smiled. "What he did to me. When my belly got big I started vomiting and my mother got mad. My father was a proper man. When he found out he came at me with a knife. He just wanted to know who it was so he could put an end to him. He gave me this scar over the knee. The knife slipped."

Why was she showing her thighs? Francisco wouldn't go with a woman who'd been his brother's because it was bad and it could bring down punishment.

"I was out on the street. A family, my godfather's, gave me work. One day I was serving table when I got the pains..."

Then Mr. Francisco understood:

"Guma?"

"It was Gumercindo, yes. It was my godfather who named him. The same name as his. I got some money together, brought him here to Frederico. He already had another woman. He kept the child but didn't want to have anything to do with me."

They were silent again. Francisco was only nosing to see what she could be after. Money he didn't have, not since that day. Sleeping with a woman who was his brother's was something he wouldn't do.

"I stayed right here, then, ashamed to go back. People may be poor but they've got pride, isn't that so? I didn't

want to be a streetwalker in my own town... My father was
a man of position, one of my brothers even got to be a med-
ical doctor. So I wandered around then. It was so long
ago..."

She stretched out her hand, looked at the sloops. From behind the market came the noise of conversations, arguments, loud laughter.

"I only got in from Recife three days ago. It was just to
see the boy, someone I knew told me Frederico had died,
two years ago. Now I've come for my son... I'm going to
raise him..."

Francisco couldn't hear the noise coming from the market
anymore. He only heard the woman there who said she was
Guma's mother and had come for him. He didn't like fighting with a woman. An argument with a woman never had
any end, but he had to argue because he didn't want to give
up Guma, who was so good at the tiller of a sloop now and
could already carry a sack of flour in his boyish arms. Francisco was used to arguing with rough men from the docks,
strong sloop masters that he could offend because they knew
how to defend themselves, letting an ugly name slip wasn't
so bad. With a woman, now, and with a woman like Guma's
mother, perfumed, dressed in silk, with a parasol on her arm
and a gold tooth, he didn't know how to fight. If he let out a
bad word she was capable of crying, and he didn't like to see
women crying. Besides, his brother hadn't done right by
her. But can sailors go around thinking about the women
they left in port? Isn't it worse when they get married and
leave widows or have them die of a heart attack when they
see them come back safe out of the storm? It's much worse.
Guma won't get married. He'll always be free on his sloop.
He'll go with Iemanjá whenever she gets the notion. He
won't have any anchors holding him to the land. A man who
lives on the sea has to be free. But if that woman took Guma
away, what would become of the boy? He'd be a cabinet-
maker, a stonecutter, maybe a doctor or even a priest,
dressed like a woman, who knows! And old Francisco's
face would be covered with shame over the fate of his

nephew and there'd be nothing left for him but go meet Janaína himself at sea some night. No, he wouldn't let that
woman take Guma away for anything.

The woman was already puzzled by his silence. Voices
were coming from the market:

"It costs so much it scares me..."

And a conversation in the distance:

"Two shots popped then and you should have seen the
guy run. But a man's a man and I screwed up my courage
and shot back..."

Old Francisco laughed:

"You know, ma'am? You won't be taking the boy away,
no. What can you do for him?"

He stood looking at the woman, waiting for an answer.
But his face was saying there wasn't a force in the world that
could make him give up Guma. The woman waved her hand
in that vague gesture and answered:

"I really don't know... I want to take him because he's
my son and hasn't got any father... The life of a streetwalker, you know what it's like... Here today, there tomorrow... If he stays he'll end up like his father, drowned
someday..."

"And if he goes off with you, ma'am?"

"I'll put him in a private school, he'll learn to read,
maybe he'll become a doctor like his uncle, my brother...
He's not going to drown..."

"Oh, missy, fate is something that's decided up there. If
he's meant to belong to Janaína, there's no way to free him
from it. If he stays here he'll become a real man. If he goes
with you he'll end up a weakling, like those cabaret people..."

"That's what you say, sir."

"Where will you get the money so he can study? I know
all about women of the streets: Today you have it, tomorrow
you don't... You yourself said here today, there tomorrow... And the son of a streetwalker is lower than a dog,
you know that..."

She dropped her head because she knew it was true. Taking her son away would be giving him the supreme humiliation of letting other people know his mother was a prostitute. No matter where he went, in the street, at school, anywhere, he wouldn't be able to say anything because he was up against the greatest insult of all. Out of the market came the voice of a man talking about an episode:

"...all I could see was the knife, shining like it was cleaning a fish. I lifted up my elbow, put my knee forward. It was an ugly scene..."

(It really would be better for him to stay there, learn how to sail a sloop to different ports, make children in unknown women, knock knives out of men's hands, drink in bars, tattoo hearts on his arm, go through storms, go off with Janaína when his day came. No one would ask who his mother was there.)

"But can I see him from time to time?"

"Whenever your heart desires..." Francisco felt pity for her now. There's no mother, no matter how bad she is, who doesn't love her children. Even the whale, who's a beast and can't think, defends her children from fishermen and even dies for them.

"You can see him right now. He's coming in tonight on a sloop from Itaparica. We can go see him then..."

Her face showed fear:

"Is he going out in a sloop alone already?"

"Only between here and Itaparica. So he can learn. And he's already a man."

Her face was full of pride now. Her son, who was only eleven, already knew how to sail a sloop, was crossing the waters now, could pass for a man. With the voice of a child that came out of the depths of her heart she asked:

"Does he look like me?"

Old Francisco looked at the woman. In spite of her rotting teeth, she was pretty. She had a gold tooth to make up for it. She gave off a perfume that was out of place on that dock, which smelled of fish. Her painted mouth was the color of blood, as if she'd been bitten. Her fleshy arms were hanging down alongside her body. Mistreated by life, she was still youthful, and she didn't look like Guma's mother either. But she'd been on the street for eleven years, meeting men, sleeping with them, beaten up by a lot of them. In spite of that she was still tempting. If she hadn't slept with Frederico...

"Yes, he looks like you. His eyes are just like yours. And his nose a little too..."

She smiled, and that was certainly her happiest moment. One day when her good looks would be all gone, when men would have worn her out completely, then she would have a guaranteed old age, she would come to her son, cook for him, and wait for him to come back out of the storms. She wouldn't need any excuses with him. Children know how to forgive completely tired old mothers who appear suddenly. And the woman let herself be lulled by that happiness and she was smiling with her mouth, her eyes, her gestures were happy, and even the strange perfume that reminded a person of cabarets had disappeared and all that was left was the smell of low tide and salted fish.

● Around nine o'clock Guma arrived on the sloop, which was the *Valiant*. He stopped at the small dock, put his hands to his mouth, and shouted:

"Uncle! Ahoy, uncle!..."

"I'm coming..."

Guma heard the voices coming closer. Someone was coming with his uncle, a stranger, because he could recognize voices from far off. Master Manuel shouted from his sloop:

"You've got company coming, boy."

Who could be coming with his uncle? By the voice it was a woman. Could his uncle be bringing a woman to go to bed with him? It had already been some time since Francisco and other dockside men had begun to hint about dealings with women, and his uncle had been threatening to bring one to leave for him alone in the sloop in the middle of the sea:

"I'd only want to see what you'd do, you devil..."

The men all laughed loud, rolled their eyes to each other.

"Guma's a man now," said Antonico, master of the *Faith in God*, who couldn't seem to think of anything else to say.

"He's got to prove it." And Raimundo clapped his hands, laughing loud and long. "My Jacques has already tasted the fruit..."

Guma knew it meant going to bed with a woman, satisfying those desires that penetrated him in his dreams and left him feeling as if he had been beaten. Many times in the small towns where they stopped he would walk past the streets where the prostitutes were, but he never had the courage to go down them. No one would take him for less than fifteen, in spite of the fact that he was only eleven. There was nothing to fear on that side. But a certain caution stopped him from going in. He was sure he would die of shame when the woman wouldn't accept him, would treat him like a child, a fatherless child lost on the street. She wouldn't guess that he could already sail a sloop and lift a sack of flour. Maybe she'd laugh at him. And he never went in. Now his uncle was bringing the promised woman. He was going to be ashamed in front of her. Francisco had probably told her that he'd never known a woman, that he was a simpleton, timid, in spite of the knife in his belt. He would end up without any urge as he faced the woman. And if his uncle tried to help, just for a laugh, enjoying his discomfort, then he would go off, run away from the docks in shame, he wouldn't sail those waters anymore. And it's with real terror that Guma hears the voices approaching. He's trembling and yet he wants them to get there quicker too because he wants to be a man as quickly as possible and sail away alone on the *Valiant* up all rivers, to all ports, through all channels.

The voices get closer. It's a woman, yes. His uncle is coming to keep his promise. He must be ashamed by now of the nephew who still isn't a man, who hasn't known a woman. And since Guma hasn't got the courage to go into one of their houses, his uncle is bringing one, the way they bring food to a blind man, the way they give water to a cripple. It's really one more humiliation, but he doesn't want to think about that now. He thinks that in just a little while beside him he'll have the body of a woman, a body that knows all secrets. He'll ask his uncle to go away, leave him alone with her, and he'll take the sloop out into the middle of the bay. Music is coming from the old fort or from another sloop. He'll make love, he'll feel the mystery of everything, and then he'll be able to take his sloop all alone to the lands around the bay, when his day comes he'll be able to look at the face of Iemanjá without fear and will be able to love her because he's learned those secrets that men talk about so much now. That's why he's chilled even though the night is warm and the wind that blows is hot, a breeze that barely rocks the sloop. The truth is, he's afraid. The voices are getting closer and closer. He can already hear what they're talking about:

"He's still a boy, but he's already got the face of a grown man..."

And his uncle is the one talking. The woman, naturally, is asking what he's like. She wants to know how to treat him. But he'll show her he's a strong man, he'll squeeze her until she cries out, until she tells him he's just like a man she's known in her life. Now he can hear the voice of the woman:

"I want him to be a handsome and brave man..."

Guma's heart fills with happiness. He already loves that woman he still doesn't know, that his uncle is bringing to his bed, and he makes plans to take her to all the ports around the bay, go up the rivers with her. He won't let her go back to her life. She'll be completely his forever. She must be pretty because his uncle knows women, the men on the docks always say. The women he brings to the sloop for nights of love are always beautiful. On those nights Guma can hear the sounds of the bodies, hear the moans, the kisses, and the laughter. When he doesn't run away he stays with his ear fixed, a crazy wish to spy, a fear that holds him back. One night he heard a sharp cry of pain. He ran to where they were, certain that Francisco had struck the woman. But they made him go back. Only much later did he learn what that splotch of blood left on the deck of the sloop meant. That little mulatto girl came back many times, and never again did he hear a cry from her mouth. Her complaints grew to be just like the others. That woman who was coming there certainly won't cry out either. It won't be the first time for her. One day, however, he'll make a woman cry out on the sloop the way his uncle did with that little mulatto girl. He hears Francisco's voice:

"Guma!"

"Here I am…"

The sloop is quite close to the pier. It's just a matter of crossing through the mud and they'll find the anchor that's hooked to the dock. His uncle is close by with the woman. He leaps inside the sloop, puts out his hand to the woman, who jumps, showing her thighs. Guma looks and a violent desire comes over him, captures him completely. She's pretty, yes. Now Francisco can go away, leave him alone with her, he shouldn't get mixed up in it because Guma will show he's up to it. The woman looks at him, she really likes Guma. Yes, he does look like a man even though he's only eleven. Guma smiles, showing his white teeth. Francisco doesn't know what to do, waving his hands. The woman smiles. Guma looks at the two of them and his laugh is one of complete satisfaction. The woman asks:

"Do you know who I am?"

He knows her, yes. He's been waiting for her for a long time. He looked for her on the street of lost women, at the edge of the docks, in all the women who looked at him. Now he's found her. She's his woman. He's known her for a long time, ever since desire penetrated his nerves, disturbed his dreams.

Francisco speaks:

"It's your mother, Guma."

But the desire doesn't go away. She couldn't be his mother, the mother that nobody talked about, the mother he never thought about. A trick of his uncle's, obviously. The one there was a woman of the street who'd come to go to bed with him. Francisco shouldn't have compared her to his mother, who must have been soft and sweet, far removed from the thoughts he was thinking. But the woman comes up to him and kisses him the way mothers must kiss. Prostitutes must kiss in a different way. The woman's voice is pure:

"I left you so long ago... I'll never leave you again..."

Then Guma begins to weep, and he himself doesn't know whether it's because he's found his mother or because he's lost the woman he was waiting for.

He didn't know what that phrase meant. Why had she come? Where had she come from? Why was she hugging him like that? She was a stranger to him. He'd never remembered his mother. They'd never spoken to him about her during those eleven years. And when she came she got all mixed up with desires, she came along with the temptation of another woman, she was bringing something he desired. She was his mother and yet she seemed more like the woman he was expecting, because the perfume that came from her was the perfume used by those women, and no matter how much effort she made, she kept using words he didn't want to hear on the lips of his mother and gestures he didn't know in women on the docks. She was his mother, but Francisco had his eyes fixed on her, on the bits of white flesh that appeared over the bulge of her breasts, on the thighs that rose up from under her dress when the wind lifted it. Guma had only one desire: to cry. Crying is something men don't do, everybody knows that. A sailor knows it more than anyone. Women cry enough already. A sailor mustn't cry. That's why Guma bites his lips and remains silent, waiting for her to leave and for that dream to end. Francisco is tempted. He thinks that she slept with his brother, that she's Guma's mother, but he sees her flesh and a thought pursues him. And he begins to talk fast, saying that it's late and they should be going:

"You still have to cross through all the docks. Night's coming on..." She says goodbye to Guma:

"I'll come to see you, my son..."

Francisco goes with her. Guma stays looking from up on

the sloop. He hasn't felt her as his mother for a single moment. And now the one who's going to sleep with her is old Francisco. In the sloop, all alone, he began to weep. For the first time he heard the music saying that "it's sweet to die in the sea." And for the first time he thought of going out to meet Iemanjá, Janaína, who at the same time is mother and wife of all who live on the sea.

Old Francisco came back like a wild animal. His face tight, his eyes small. He jumped into the sloop, he didn't want any conversation, he stretched out on the bow, his pipe lighted, looking at the sea. Guma smiled: He hadn't had a woman either that night. Frederico's woman didn't want to go with her man's brother. They have their code of honor too. Only then did Guma feel a certain tenderness for that woman.

But the moon came out and Janaína's hair spread out over the sea. Then music came from the sloops, from the old fort, from the canoes, from the wharves, greeting the mother-of-water, the mistress of the sea, whom all fear and desire. She was mother and wife. Only she knew of their desires and only she consoled them all. The women were praying to Iemanjá now. Everybody asks for things. Guma asked for a pretty woman, a good woman without the strange perfume that his mother had on her throat, he asked Iemanjá to give him a woman who was new and virgin like him, almost as pretty as she was herself. Maybe in that way he would forget the image of the lost mother, of the mother who gave herself to men, tempting his uncle, tempting Guma, her own son.

Iemanjá, whom the canoemen call Janaína, is good for men of the sea. She attends to their desires.

His mother never came back again. She must have gone off to other places, because a lady of the evening is just like a sailor, she has no stopping place, she lives from port to port, wherever there's money to be made. For a long time, however, her image, her strange perfume disturbed Guma's sleep. He wanted her to come back, but not as his mother, not with soft words of affection, but as a woman of the streets, with her lips open for kisses of love. He no longer had any respite. In his young heart he mingled the image that everyone considered purity itself—the image of mother—with that of the women who gave themselves for money, the ones who make love their trade. He'd never had a mother. And when he found her it was to lose her immediately, desiring her without loving her, almost hating her. There is only one woman who can be wife and mother at the same time: That is Iemanjá, and that's why she is loved so much by the men of the waterfront. In order to love Iemanjá, who is mother and wife, you have to die. Many times Guma thought of jumping off his sloop on a stormy day. Then he could travel with Janaína, he could love mother and wife.

One night, however, old Francisco left a mulatto girl on the sloop when he was away. When Guma arrived, pants rolled up, legs dirty with dockside mud, she was stretched out seductively, her eyes on the moon. He understood. Two years had already passed since his mother had appeared. The one there now was the one who should have come in her place. It would have been better that way.

And when the great clouds swallowed up the moon he sailed the sloop to the middle of the bay, the breezes went with him, music sang out from the old fort. Shouts of pride came from Guma's chest. It mattered little that old Francisco and others were laughing and making comments on shore. He was a man now, a woman was curled up at his feet. Now he would be able to go out alone with the *Valiant*, to all ports like a real sloop master. He came back in the middle of a storm that had struck. The mulatto girl was clinging to his chest in fear. He smiled, thinking that Iemanjá must be jealous and was unleashing the wind and lightning against him.

One day, other years had passed, other women, old Francisco almost ran the *Valiant* onto some shoals in the river. If Guma hadn't put his hand to the tiller it would have been goodbye sloop. The old man lowered his head and didn't smile anymore during the trip. He didn't crack any jokes at the bar in Maragogipe, he didn't tell any stories in the saloons in Cachoeira. On the return trip he turned the tiller over to Guma and stretched out on the deck of the sloop. He let the late-morning sun warm up his body. He spoke to Guma:

"I've been sailing these waters for more than thirty years..."

Guma looked at his uncle. The old man knocked the ashes out of his pipe: Frederico hadn't been that type of man, content in going up and down the river. He thought it would be nice to be a sailor on a ship, getting to know all countries... Everybody has his own way...

The sun was beating down on the calm waters. The rocks in the shoals were glistening. Guma consoled the old man:

"You've had four sloops, uncle..."

"It was on a trip that Frederico made you. Going on eighteen years... He was traveling as a sailor. First he sailed on those coastal boats of the Baiana Line, then he went on a big ship, went out into the big world. You stayed with us people until he came back one day..."

"I remember, uncle. One night, all of a sudden."

"He wouldn't say why he came back. I think it had something to do with women. The rumor was he'd cut somebody's guts out. He was a tough mulatto. He wouldn't take any insults..."

Guma smiled, remembering his father dressed in a black rain cape, the raindrops dripping down, embracing Francisco:

"I'm back, brother..."

First Guma was afraid. He even avoided his father's kisses, his big mustache. Now he found a great pleasure remembering that scene, his father, all of a sudden, after having cut the guts out of a guy over a mulatto girl. That father who'd known different places, who'd sailed on big ships.

Old Francisco went on:

"He stayed on with me sailing the sloops. His was the *Morning Star*..."

"I remember... A lively man."

"Till that stormy night in August. He was even laughing the moment he gave up his soul. He was a brave skipper. My old lady went that night too... It was her heart. I even called a doctor. It wasn't any use. It was her heart."

Guma wondered why old Francisco was remembering all that. He had a lot of stories to tell, why tell his own story? He found it awkward and it saddened him.

"I should have stopped sailing that day. I had nothing more to do... But I had you and I had to teach you how to handle a boat... Now you've learned..."

The old man smiled. Guma too. He already knew what it was to run a boat. The one who didn't know anymore was old Francisco, who'd given everything he knew to his nephew.

"I'm an old man... I'm all through... The fish don't even want me anymore because I'm all bone..."

He was silent for a moment, as if gathering strength:

"Did you see? Going upriver, I almost put the *Valiant* onto the rocks..."

"Come on, uncle, you missed by a mile."

"That's because you grabbed the tiller. My eyes are giving out on me. The light on the sea eats up people's eyes..."

He looked at Guma like someone who had something very important to say. The sun was punishing, but he was like an old animal warming up in it. He lifted a hand:

"I'm an old man, I'm all through. But I don't want those blacks on the docks to laugh at me. Old Francisco, after thirty years, ran his sloop onto the rocks. The fish don't even want me anymore..."

His voice was growing anguished. There was some kind of finality in it; an anguish that couldn't be expressed. Guma didn't know what to say. Old Francisco went on:

"Don't you say anything... Nobody should want to see my shame..."

The rest of the trip passed in silence, and that was old Francisco's last trip.

Now he was the only one who sailed the *Valiant* over those blue waters. Old Francisco mended sails, drank cane liquor, told stories. Everything had ended for him, valiant as he was, the sea hadn't wanted him. He'd seen Iemanjá smiling, he didn't have to die to see her.

Guma stayed with the sloops, stayed on the docks, but his father's way tempted him, he loved the big ships that tied up at the piers, he listened in fascination to the strange languages the blond sailors spoke, he heard the tales the black stokers told and said to himself that someday he too would go off on one of those ships, see other moons and other stars, sing the songs of his docks in ports where the men wouldn't understand his talk, and they would lower their voices and listen to his songs, just the music, just because they knew that a sailor's song, no matter what the language, talks about the sea, misfortune, love. One day he would go on board one of those ships, look at the tiny little sloops, exchange the calm waters of the bay and the Paraguaçu River for the stormy waters of the limitless sea, the endless road that led to the most distant lands. Oh, to sail off on a black ship, live the stories that he'd heard, that was his desire. A few sloop men had already gone. They would come back sometimes, tell of terrible things, amorous adventures, adventures in storms and shipwrecks, fights with yellow men on the other side of the earth, speak a language that was a mixture of all others. But it happened too that they didn't come back sometimes. Chico Tristeza (Francisco Sadness, who didn't remember him?) signed on a German freighter while still a boy. He was a sturdy black man who never smiled. He lived looking at the waves, the ships, and all he talked about was going away. It seemed that his land was different, it was on the other side of the sea. One day the ship Chico Tristeza had signed on arrived on a return trip. Even his old mother who sold coconut cakes in the center of the city appeared, and nobody knew how the news had got to her. But they all went back, because Chico Tristeza hadn't come on his ship. He'd transferred to another and was a stoker now. From that other one, the Germans said, he'd gone to a third one, and nobody knew what part of the world Chico Tristeza was traveling in. When they talked

about him there were those who said he'd died, but nobody
believed it. A sailor comes back to die in his own port, beside his sloops and his seas. Unless he dies at sea. Even then
he comes later with Iemanjá to see the moon over his docks,
to listen to the songs of his people. Chico Tristeza hadn't
died.

Guma didn't know him very well, he was still a boy when
he left. Guma loves him and wants to be like him. Those
black ships tempt him. There's mystery in them, in their
whistles, in their anchors, in their masts. One day Guma
will leave for the Lands of the Endless Way. Only old Francisco holds him back to his dock, he is his anchor. He has to
earn keep for his uncle, who taught him everything. When
the old man becomes weary of the shore and goes to see Iemanjá, then he'll leave, his way will no longer have limits,
his sloop will be an enormous black ship, they'll tell stories
about him on the docks.

He'd stayed on the *Valiant* by himself, and he considered
his adolescence at an end. His childhood had been over very
early too, because he'd been a man for a rather long time already, even before making love to that mulatto girl that old
Francisco had left lazing on the sloop for him. One day his
mother had come, and that had been a long time before the
mulatto girl, it had been years before, and on that day he'd
taken the sloop as far as Itaparica and already felt the desires
of a man in his body. On that day he'd smiled crudely like a
man; it was on that day that sin had entered his heart and the
desire to leave began to live inside him. From that time on
he was a man.

He carried very few things from his childhood as a boy of
the sea whose lot had already been drawn by the lot of his
father, his uncle, his companions, everybody around him on
that shore: His lot was the sea and it was a heroic lot. Perhaps even he didn't know that, perhaps he hadn't even
thought that, like those men who shouted ugly names on the
sloops during the day and sang love songs with soft voices at
night, he would be a hero risking his life on the waters, rain

or shine under the skies of Bahia, the Bay of All Saints. He had never thought that his lot was heroic or that his life would be beautiful. Nor had his childhood been carefree, because he had much to look after, thrown into the bow of a boat at an early age, getting his eyes used to the reefs that were barely visible on the surface of the water, getting his hands callused from fishing lines and the wood of the tiller.

He had gone to school, yes. It was a crude building behind the docks, the teacher rhyming love sonnets (maybe love had come to her on a ship in the always-mysterious night of the sea, maybe it had never come, and she was languid and had the cool voice of a disenchanted person), the kids telling stories about fishing, talking the strange language of maritime people, making bets on boat races.

He hadn't spent much time in school. He and the other sons of sloop masters and canoemen didn't spend any more time than was needed to learn to decipher a letter and to scribble out a note, making an effort to put a flourish under the last letter of their signature. There was a lot to be done waiting for them at home or at sea, they would soon go. And when the teacher saw them (her name was Dulce), she didn't recognize them anymore, they were little men, their chests bare and their faces burned. They still came by to see her, timid, their heads down, and they still loved her because she was good and weary of everything she saw along the shore. She saw sad things, that girl who had come from Normal School to teach there in order to help a poor mother who'd been rich once and a drunkard brother who'd been her hope, the mother's, and of the father too, a gentleman with a bass voice and mustache who had died before everything had become so ugly in the world that was his home. She had come to take the place of an old maid who slapped and shouted hysterically, and she tried to make her schoolroom a happy house for the children of the waterfront. But she saw such sad things beside the ships, in the fishermen's rough houses, in the bows of the sloops, she saw the misery close up and she lost courage and lost her joy and no longer looked at the sea with the enchantment of her early days, no longer waited for a fiancé, had no more rhymes for her poetry. And, as she was religious, she prayed, because God, who was good, would have to put an end to so much misery, unless it was the end of the world. From the window of her school the little teacher would look at all those shabby boys, dirty with mud, who went out without books or shoes, boys who went from there to work, to hanging around bars, to cane liquor, and she didn't understand. They all said she was good, and she knew that. Only in the beginning, however, did she feel worthy of the description, when she said words of consolation and hope in God to those disillusioned people. But that hope had really ended many years ago and now it was only a formula, it was all external, nothing more could come from such a wounded heart. She was tired of waiting too. And she had no more words of comfort or tender words of hope. She could do nothing for those people who sent her their children for six months. She didn't deserve their description as good, because she couldn't help them at all, she didn't have any word to tell them that made sense. And unless a miracle happened, suddenly, just the way storms arrived, then she would die of sadness, of the sadness of being unable to do anything for the men of the sea.

In her school Guma had learned to read and write his name. She tried to teach him much more, he wanted to learn much more. But old Francisco called him to the sloop, for his lot was there. No doctor ever came out of the docks. Machinists and stokers had, however, and one had even gone so far ahead as to be radio operator on a passenger ship.

He didn't leave school with sadness, nor did he leave it with joy. He liked the teacher, it hadn't been so hard to learn how to read, he liked Rufino, a little black boy who made tattoos with the tip of a pen and never knew the lesson. But he also liked to go out to sea on a boat and follow his destiny. Dulce gave him a medal the day he left.

From the window she watched Guma leave. He was eleven years old and there he went, ready for life the way young doctors and lawyers were at twenty-three and twenty-five. He was entering life too, he was starting his profes-

sion, but there was no party, no ceremony, only the relief of
not having to wash his clothes so much, because in school
he had had to keep himself cleaner. There was no hope in
that breast either. No idea of great conquests, great discov-
eries, marvelous inventions, eloquent or sweet poems. She
knew that Guma was intelligent, and she had met few col-
leagues at Normal School or among her academic friends
who were as intelligent as he. They, however, always
thought about doing great things, charting their destinies.
The children who left her school never had any of those
thoughts. Destiny had already been charted for them. It was
the bow of a sloop, the oars of a canoe, at best the engine
room of a ship, a grand ideal that few nourished. The sea
was in front of her and had already swallowed up many of
her pupils, and had also swallowed up her girlhood dreams.
The sea is beautiful and terrible. The sea is free, they say,
and free are those who live on it. But Dulce knew quite well
that it wasn't that way, that those men, those women, those
children weren't free, they were chained to the sea, they
were fettered like slaves, and Dulce didn't know where the
chains that held them were, where the leg irons of slavery
were.

There went Guma, who'd learned to read so quickly. He
could have got into the Polytechnic School, been a great en-
gineer, and maybe have invented a machine that would improve the lot of the sailors on the unstable sea. But
waterfront children don't go to the university. They go to the
sloops and canoes. They will sing at night and the voices of
some will be beautiful. The songs are sad, however, like the
lives they lead. Dulce doesn't understand.

But Dulce is waiting for a miracle. It will come just like
that, suddenly, like a storm. Everything will change and it
will be beautiful. It will be beautiful like the sea. What if one
day it is she who knows the word that brings on the miracle
and she who says it to those people on the waterfront? Then
she really will deserve their calling her good and their bringing out the best they have at home when she visits them.

* * *

When he saw Dulce or when the sea made the medal he wore on his chest sway, Guma remembered school and his fleeting childhood. It had all been so swift.

One day, a day that was very far away now, it had been raining on the city and the sloops weren't moving and old Francisco was telling his wife and Guma the story of a shipwreck, when the door opened and a man entered wrapped in an oilskin cape, dripping rain. Almost all he saw was the man's big mustache, but he never forgot the voice that said to old Francisco:

"I'm back, brother..."

Guma had been afraid. But the man strode over to him and kissed him, with his great mustache, and chuckled with satisfaction, looking into Guma's face. Then he chatted on with old Francisco, telling him a story about a fight, about a "man he sent down to the depths..." That was how his father appeared on his return trip after having traveled through unknown lands and seas. He'd come back with someone's life on the tip of his dagger and unable to leave his own waters again. But since what his father loved was traveling and he couldn't do that, he didn't last long on the sloops; he stayed with the *Morning Star* at the bottom of the sea after saving his brother. Only in that way could he continue his interrupted trip, and he went away with Iemanjá, who loves brave men.

Guma vaguely remembered his father, but he always remembered his coming into the house on that stormy night, with the black oilskin cape dripping rain, still carrying the knife that had taken the life of a man. It must have been over a woman, old Francisco would say, every time the subject came up. Frederico had always been a woman-chaser...

On the night he died, Aunt Rita, Francisco's wife, died too. When the storm broke she ran to the docks and took Guma with her, wrapped under her shawl. They'd waited there in vain. Later they went back home, because dinnertime was approaching. She prepared the fish for the men. Maybe at that very moment they were the ones who were dinner for other fish. She waited, walking back and forth, praying to Our Lady of Monte Serrat, making promises to Iemanjá. She would carry bars of soap to the feast of Dona Janaína and two candles for the altar of Our Lady of Monte Serrat. In the middle of the night Francisco arrived. She ran to his arms and left her life there. She didn't have the strength for so much happiness. Her heart burst and Guma was left alone with old Francisco.

He went to the feasts of Dona Janaína, he met Anselmo, the sorcerer of the Dam district, the one who had power with the mistress of the sea, he met Chico Tristeza, who went away on a ship. He was still a small boy when the black man ran away from home. But he'd seen him many times beside the docks, looking out toward the end of everything, toward the blue line where everything ends. Chico's land must have been far away, it was to the Lands of the Endless Way that he'd gone. He'd been looking for it up till now and he would have to return one day because he was a sailor from that port and he had to die in it. He would still have to see Dona Dulce again, he'd learned to read from her and she always spoke of him. When he came he'd have a lot to tell and the men would sit down around him, even the oldest ones on the docks, to hear his stories. There was no doubt that he would be back. Ships have the name of their port written on the stern, above the propellers. In the same way sailors have the name of their waterfront on their hearts. Some even have that name tattooed on their chests alongside the names of their sweethearts. It can happen that a ship goes down far from its port. In the same way a sailor can die far from his waterfront. But later on he will come with Iemanjá, who knows where they all come from, to see his people and his moon before going through the unknown. Chico Tristeza would return. Then Guma would learn a lot of things from him, and he would go away too, because the broad paths of the sea tempted him.

Of all his childhood memories, that of Chico Tristeza leaving suddenly on a ship was the one he recalled most. One day he would do the same.

During the nights of his childhood many times he slept on

the quarterdeck of the sloop moored to the small dock. On one side, huge and illuminated by a thousand street lamps, was the city. It went up the hillside and its bells tolled, happy music came from it, the laughter of men, the sound of cars. The light on the elevator went up and down, it was a gigantic toy connecting the port to the upper city. On the other side was the sea, the moon, and the stars, all lighted up too. The music that came from it was sad, and it penetrated more deeply. The sloops and the canoes arrived noiselessly, the fish passed under the water. The bustling city was a bit calmer then. There were beautiful women there, different things, movies and theater, bars and lots of people. On the sea there was none of that. The music of the sea was sad and spoke of death and lost love. In the city everything was bright and without mystery, lighted by the street lamps. On the sea everything was as mysterious as the light of the stars. The paths of the city were many and well paved. At sea there was only one path and it wavered, it was dangerous. The paths of the city had been well conquered already. That of the sea had to be conquered daily, it was an adventure every time a person went out. And on land there is no Iemanjá, no feasts to Dona Janaína, there is no music that is so sad. Never had the music of the land, the life of the land tempted Guma's heart. On dockside there was never a story told about the case of a sailor's son being tempted by the peaceful life of the city. If anyone spoke of that to the old sailmakers they wouldn't understand and would have to laugh. A man might well be tempted to go see other lands, that, yes. But to leave his sloop for the life of the land, that would be heard only with a guffaw and a drink of cane liquor.

Guma was never tempted by the land. There was no adventure there. The path of the sea, broad and wavering, that tempted him, yes. His destiny was the sea.

. It was on such a night that his mother had come. No one had spoken to him about her and she came from the land, she was of the land, she had nothing of the women of the sea, she had nothing in common with him, he thought she was the prostitute he was expecting. She only came to make him suffer. And she hadn't returned. Other women had come from the land to his boat, first prostitutes who came for money, then mulatto girls, young black girls from the houses near the docks, and they came because they found him strong and knew his love would be good. The first reminded him of his mother. They had the perfume she wore, they talked the way she talked, except they didn't know how to smile the way the waterfront women smile at their children, and in that way she was half mother, half prostitute, making him suffer all the more.

She hadn't returned. She was probably wandering through other ports with other men. Who knows, maybe at night, when the last man had gone and she was alone, she remembered that son who lived on the sloops and hadn't known how to say a single word to her. Who knows, maybe she was intoxicated with love for that son who was lost to her. But if the music comes from the sea and crosses through the fort, the sloops, the canoes, and speaks of love, Guma forgets everything and lets himself go in the soft rocking of that ever so beautiful melody.

His childhood had been quick and he'd had almost no toys, but he'd begun to feel his first strength in it. The large cut he had on his hand was from a fight in his fourteenth year. The others were Jacques, Rodolfo, Wall-Eyes, and Maneca One-Hand. He was alone with Rufino and the fight was because of a dumb trick, because Maneca One-Hand had peeked at the thighs of Rufino's sister, a small black girl, a little over ten. He was talking about trifles with the black boy when Maricota came up crying:

"He was peeking under my skirt..."

Rufino went looking for One-Hand. Guma wasn't a man to let a buddy down at a moment like that, and the law of the docks says the same. They went together and found the four of them, still laughing. Rufino swung his fist, because he wasn't one for arguments or curses, and the fight was ugly. It was on the sand that the morning sun was lighting up and they rolled around, punching. Maneca One-Hand, who had a withered arm, was laid out by a punch from Rufino. But it was still three against two, and halfway through the fight Rodolfo, who wasn't good for much, pulled out a knife and it got bloody. Rufino was cut under the jaw and when Guma went to his aid he was only able to brush aside with his hand the blade that was aimed at his face. In spite of the knife and their being three, they ran away. Black Rufino cleaned off the blood and promised:

"That Rodolfo's going to pay me back for this. I'll teach him a lesson someday…"

Guma didn't say anything. He loved the law of the docks and it didn't permit anyone to pull a knife unless the enemy were greater in number. Anyone who didn't obey the law of the docks wasn't worth anything in his eyes.

A week later Rodolfo was found with his face smashed, stretched out on the sand with no knife and no pants. Rufino had kept his promise.

He'd liked Rufino ever since school. Without a father, reared by his mother, Rufino hadn't stayed in school long. What he'd learned was almost nothing: tattooing anchors and hearts on his comrades with a pen and blue ink. Dona Dulce scolded him, but the black boy laughed with his peaceful eyes and broad teeth and Dona Dulce smiled too. He left school, went off to support his mother and sister. He hired out his huge arms to all canoemen. He was a strong rower because there was nobody dockside who had more faith in Iemanjá than he. One day he would have a canoe of his own, without doubt, which he'd already asked for on the feast day at the Dam, and he'd sent a vial of perfume so the Princess of Aiocá (that's what the blacks call Iemanjá) would always have scented hair. She would give him a canoe because he was the most enthusiastic at her festivals, and someday he'd be an *ogā*, an acolyte in her *candomblé* rites. Black Rufino laughed a lot. He drank a lot, too, and he sang in a bass voice that drowned out all others.

Rodolfo had never looked like a man from those parts.

His father had arrived one day and opened a store, which failed. In spite of that he didn't leave the waterfront, but set up a booth in the Market and sold things at the fair in Água dos Meninos. Rodolfo was born, a handsome white boy with very straight hair that he wore smoothed down with grease. When he grew up he abandoned the rudder of the sloop his father had got for him, deserted the water, and would appear and disappear. Sometimes he would show up with lots of money, buy drinks all around, start fights, at the Beacon of the Stars. Other times he would show up broke, begging ten cents, drinking at the expense of others. On the waterfront they looked a little askance at him and said he was "shifty."

Jacques grew up on the sloops like Guma. He married and then died in a storm one night. He died like his father and left a wife with a child in her belly. Maneca One-Hand was still on the sloops, with his crippled hand but knowing how to sail a boat like nobody else. Even Master Manuel, so old on the docks and always young, respected him.

These had been his childhood friends. There were a lot of boys like them on the docks, men in their sloops now. They didn't expect much out of life: sailing over the waves, having a sloop of their own, drinking at the Beacon of the Stars, making a son who would follow their lot and go off with Iemanjá someday. Even though a voice on the waterfront on the most beautiful nights sings:

*"It's sweet to die in the sea…"*

Dona Dulce, who is getting old and wears glasses now, hears the music and knows they will die without fear. In spite of that she feels bitterness in her heart. She fears for them, she's sorry for those men. Old Francisco, who no longer goes out, who stays on shore waiting for a peaceful death, free of storms, treacherous waves, also knows they will die without fear. But, unlike Dona Dulce, old Francisco envies them. Because they say that the trip that shipwrecked sailors make with Iemanjá to the Lands of the Endless Way, under the seas, swifter than the swiftest ships, is well worth the rotten life they live on shore.

# ROSA PALMEIRÃO'S LULLABY

Rosa Palmeirão sounds good to the waterfront people. They tell a lot of tales about that mulatto woman. Old Francisco knows any number of them, in prose and in verse, because Rosa Palmeirão already has one of those ABC ballads, the kind in which each verse begins with a letter of the alphabet, about her and even in the backlands blind men sing about her carrying on. The men of the docks, who know her, like her and no one will refuse her a light for her pipe and a long handshake. And alongside Rosa Palmeirão nobody can talk about brave deeds.

On nights when not many sloops are out, old Francisco tells tales. It's quite true that old Francisco will blow up the tales he tells, invent whole sections, but no matter how much he blows things up he will never be able to tell the whole truth about Rosa Palmeirão. No storyteller in the world (and the best can be found at dockside in Bahia) can tell everything Rosa Palmeirão has done. She's done so many things that old Francisco with his guitar sings to those around him:

> *"Rosa Palmeirão keeps a razor 'neath her skirt,*
> *A ring in her ear and a dagger by her breast.*
> *She's not afraid of a ray-fish tail.*
> *Rosa's body's the best of the best."*

Oh! she wouldn't amount to anything if her body wasn't the best. Her fame has gone out now, spread over the world, every sailor knows her. They're all afraid of the razor under

her skirt, the dagger by her breast, her clenched fist, but
even more afraid of her body that's the best. She does a lot
of tricking. She passes by, body swaying, really calling, it
doesn't look like her. The sailor follows, the sand is soft and
the moon is beautiful over the sea. On the docks people sing
that the night is for love. She goes along, her body swaying,
rocking as if she too belonged to the sea. The sailor doesn't
know. He follows her. The sand is waiting. And she doesn't
seem to be Rosa Palmeirão, she's so pretty. Poor sailor if
she doesn't like him or doesn't want to make love that night.
Rosa Palmeirão keeps a razor 'neath her skirt, a dagger by
her breast. Rosa Palmeirão has already hit six cops, seen the
inside of twenty jails, hit a lot of men. Old Francisco sings:

> *"Rosa beat up six cops,*
> *All on Saint John's Eve.*
> *They called their inspector up,*
> *He said I'm not going, won't leave.*

> *All of the cops came at her,*
> *She made a grab for her knife.*
> *The row was a terrible matter,*
> *A night for losing your life."*

She downed a man, chased off all the police. She was valiant and she was beautiful. Old Francisco sings of Rosa Palmeirão's deeds and they all applaud:

> *"The order said bring her in,*
> *Palmeirão dead or alive...*
> *She pulled out her razor thin,*
> *Men all around taking a dive..."*

They listen and they applaud. Guma is among the ones
applauding the most. He doesn't remember Rosa Palmeirão.
It's been a long time now since she left that port. First she
went all around the bay, then she traveled to the southern
part of the state, became involved with a landowner, gave

him a fearful thrashing, and disappeared in that world without end. One day she passed through Bahia again, but almost nobody saw her, she arrived on one ship and left on another. They say she hadn't aged at all, that she was just the same. The flower that she always wore on her dress (a palm rose, a *rosa palmeirão*) was there. But she went away again and all that was left of her on those nights was her ABC ballad and the tales men told under the shade of the Market overhang. She had a beautiful body and still hasn't lost anything. When she loved a man she was a woman like no other. Then her rose would become even prettier, she would give off an aroma through her hair. Whoever got involved with her when she wanted a lover had no way out: Rosa Palmeirão was a one-man woman. Old Francisco sang:

> *"If she was brave in the day,*
> *Brave as only she could be...*
> *At night she had a different way,*
> *Feeling sorry for men was she..."*

The image of Rosa Palmeirão passed through the memory of the men of the docks. Some of those there, Brígido Ronda, for example, had loved her. Almost all had been present at Rosa Palmeirão's fights, that's why they liked to hear her ABC and the tales of her fights. Where could Rosa Palmeirão be wandering? She'd been born on that waterfront, she went out into the world because she didn't like staying in just one place. No one knows where she's wandering. Wherever she is there'll be trouble. Because she carries a razor 'neath her skirt, a dagger by her breast, and because her body's the best of the best.

One night she came down the third-class gangplank of a ship that had arrived from Rio. Number 35 picked up her baggage and carried it to a room in the Beacon of the Stars free of charge. Five minutes later everybody on the waterfront knew that Rosa Palmeirão had come back and was just the same, hadn't grown old. Rosa's body's the best of the best, the line could still say. No sloop went out that night. Cargoes of fabrics, oranges, pineapples, and sapodillas waited for the following morning. Rosa Palmeirão had come back and after many years of absence. The sailors from a Baiana Line ship ran to the Beacon of the Stars. The canoemen came too. Old Francisco brought Guma.

The sound of glasses came from the barroom. A red spotlight illuminated the scene with a dim light. When they entered Rosa Palmeirão was sitting at the bar and laughing long and loud, her arms open, a glass in her hand. When she caught sight of old Francisco, she leaped down, threw her arms around his neck:

"Just look at old Francisco... Look at old Francisco... They're right when they say a no-good glass never breaks..."

"That's why the pair of us are still alive..."

She laughed, shook old Francisco:

"You didn't stay at the bottom of the sea, eh, you old devil? Who would have thought..."

She noticed Guma:

"Who's this cabin boy? He's got your look..."

"It's my nephew Gumercindo. The people call him Guma. You saw him when he was just a tot..."

She was remembering. Then she smiled:

"Is he Frederico's boy? Tighten up those bones, kid... Your father was a man and a lot more..."

"He was my brother," Francisco laughed.

"There were two brothers who didn't look at all alike. He didn't have the face of a dead fish."

They all laughed, because Rosa Palmeirão was really quite funny, she waved her arms, talked like a man, drank like few people could. Old Francisco clapped his hands and said:

"Good people, let's us all have a drink because this old leather pouch has come home... I'm buying all around..."

"I'll buy another round..." shouted Master Manuel, who wasn't living with Maria Clara yet at that time.

They sat down and drained their glasses of cane liquor. Mr. Babau, the owner of the Beacon of the Stars, was going back and forth with a bottle of booze in his hand, keeping count of the number of glasses drunk. Rosa Palmeirão came over and sat down beside Guma at a little corner table. He was looking at her. Her body was the best of the best. Her large buttocks rolled like the prow of a sloop. She drank the cane liquor, made a face:

"I knew your father, but I'm not all that old..."

Guma laughed, looking into her eyes. Why didn't the ABC say anything about those green eyes that looked like a stone from the bottom of the sea? More than the razor, the dagger, the body that was best, the sloop behind, those eyes brought on fear, deep and green like the sea. Who can say that they don't change color with the sea, a blue sea, green, a lead-colored sea on heavy nights of calm?

"I knew old Frederico too and I'm only twenty years old ..."

"I'm not such a baby either... But I pissed in Frederico's drawers a lot. You, it's like seeing him..."

Now it was Master Manuel who was paying for the round of cane liquor. He shouted to Rosa Palmeirão:

"I'm the one paying now, you she-devil..."

She turned in her chair:

"Don't I deserve it?"

"You're getting to be an old leather pouch, Rosa," old Francisco laughed.

"Shut your mouth, you swamped canoe. You don't understand these things..."

"That's the way, Rosa. You can still turn a person's head," Severiano came to her support.

Rosa Palmeirão spoke to Guma:

"Am I really an old leather pouch like your uncle says?" and she laughed and looked him straight in the eyes. She had daggers in her eyes too.

"Oh, no... There's nobody can resist you..."

Rosa Palmeirão's eyes smiling. Why this barroom when the sand by the docks is smooth and the passing wind is warm? Rosa Palmeirão's eyes are the color of the sea.

But Rosa Palmeirão doesn't belong to one man alone

now. She belongs to all the men on the docks who want to know what she was doing away from her land for such a long time. Where she went, what fights she had, what jails she'd been in. On all sides they demanded that she tell:

"I'm only going to say one thing to all of you... I covered this big old world, with God's help. I went to so many places I can't remember them all. I saw big cities, cities that could hold ten Bahias..."

"Did you get to Rio de Janeiro?"

"I got there three times... I've just come from there."

"Is it nice?"

"It's a beauty... All that light and all those people, so pretty that it hurts..."

"Lots of big ships?"

"All of them whoppers, too big to dock here. They've got some that from stem to stern measure from the dock to the jetty..."

"Couldn't be that big."

"Did you see them? Well, I did. You just ask a real sailor. Or do you think a canoeman is a sailor?"

Master Manuel cut in:

"I heard talk too... They say it's exaggerated..."

"Didn't you fall for any man there, Rosa?" Francisco asked.

"The men there aren't men. They're not even worth the trouble. I lived in the *favelas* on the hills there, I was respected like nobody else. Don't ask. Once a dude tried to cut in front of me in a dance hall. I hooked my anchor onto the guy's throat, he ran aground on the floor. Everybody laughed..."

The men were satisfied now. Out there, in Rio, in other places, she'd shown who she was. Rosa Palmeirão looked at Guma and said:

"They even said if a woman from Bahia is like that, what can the men be like?"

"You were famous, eh Rosa?"

"I had a neighbor and I don't know what got into him, to make him jump on me one day. I was crazy about a mulatto who did sambas, I didn't dare. One night he came by for small talk in my room. He was talking, looking at the bed, and he jumped on top of me. I said to him: 'Brother, get your ass up and out of here.' He was making himself to home, anchored there like it was his home port. His eyes popping out at me. I warned him that my man would be back at any time... He only said he wasn't afraid of any man. I asked him what about a woman, are you afraid of a woman? He said only for witchcraft. And with those eyes bugging out at me. I said it would be better if he left. But he didn't want to, no way. He was even taking off his pants, and I couldn't take that, see?''

The men smiled, savoring the ending:

''What did you do?''

''I grabbed him by the neck, threw him out the door. He was sprawled out on the ground there, looking up with a dumb face.''

''Good deal, girl...''

''You all haven't seen the rest of it. I thought the song was over too. But no way. My mulatto came home then, I wasn't upset. But I'd got the little man mad and round about midnight he broke into the house with a half-dozen people. My mulatto was a good man and people shouldn't have any doubts: It was a wild brawl... The men, poor things, thought it was just a matter of beating up Juca, grabbing me, and setting sail. When the whole business got down to its last letter one of them had his face opened up and me with the old war razor in my hand. It was a bloody mess, it looked like a regular spear-fishing expedition. When we least expected it, lo and behold, the police at the door. Everybody to the station house.''

''Did you do time in Rio?''

''I did nothing. I got there, told everything to the inspector, I said Rosa Palmeirão wouldn't stand for anything like that, no sir. The inspector was a lawyer from Bahia, he laughed, said he'd heard of me already, and let me go. I asked about Juca too and he let him off. The others stayed, there was one they sent to the hospital, tattooed all over.''

"You were lucky to get that inspector!"

"But when I went to get Juca, where was he? I never saw him again. He'd become scared of me..."

The sailors laughed. The glasses of cane liquor were emptied all together. Master Manuel was paying. Who was it said Rosa Palmeirão was an old piece of leather? Guma couldn't take his eyes off her. She had an ABC and she knew how to fight. But her body was the best and she had deep eyes. Rosa Palmeirão told him:

"I never fought with men I liked... Ask any of them..." But she didn't see any fear in his eyes.

They left the bar late. Old Francisco went away, even Master Manuel got tired of waiting. Mr. Babau said to Rosa Palmeirão:

"Aren't you ever going to bed?"

"I'm going to take a look around outside first."

It had been a long time since she'd made love to a man on that sand. A lot of people thought that all she knew how to do was fight, that life was a riot for her, the tip of a knife, the edge of a razor. If brave men turned into stars in the sky, she would be there among them someday. But life for Rosa Palmeirão wasn't only a riot. What she liked most, more than fighting, more than drinking, more than talking, was being like that in Guma's arms, stretched out on the sand, dominated, a woman, very much a woman, running her fingers through his hair, snuggly. Her eyes are deep like the sea and, like the sea, they change. They're green, green with love on nights on the sand. They're blue on calm days, and lead-colored when the calm is only the prelude to a storm. Her eyes glow. Her hands that manipulate knives and razors are soft now and hold up Guma's resting head. Her mouth that gives off curses is tender now and smiles with love. They never loved her the way she wanted. They were all afraid of her, of the dagger, the razor, her body that was the best. They thought about the day when she would get angry and the dagger and the razor would appear and the body disappear. They'd never loved her without fear. She'd never seen eyes as limpid as Guma's now. He admired her, he

didn't fear her. Even those who'd had the courage to see her
well-built body, in spite of the dagger and the razor, had
never looked her in the eyes, had never discerned the tenderness in those sea-eyes, wanting love, the tender eyes of a
woman. Guma looked into those eyes and understood.
That's why Rosa Palmeirão's hands stroke his hair, her lips
smile and her body quivers.

Three nights later the *Valiant* was slipping through the
waters of the Paraguaçu River. A smell of fruit came from
the hold. The wind was carrying the sloop along and no one
was needed at the tiller, the river was so calm. The stars
were shining in the sky and on the sea, Iemanjá had come to
see the moon and had spread her hair over the calm waters.
Rosa Palmeirão (razor 'neath her skirt, dagger by her
breast) was speaking into Guma's ear:

"You're going to laugh at me, think I'm silly... Do you
know what I wanted to have?"

"What?"

She lay staring into the water of the river. She tried to
smile, bashful:

"I swear that I wanted to have a son, a little son I could
take care of and raise... Don't laugh, please..."

And she wasn't ashamed of the tears that rolled down
over the dagger by her breast, the razor 'neath her skirt.

# LAW

The fishing boats returned to the docks. Some had barely begun their fishing and hadn't even covered expenses yet. Rufino came back in his canoe from the middle of the bay. Sloops that had their sails already unfurled and their anchors weighed dropped anchor and pulled in their sails. But the sky was blue and the sea was calm. The sun was brightening everything, brightening it too much. For that very reason the fishing boats had come in. Rufino brought his canoe to the Firewood Dock, the sloops struck their sails. The water was changing color, from the blue it had been it was turning the color of lead. Severiano, a resolute canoeman, came alongside the sloop docks. Seeing that the sloops weren't going out, several people had left the Market and taken the elevator. Most, however, decided to stay because the weather was good, the sky blue, the sea calm, and the sun bright. As they saw it, nothing was going to happen.

Severiano came over and spoke to Master Manuel and Guma:

"It's going to be a rough one today..."

"Anyone who goes out is crazy..."

They put tobacco in their pipes. People were entering and leaving the Model Market. The sun glistened on the small pavement stones. At the window of a house a woman was laying out a towel. Sailors up on the deck of a ship were swabbing it. The wind began to run, stirring up the sand that flew about. Severiano asked:

"Are many people out to sea?"

56

Master Manuel looked around. The sloops were bobbing on the small waves.

"Not as far as I know... Whoever is will stay in Itaparica or Mar Grande..."

"I wouldn't want to be out in weather like this..."

Old Francisco joined the growing group:

"It was on a day like this that João Pequeno, Little John, had his drink of water..."

Yes, João Pequeno was a sloop master famous all up and down the waterfront for his professionalism. His fame was respected in faraway places. Men talked about him in Penedo, Caravelas, Aracaju. His sloop traveled farther than all the others, and he wasn't afraid of storms. João Pequeno understood that harbor so well that one day he was invited to be a pilot. He brought the ships in on stormy nights. He went out to meet them, rising over the waves, and he brought them in, avoiding the dangers of the difficult harbor entrance on stormy days.

Yes, on a night like that, calm, except that the sea was copper-colored, he ventured out. A ship didn't know its way, it was coming to Bahia for the first time. João Pequeno didn't come back from his adventure. The government gave his wife a pension, but they cut it off later for reasons of economy. Today all that's left of João Pequeno is his fame along the waterfront.

Old Francisco, who knew him, had told the story of João Pequeno more than a hundred times already. And those who hear it listen with respect. They say that João Pequeno appears on stormy nights. A lot of people have already seen him sailing over the sloops, looking for the ship that was lost in the fog. Even today João Pequeno is still looking for the ship. And he won't rest until he brings it into port. Only then will he begin his well-deserved trip with Iemanjá to the Lands of the Endless Way.

That was a night for him to appear. When the wind swirls and hums as it shakes the houses, when night falls over the waterfront, he comes in search of the route of the lost ship. He will sail over the sloops, put fear in those who are at sea.

A sloop approaches the docks. With the strong wind blowing, it careens along wildly. The sails are filled to the limit. The men look:

"It's Xavier coming…"

"That's right, it's the *Black Owl*…"

The sloop is arriving and its name can be read in black paint: *Black Owl*.

"I've never known an uglier name for a boat," Manuel says.

"He must have his reasons," Francisco puts in. "Nobody knows anything about other people's lives."

"I didn't mean anything by it. I was just saying…"

The wind was growing stronger at every moment and the waters were no longer calm. From far away came the whistle of the strong and pitiless wind. In a short while the docks are deserted. Xavier tied up his sloop and came over to the group:

"Things are getting ugly…"

"Are there many out?"

"I only ran into Otoniel, but he was pretty close to Maragogipe…"

The sea was moving, the waves were big now, the sloops and canoes were going up and down. Manuel turned to Xavier:

"If you'll excuse my asking, brother, why did you lay such a scary name on your boat?"

Xavier's face tightened. A stocky mulatto, he wore his hair slicked down:

"People do things… Everything's crazy, right?"

The storm had broken over the city and the sea. Nobody was seen around the market now except for them, forming a group in oilskin capes with the rain pouring off. The wind was deafening and they had to talk in loud voices. Manuel shouted:

"What did you say?"

"You want to know? It had to do with a woman… A long time ago, in a different port, down south there. Everybody's crazy, it doesn't pay, does it? Nobody can guess what women mean. Why did she call me Black Owl? Only she could have said, and she never did, she just laughed, laughed a lot... It was enough to drive you crazy, that was it..."

The wind carried off his words. The men leaned over to hear better. Xavier lowered his voice:

"She called me Black Owl... Why, I don't know. She would laugh every time I asked... The boat became the *Black Owl*..."

There was no reason for the others to be surprised. He put on an angry face and shouted:

"Didn't you people ever love a woman? If you didn't you don't know what trouble is... I'd rather have a storm like this a thousand times more, God forgive me,"—and he put his hand over his mouth—"than have a two-faced woman, the kind that's always laughing... She called me Black Owl, the devil only knows why. Why did she leave me? I hadn't done anything to her. One day when I got back she'd been swallowed up in the world, she left all her things behind... I even looked for her at sea, she could have drowned... Let's have a drink."

They went off to the Beacon of the Stars. The voice of Rosa Palmeirão who was singing was coming from there. The wind was picking up sand. Xavier spoke:

"It doesn't pay... But people keep on thinking... I put the name *Black Owl* on the boat. She'd even told me, it wasn't too long before, that she was going to have a child of mine... She went off with the kid in her belly."

"She'll come back someday," Guma consoled him.

"Child, you belong to a different day and age... If she does come back I'll tear her limb from limb..."

"The name of the boat... I imagined..."

"If I hadn't done it, it would have been to my shame..."

He said something else that was carried off by the wind. They couldn't hear Rosa Palmeirão's voice singing anymore. The darkness dominated everything. They could hear voices again only when they went into the Beacon of the Stars.

The man in the raincoat was shouting at Mr. Babau:

"I thought there were men here... All we've got are cowards..."

The room was empty. Only Rosa Palmeirão was listening attentively. Mr. Babau was holding out his hands, he couldn't find excuses:

"But this storm isn't child's play, Mr. Godofredo..."

"Big cowards. The time of brave men on this waterfront is over. Where are the likes of a João Pequeno?"

They went over. It was Mr. Godofredo from the Baiana Line, who was acting like a man possessed:

"What's all the trouble, Mr. Godofredo?" Manuel asked.

"What's the trouble? Well, don't you know? The *Canavieiras* is out there and can't come in..."

"Doesn't the captain know the way?"

"He doesn't know his own face... He's an Englishman who just got here. He doesn't know anything yet. I'm looking for someone to serve as pilot..."

He spat with rage:

"But the days of brave sloopmen on this waterfront are over..."

Xavier went forward. Francisco, who thought he was going to volunteer, tugged on his cape.

"You mentioned João Pequeno? What did he get? Not even a rest in hell. He lives out there scaring people. What did he get? They gave a monthly allowance just to shut things up... Then they took it away... People are only brave when they die..."

"But there are families on board the ship..."

"We've got families too... What do they get?..."

Mr. Godofredo changed the subject:

"The company will pay two hundred *milreis* to the man who'll go..."

"Life is cheap, eh?" Xavier sat down and asked for a drink of cane liquor.

Rosa Palmeirão laughed loud:

"Is your wife arriving on that ship, Godô? Or is it your mistress?"

"Shut your mouth, woman, can't you see that the ship is full?"

They didn't like Mr. Godofredo on the waterfront. He'd begun as a midshipman on a Baiana Line ship, no one knows how he got to be captain. No one ever understood that, all he knew was how to mistreat sailors. After he'd almost run the *Maraú* aground at the harbor mouth of Ilhéus, the company gave him a good spot in its office. And he mistreated sloopmen, canoemen, and stevedores as much as he could.

"It's full of people. Where are the men on this waterfront? In the old days a ship wouldn't be lost like that..."

"Do you have somebody on board the *Canavieiras?*"

He looked at Francisco:

"I know you all hate me..." He smiled. "I'd only be capable of asking you to save someone of mine, is that it? But I'm not asking for that, no. What I'm doing is paying. Two hundred *milreis* to whoever wants to go..."

Other men were arriving. Godofredo repeated the offer. They looked at him with disbelief. Xavier was drinking at a table:

"Nobody here wants to get killed, Mr. Godofredo. Let the Englishman take care of himself."

Guma asked:

"Why don't they send out a tug?"

Mr. Godofredo shuddered:

"They ought to, yes... But the company says it's too expensive... I need a man with courage. The company will pay two hundred *milreis*..."

The wind was shaking the door of the Beacon of the Stars. For the first time they could hear the ship's whistle asking for help. Mr. Godofredo lifted his arms (he looked so short in that oversized coat) and said almost lovingly to the men:

"I'll give another hundred *milreis* out of my own pocket... And I swear I'll take care of the man who goes..."

They were startled, but nobody moved. Mr. Godofredo turned to Rosa Palmeirão:

"Rosa, you're a woman but you've got more courage than a lot of men... Look, Rosa, my two children are on board. They went to spend their holidays in Ilhéus... Didn't you ever have a child, Rosa?"

Francisco whispered into Guma's ear:

"I told you he had somebody on the ship..."

Godofredo extended his arms to Rosa. Now he was ridiculous, short in his expensive coat, his face anguished, his voice heavy:

"Ask them to go, Rosa... I'll give two hundred *milreis* to whoever goes... I'll take care of him for the rest of his life... I know they don't like me... But they're my children..."

"Your children?" Rosa Palmeirão was looking at the dark afternoon.

Godofredo went over to a table. He leaned his head onto his manicured hands and his shoulders went up and down. They looked like sloops at sea.

"He's crying," Manuel said.

Rosa Palmierão got up. But Guma was already beside Godofredo:

"Leave off, I'm going..."

Old Francisco smiled. He looked at the arm where the names of his brother and his two sloops were. There was still room for Guma's name. Xavier put down his glass:

"It's crazy... And it won't do any good..."

Guma went out into the darkness. Rosa Palmeirão's eyes were gleaming with love. Godofredo held out his hand:

"Bring in my children..."

He disappeared into the night that had fallen, turned the sloop into the wind. He could still see the shapes of the ones who had gone with him to the docks. Rosa Palmeirão and old Francisco were waving. Xavier shouted:

"Regards to Janaína..."

Master Manuel turned with hate:

"No one should ever say that a man is going to his death..."

He raised his eyes, saw the shadow of the sloop going off into the lead-colored sea:

"He was still a child..."

The stars had disappeared. The moon hadn't come out that night either, and that's when there were no songs at sea, no talk of love. The waves ran one on top of the other. All that inside the harbor, even before the breakwater. What could it have been like out there, beyond the entrance, where the sea was open?

The *Valiant* has trouble leaving its moorings. Guma is trying to see what's in front of him, but everything around is black. The hard part is crossing that little patch of sea against the wind. Then it would be a mad race, with the wild wind in back of him, through a sea that no longer belongs to sloops and canoes, the sea of great ships.

Guma can still make out the shadows on the docks. The one waving is Rosa Palmeirão, the bravest and softest woman he has ever known. Guma is only twenty but he's already loved many women. And none of them ever knew how to be like Rosa Palmeirão, so affectionate in his arms. The sea is like Rosa Palmeirão on her riotous days. The sea was the color of lead. A fish leaps up over the waves. For him the storm is of no importance. It even hinders the fishermen in their chores. The sloop quickly covers the water by the docks. The breakwater is close by. The wind runs around the old fort, goes in through abandoned windows, plays about the old useless cannons. Guma can no longer see the ships on the docks. Maybe Rosa Palmeirão is weeping. She's not a woman for weeping, but she wanted to have a son and she forgot that it was too late for that. She'd made Guma into her lover and her son. Why, at that hour of death, does he think about his mother who had gone away? Guma doesn't want to think about her. Rosa Palmeirão has something of a mother in her love. She's no longer a lover but fondles him as she would a son, a lot of times she forgets

about the mad kisses of desire and kisses him softly with
maternal lips. The sloop leaps over the waves. It goes forward with difficulty. The breakwater always seems to be the
same distance away. So near and yet so far. Guma takes off
his drenched shirt. The wind crosses the sloop from one side
to the other. What must it be like outside the entrance? Rosa
Palmeirão wants to have a son. She was tired of dealing with
the police, of doing time in jail, of the razor 'neath her skirt,
the dagger by her breast. She wants a son to caress, to sing
cradle songs to. Once Guma fell asleep in her arms and Rosa
sang:

> "Sleep, sleep, little baby,
> Bogeyman's on his way..."

She was forgetting that he was her lover and was making a
son of him, snuggling him at her neck. Maybe that was what
had unleashed the wrath of Iemanjá. Only Dona Janaína can
be mother and wife. And she is that for all the men of the
waterfront, she is the protectress of all women. Now Rosa
Palmeirão will make promises to her so Guma will come
back alive. Maybe she'll even promise (what isn't love capable of?) the razor 'neath her skirt, the dagger by her
breast. Another wave washes over the sloop. The truth is—
Guma thinks—it's going to be hard to get back alive. Today
will be his day. He thinks this without any fear. It came
sooner than he had thought, but it had to come all the same,
he wouldn't escape. He was only sorry that he still hadn't
loved a woman the way he'd asked Dona Janaína on a certain night. A woman who would give him a son to inherit the
sloop, to listen to old Francisco's stories. Nor had he sailed
to other ports as he'd thought he would. He hadn't gone out
over other seas like Chico Tristeza to the lands of the endless
way. Now he would go with Iemanjá, Dona Janaína to the
canoemen, Princess of Aiocá to the blacks, running under
the water. Maybe she would take him to the land of Aiocá,
which was his land. It's the land of all men of the sea, where
Dona Janaína is princess. Lands of Aiocá, distant, lost on

the horizon line, where Iemanjá comes from on moonlit nights.

Where is the breakwater that the sloop never reaches? Guma grips the tiller, and even so it's hard to hold the boat against the wind. He passes under the shadow of the old fort. There, outside the harbor entrance, is a ship that's whistling. The wind brings the cry of the ship full of people. It's not for the money that Guma is going out on the *Valiant* in an attempt to bring that ship to port. He's not sure himself why he's facing the storm like that. It's not for money certainly. What will he do with those two hundred *milreis,* which will be even more if Godofredo also gives what he promised? He'll buy gifts for Rosa Palmeirão, new clothes for Francisco, maybe a sail for the *Valiant.* But he would have gone through all that anyway, and a man doesn't go to his death for two hundred *milreis.* Nor is it because Godofredo has two children on the *Canavieiras* and is weeping like an abandoned child. Not for that, no. It's simply because a sad whistle comes from a ship, a call for help, and the law of the sea ordains that a person attends to those who ask for help at sea. So Iemanjá will be pleased with him, and if he comes back alive she'll give him the woman he asked for. Guma can't answer the ship's whistle. It must be near the headland light, waiting for help most certainly, the men on board trying to console the women and children. A ship off course, lost near its port. That's why Guma is going. Because a ship, a canoe, a sloop, a raft, anything at sea is the home of those waterfront men, Iemanjá's people. They themselves don't know that in the timbers of ships, in the broken sails of sloops, lies the land of Aiocá, where Janaína is princess.

He passed the breakwater. In the old fort a light wavers, moves about like a ghost. He shouts:

"Jeremias! Ahoy, Jeremias!"

Jeremias appears with a lantern. The light falls onto the sea and sways with the waves. Jeremias asks:

"Who goes there?"

"Guma..."

"What the devil's got into you, boy?"

"I'm going to bring in the *Canavieiras,* it's outside the entrance…"

"Couldn't it wait till tomorrow to come in?…"

"It's whistling for help…"

He passed the breakwater. Jeremias is still shouting and the light of the lantern waves:

"Good luck! Good luck!"

Guma works the rudder. Jeremias has no hopes of seeing him again either. He doesn't expect to see the *Valiant* crossing by the breakwater. Jeremias will never again sing for Guma. It's Jeremias who says at night that "it's sweet to die in the sea." Now it will be a mad run. He has the wind behind him. The sloop almost capsizes in the maneuver of changing course. Now the wind drags the sloop along, throws water over it, soaks his hair, sings in his ears. The wind goes back and forth across the sloop. It puts out the lantern. The lights of the city, more and more distant, pass by swiftly. Now it's a run with no end, leaning completely to one side, clutching the tiller. Where is this wind dragging him? The rain wets his body, lashes his face. He can't make anything out in the darkness. Only the whistle of the *Canavieiras* is his direction. He could pass far away from it, he could run aground at Itaparica or onto some rock in the middle of the sea. No one had the courage to come out. Even Jeremias was astonished when he passed. And Jeremias is an old soldier. He's lived all alone there in the fort like a rat ever since he was discharged because of old age. He came to live there in the midst of the waters, in an abandoned fort, so as not to leave the cannons, the things that reminded him of barracks and arms. He followed his destiny to the end. In the same way Guma was following his, which was his sloop. He was in a headlong run. Maybe he would never arrive and tomorrow the men would look for his body. Old Francisco would engrave his name on his arm, tell about his madness to the other men on the docks. Rosa Palmeirão would forget about him and love another and think about a son. But in spite of that, the law of the docks had to be obeyed and his story would be an example for other times.

He can't hear the whistle of the ship. The lights of the city are almost invisible. In spite of his efforts the sloop has gone far off the course it should be following. It's much farther out to sea, the shores of Itaparica are nearby. He forces the rudder and continues his run, trying to orient himself. How long will it last, how many hours will it take? It's already getting to be time for it to end. Why doesn't the time for seeing Iemanjá come right now, since he can't find the *Canavieiras*?

He's much too young to die. He still wanted a fresh woman (just like Dona Dulce when he was in school) who would be only his. He wouldn't leave a son and his sloop would be broken up. He doesn't fear death, but he thinks it's still too soon to die. He wanted to die after having left a story that could be remembered on the waterfront. It was still too soon to die. It was still too soon to go with Dona Janaína. He still wasn't an *ogã* in her *candomblé*, he still hadn't sung her chants, he couldn't wear her green stone around his neck.

What he wears around his neck is the medal that Dona Dulce had given him. Dona Dulce will be sad when she finds out that he died. She doesn't understand their lives, their hard lives, alongside death all day and waiting for a miracle. Who knows, maybe it will come. That's why Guma doesn't want to die. Because on the day that miracle comes everything will be more beautiful, there won't be so much misery on the docks, a man won't risk his life for two hundred *milreis*.

He's back on the correct course. He can hear the ship whistling, calling. But a wave comes that's too strong and it pulls Guma away from the tiller. He swims toward the sloop, which is out of control, spinning in the wind. Maybe it's all over and he doesn't have a name to call at that moment. His moment of death hasn't come yet. Because *his woman* hasn't come yet. He swims desperately, reaches the side of the sloop, grabs the tiller, turns it toward the ship that can be seen in the distance. He fights against the wind, against the water, against his body that trembles with cold.

The run begins again. His teeth are clenched. He feels no fear. He wants to get it all over with once and for all. Close, very close by, the illuminated ship glows. The rain is falling heavily. The wind splits his sails, but he's already shouting, alongside the hull of the *Canavieiras:*

"A ladder!"

The sailors come running. They throw down a line, which is tied to the *Valiant*. Then it's the adventure of going from the sloop to the swinging boarding ladder. Twice he was about to fall, and then there would have been no rescue, he would have been crushed between sloop and ship.

He smiles. He's soaked and happy at the same time. On the docks they're probably thinking at that moment that he's dead, that his body is traveling with Iemanjá.

He goes up to the bridge, the Englishman turns the ship over to him. The men in the engine room start up the engines and the stokers build up the fires, the sailors steer. Guma is in command. He gives the orders. Only in that way can a man from the waterfront ever get to be captain of a ship. Only through the wiles of Iemanjá. It will be a singular night. Tomorrow neither the Englishman nor Mr. Godofredo will recognize him when he passes on the *Valiant*. No one will call him hero. Guma knows that. But he knows that it was ever thus and that only a miracle, as Dona Dulce hopes, can change that law.

Two hours later—the storm still dominates the city and the sea—the *Canavieiras* was docking. The sails of the *Valiant* were torn, its hull cracked from pounding against the ship, its rudder in pieces.

On the docks they say that João Pequeno never appeared again because the ship had found its way to port now. And from that day on they began to talk about Guma on the waterfront of Bahia.

# IEMANJÁ OF THE FIVE NAMES

No one on the docks has just one name. Everybody has a nickname too, or the name is shortened, or lengthened, or something is added that recalls a tale, a fight, a woman.

Iemanjá, who is mistress of the docks, of the sloops, of the lives of all of them, has five names, five sweet names that everybody knows. She is called Iemanjá, she has always been called that and it is her real name, as mistress of waters, lady of the oceans. Canoemen, however, like to call her Dona Janaína, and the blacks, who are her favorite children, who dance for her and fear her more than any others, call her Inaê, with devotion, or they make their entreaties to the Princess of Aiocá, queen of those mysterious lands hidden behind the blue line that separates them from other places. The women of the docks, however, who are simple and valiant, Rosa Palmeirão, women of the evening, married women, virgins awaiting their betrothed, call her Dona Maria, because Maria is a pretty name, it's even the prettiest of them all, the most venerated, and so they give it to Iemanjá as a gift, the way they take boxes of soap to her stone by the Dike. She is a siren, she is the mother-of-waters, the mistress of the sea, Iemanjá, Dona Janaína, Dona Maria, Inaê, Princess of Aiocá. She dominates those seas, she adores the moon she comes to see on cloudless nights, she loves black people's music. Every year the feast of Iemanjá is celebrated by the Dike and at Monte Serrat. Then they call her by all of her five names, give her all her titles, bear her gifts, sing for her.

The ocean is large, the sea is a road without end, waters

69

make up more than half the world, they are three-quarters of it, and all that belongs to Iemanjá. Where she lives, however, is in the stone by the Dike on the waterfront of Bahia or in her grotto in Monte Serrat. She could live in the cities of the Mediterranean, the China seas, California, the Aegean, the Gulf of Mexico. In ancient times she lived on the coasts of Africa, which they say is near the lands of Aiocá. But she came to Bahia to see the waters of the Paraguaçu River. And she stayed to live on the waterfront, near the Dike, in a stone that is sacred. There she combs her hair (beautiful slave girls come with combs of silver and ivory), hears the prayers of the women of the sea, unleashes storms, chooses the men she is to take on the bottomless journey to the depths of the sea. And it is there that her feast takes place, much more beautiful than all other processions in Bahia, more beautiful than all *macumbas*, because it belongs to the most powerful *orixás*, it belongs to the first ones, the ones from whom all others came. If it weren't too dangerous, one might even say that her feast is more beautiful than that of Oxolufã, Oxalá the Elder, the greatest and most powerful of *orixás*. Because the night of the feast of Iemanjá is a thing of beauty. On those nights the sea is of a color between blue and green, the moon is always in the sky, the stars accompany the lanterns on the sloops, Iemanjá slowly spreads her hair out toward the sea and there is nothing in the world as beautiful (sailors on big ships that travel all over always say) than the color that emerges from the mingling of Iemanjá's hair with the sea.

The *pai-de-santo* Anselmo was the priest and spokesman for sea people before Iemanjá. A *macumba* leader on the waterfront, he'd been a sailor before, had traveled to lands in Africa, where he'd learned the real language, the meaning of those festivals and saints. When he returned he left his ship immediately and stayed on the waterfront in the place of Agostinho, who had died. Now he was the one who presided over the feast of Iemanjá, who directed the *macumbas* on Monte Serrat, who, by order of Dona Janaína, cured illnesses, gave the sloops good winds, sent the frequent storms away. There was no one on that waterfront or in that great water world who didn't respect Anselmo, who had already traveled to Africa and could pray in the Nagô language. His white hair was enough of a signal for all the men from the docks and the canoes to take off their hats.

It wasn't that easy to belong to Pai Anselmo's *macumba* and it was necessary for a black man to be a good sailor in order to sit among the *ogãs* of Iemanjá, surrounded by the *feitas*, the possessed dancers. Guma, a light mulatto with long, dark hair, would soon sit in one of the chairs placed around the *pai-de-santo* in the *candomblé* chamber. Ever since he had brought in the *Canavieiras* on that stormy night his fame had gone from mouth to mouth, and it was proof that Iemanjá favored him. It wouldn't be long therefore before he would be sitting among the *ogãs*, surrounded by the *feitas*. At the next feast of Iemanjá he would already be wearing her stone (which is green and is found at the bottom of the sea) and would take part among the *ogãs* in the initiation of the *feitas*, the *iavôs*, who are the black priest-esses.

And along with him black Rufino would also wear the stone of Iemanjá. They would be dedicated together at the same time to the mistress of the sea, the woman with five names, mother of them all, who one day, only one day in all their lives, is also wife. Black Rufino even sang as with his strong arms he drove his cargo-laden canoe up the river:

> *"I'm called Ogum with good reason*
> *I won't deny what I am*
> *I'm the son of clear ocean waters*
> *Grandson of Iemanjá..."*

He was jet black but had come out of clear waters, Iemanjá was his grandmother, the mother of his father who'd been a sailor like his grandfather and the elder ones before, whose memory had been lost.

The feast of Iemanjá is drawing near. On that day Guma will go to ask for his wife, the one who looks like her and

will be a virgin and beautiful, dazzling the waterfront of Bahia, the Bay of All Saints. Because Rosa Palmeirão is already talking about leaving, about weighing anchor for
other lands. She'd hoped to have a son by that valiant young
man, a son she could rock in those arms of hers that were
accustomed to fighting, to whom she would sing lullabies
with those lips trained for curse words. But Rosa Palmeirão
had forgotten that it was too late for that now, that she'd
wasted her youth in fights, and all she had left was the tenderness she'd never used up, the wish to caress. And since
the son wouldn't be coming, she would go looking for trouble in other lands, drink cane liquor in other bars, travel over
the waters of other seas. But never before the feast of Iemanjá, because otherwise she wouldn't have a fair wind, she'd
find storms along her way.

That's why, since Rosa Palmeirão is going away, Guma
will remind Iemanjá that the time to give him what was
promised has arrived. In addition to a comb for her locks, he
will bring her as a gift a piece of the sail of the *Valiant*, the
sail that had been torn to shreds when he saved the *Canavieiras*.

The day of the feast of Iemanjá draws near. On that day
the waterfront will be empty, there won't be a canoe at sea, a
single sloop carrying cargo, a sailor who won't find some
way to leave his ship for a minute. Everybody will go to the
dwelling place of Dona Janaína, she of the five names.

> *"Iemanjá, come…*
> *Come from out of the sea…"*

That's what they sing on that night of Iemanjá. That place
there is where the Água dos Meninos market is, the biggest
in Bahia. Farther on, in Itapagipe, is the Firewood Dock,
the canoemen's port. And between the two the dwelling of
Iemanjá, in a sea stone. The sand holds the remains of sloop
hulls. Seashells of different colors gleam in the moonlight.
In the background the dimly lighted streets. Voices coming
from far off that sing:

*"Hail the Siren and her band.*
*The Siren's come to play on the sand..."*

It's the night of Iemanjá's feast. That's why people call her, for her to come and play on the sand. The grotto can be seen clearly in the moonlight, surrounded by Iemanjá's hair as it spreads out over the sea. If she doesn't come they will go out there to fetch her. Today is the night of her feast, the night for Janaína to play:

*"Siren of the sea, rise up today...*
*Siren of the sea who wants to play..."*

Iemanjá is playing in the sea. There was a time, the eldest still remember, when Iemanjá's fury was fearsome. In those days she didn't play. Canoes and sloops had no respite, they lived a life of suffering. Storms filled the harbor, lifted the river up over its banks. In those days even children, even young girls were carried out as gifts for Iemanjá. She led them down to the depths of the waters and their bodies never appeared again. Iemanjá was in her terrible years, she didn't want chants, melodies, music, bars of soap, or combs. She wanted people, living bodies. The wrath of Iemanjá was feared. They brought her children, they brought her maidens, a blind one was even offered and she went smiling (she would doubtless see beautiful things!), a child cried on the night they carried it off and shouted for its mother, its father, that it didn't want to die. That was on a feast night to Iemanjá too. Many years had passed now. That had been a terrible year, winter had destroyed half the sloops, rare were the canoes that resisted the south wind, and the wrath of Iemanjá had not gone away. Agostinho, the *macumba* priest who conducted the feast in those times, said that what Iemanjá wanted was human flesh. They took that child because she was the prettiest on the waterfront, she even looked like Janaína with her blue eyes. The storm ran over the docks and the waves washed the stone of Iemanjá. The sloops ran over the docks and the waves washed the stone of

Iemanjá. The sloops ran alongside, and they could all hear the screams of the child who was taken along blindfolded. It was a night of crime, and old Francisco still trembles when he tells the story. The police found out about everything, some people went to jail, Agostinho ran away, the child's mother went mad. Only then did Iemanjá's wrath cease. Her festival was prohibited, and for a long time it was replaced by the procession of the Good Jesus of Navigators. But those waters belonged to Iemanjá, and after a time her festival returned, her wrath had passed too, she wanted no more children or virgins. Only by chance would one be her slave girl, like the wife of that blind man whose story old Francisco knows.

Iemanjá is terrible like that because she is mother and wife. Those waters had been born from her on the day that her son possessed her. There aren't many on the docks who know the story of Iemanjá and Orungã, her son. But Anselmo knows it and so does old Francisco. They don't spend much time on that story, however, because it would unleash the wrath of Janaína. The fact of the matter was that Iemanjá had a son by Aganju, god of dry land. Orungã, the son, was made god of the air, of all that lay between earth and sky. Orungã circled about these lands, lived in this air, but his thoughts never lost the image of his mother, that beautiful queen of the waters. She was the most beautiful of all, and his desires were all for her. And one day she didn't resist and he raped her. Iemanjá fled and in the flight her breasts broke open and in that way these waters arose and also this Bay of All Saints, this Bahia. And from the womb fertilized by her son were born the most fearsome of *orixás*, those gods who send down lightning, storms, and thunder.

Thus Iemanjá is mother and wife. She loves the men of the sea as a mother when they are alive and suffer. But on the day they die it is as if they were her son Orungã, full of desires, wanting her body.

One day Guma heard that story from the mouth of old Francisco. And he remembered that his mother, too, had come one night and he had desired her. He was like Orungã, it was a suffering that was repeated. Maybe that was why Iemanjá loved him, watched over his trips on the sloop. That's why, so he wouldn't stay like Orungã, she had to give him a pretty woman, almost as pretty as Dona Janaína herself.

Today is Iemanjá's feast day. At the Dike, where she spends some time during the year, her festival is February 2. In Cabeceiras da Ponte, Mar Grande, Gameleira, Bom Despacho, and Amoreira her day is February 2 too, and on that day they celebrate her. In Monte Serrat, however, where her festival is even greater because it's held in her own dwelling in the Grotto of the Mother-of-Waters, she is celebrated on October 20. And the *pai-de-santo* priests come from the Dike, from Amoreira, from Bom Despacho, from Gameleira, from all over the island of Itaparica. And that year even Pai Deusdedit came from Cabeceiras da Ponte to take part in the initiation of the *feitas* of Iemanjá.

The white sand is black now from the feet that tread it. It's the people of the sea arriving, calling their queen. They are all subjects of the Princess of Aiocá, they are all exiled in other lands and that's why they live on the sea, trying to reach the lands of their queen. The chant crosses the sands, crosses the sea, the canoes and sloops, the city that moves in the distance, and it surely must arrive in those unknown lands where she is hiding:

> *"Iemanjá, come...*
> *Come from out of the sea..."*

It's a huge human mass that moves over the sand. The church of Monte Serrat can be seen up above, but it's not there that those arms full of tattoos are aimed. It's toward the sea, the sea from where Iemanjá, the mistress of those lives, will come. Today is the day for her to play on the sand, for her to celebrate her wedding to sailors, for her to receive the gifts the rough bridegrooms bring her, to receive the greetings of those who will soon be their priestesses. Today is her day to rise up, spread her hair over the sand, play

with them, promise them fair winds, full cargoes, beautiful
women. They call her:

> *"Iemanjá, come...*
> *Come from out of the sea..."*

She will come from out of the sea with her long hair mysterious in color. She will come with her hands full of
seashells and her face smiling. And then she will play with
them, she will enter the body of a black woman and be just
like the black people, the canoemen, the sloop masters, a
woman like others on the waterfront, possessed by them, the
wife of those men. The dark docks of Bahia, dimly lighted
by electric bulbs, full of nostalgic music, will disappear
then, and they will be in the lands of Aiocá, where Nagô is
spoken and where all those who died in the sea can be found.

But Iemanjá won't come out just like that, with simple
chants. They have to go fetch her, bring her presents. And
all those people get into the sloops. The canoes are filled to
the gunwales, Guma's sloop can barely move, Master Manuel goes along hugging Maria Clara, with whom he had
started living a few days before, women sing aloud, the
moon lights everything up. A thousand lanterns fill the sea
with stars. Guma goes on the *Valiant* with black Rufino. Old
Francisco is singing too, and Rosa Palmeirão carries an expensive pillow where Iemanjá can rest her head.

The procession cuts through the sea. The voices rise up
and take on a mysterious sound because they come from the
boats and the canoes and are lost in the immense sea where
Iemanjá is resting. Women weep, women carry letters and
gifts, all have a favor to ask of the Mother-of-Waters. They
dance on board the sloops and look like ghosts, those bodies
of women twirling, men rowing rhythmically, that barba-
rous music that crosses the sea.

They surround the Grotto of the Mother-of-Waters. Iemanjá's hair extends over the blue of the sea far below the
moon. The women shake their gifts, recite their requests
(Don't let my man get caught in a storm... We've got two

children to raise, my holy Janaína...) and they look with wide eyes to see if they reach bottom. Because if they float it's because Iemanjá hasn't accepted the gift, and then misfortune will weigh over that house.

Now the Mother-of-Waters will come with them. She received gifts, she heard requests, she heard black songs. And the sloops make ready to return. That's when the cries of an animal come whinnying from the beach. And by the light of the moon those on the sloops and in the canoes make out the shape of a black horse on the sand. That was the promise, that was the great promise for Iemanjá. The horse has empty eyes, he can't see the sea in front of him. And the men push him. He's black, jet black, his tail shiny, his mane full. He enters the sea, he's a gift for Iemanjá. Mounted on him she will ride through her lands in the waters. Mounted on the black horse she will run through her seas, will come to glimpse the moon. The animal is shoved into the water. The men come in two canoes and guide him, because he is blind. They emptied his eyes with a branding iron, they marked him for Janaína. And they release him close by the Grotto, and the women then repeat their requests (Let my man leave that bitch of a Ricardina and come back to me...) and the procession returns. The horse struggled, swam aimlessly with his lightless eyes, and finally went to Iemanjá. Now she is riding him through the stormy nights, passing the small ports on her black horse, commanding winds, lightning, and thunder.

They get out of the sloops. Iemanjá comes with them. It's the night of her festival and she's coming to dance at the *candomblés* of Itapagipe. Even Deusdedit, the *pai-de-santo* from Cabeceiras da Ponte, came for that feast of Inaê. She comes with them, galloping on the horse they had given her today. She comes through the air, near the moon, and mounted on her black horse she doesn't even fear meeting her son Orungã, who had raped her.

And the procession continues, slowly and rhythmically, rocking like a sloop on the waves. The wind that passes carries a smell of low tide and an echo of savage sounds toward the sleeping city.

The sound of the instruments echoes through the peninsula of Itapagipe. The musicians are excited too, like all attending this *macumba* of Pai Anselmo in honor of Iemanjá. It's been months since these black women, who are *feitas* today, had been initiated. First they gave them all a bath with the sacred leaves, shaved their heads, their armpits, their pubises, so the saint can penetrate them more easily, and then came the *efun*. They had their heads and their faces too painted with bright colors. Then they received Iemanjá, who penetrated them through the head or the armpits or the pubis.

She only penetrates through the pubis when the black woman is a virgin and untouched, and it's as if she were choosing her for her slave girl, to comb her hair and tickle her body.

Then they spent all those months in seclusion. They knew no men, nor did they see any of the activities on the streets or at sea. They lived only for Iemanjá. Today is the day of the great festival when they will become real *feitas*, real priestesses of Iemanjá. They dance madly, shimmy, go completely out of joint, they dance even better than Rosa Palmeirão, who has been a *feita* for twenty years.

The mother of the temple-plot sings the chants of Iemanjá:

> "*A ôdê rêssê*
> *ô ki é Iêmanjá*
> *Akóta guê lêguê a ôio*
> *Êró fi rilá.*"

The *feitas* dance as if they had suddenly gone mad. The *ogãs*—and Guma and Rufino are among them now—move their shoulders as if rowing canoes. In the midst of the feast that has possessed all of them now (Iemanjá has been among them for a long time, resting in the body of Ricardina) Rufino nudged Guma:

"Look who's staring at you…"

Guma looks, but he can't make out the one Rufino is talking about:

"That dark girl…"

"That pretty one?"

"She hasn't taken her eyes off you…"

"She's not even looking…"

The shoulders move in an always regular cadence. Iemanjá greets Guma, who is protected by her. The mother of the temple-plot sings:

> *"Ô yiná ará wê*
> *Ô yiná marabô*
> *Mabô xá rê nun*
> *Mabô xá rê wá."*

They all dance madly. But Guma doesn't take his eyes off the people there. There's no doubt that it's the woman that Iemanjá has sent him. She has long, wet-looking hair, her light eyes are water-colored, her lips red. She's almost as beautiful as Janaína herself, and she's young, quite young, because her breasts barely show under her bright-red chintz dress. The dance dominates the room, Iemanjá dances more than any, only she isn't dancing, she only looks at Guma from time to time, with those eyes made of water, with her long, loose hair, her breasts still in the process of being born. Iemanjá has sent him his woman, the one he asked for when still a boy, the day his mother appeared. And he has no doubt at all that he will possess her, that she will sleep on his sloop, will be his companion on trips. And he sings to Iemanjá of the five names, mother of the men on the waterfront, their wife too, who comes to them in the bodies of other women who appear suddenly like that at her *macumbas*.

Where could she have come from? He looked for her when the festival was over, but he couldn't find her anywhere. He went after Rufino, who was already on his way down to the Beacon of the Stars with his guitar:

"Who's that girl?"

"What girl?"

"The one you said was looking at me."

"Wasn't she? Every look was like a spotlight..."

"Where did you meet her?..."

"I laid eyes on her today for the first time. But she's something special. Did you get a load of her keel?"

Guma felt enraged:

"Don't talk that way about a girl you don't know."

Rufino laughed:

"I'm not saying anything bad... She's got a nice behind..."

"Go find out who she is and tell me."

"You're getting to like her, eh?"

"Can't I?"

"If Palmeirão finds out, you're sunk..."

Guma laughed. They went into the Beacon of the Stars. Rosa Palmeirão was drinking, one glass after another:

"Now I'm going away, my good people, this place here hasn't got any gate to hold me back..."

Master Manuel, who was drinking with Maria Clara, very proud of his love, seeing Guma come in, shouted to Rosa:

"Somebody's going to miss you, black girl..."

"Anybody who likes me will come with me..." And she smiled at Guma.

But Guma sat down away from her. He already felt he belonged to someone else, it was as if Rosa Palmeirão had gone away a long time ago. Rosa came over to him:

"Are you sad today?"

"Aren't you going away?"

"I'll stay if you want..."

No answer came. He was looking at the night that was covering the docks. Rosa Palmeirão knew what that meant. She'd gone through the same thing with many men, she'd even given some a slap. She was old, she wasn't the woman for a young man like that anymore. Her body was still well-made, but it wasn't the body of a young woman anymore, it was the body of a failed mother. They remembered now.

For the last time the image of his prostituted mother bothered Guma. Rosa Palmeirão's big breasts, the dagger between them, reminded him of his mother's breasts, also worn-out but full of love. But from here on a new image presented itself before his eyes. It was the scarcely visible breasts of the girl who'd been at the *candomblé,* those eyes of water, limpid, clear, so different from Rosa Palmeirão's. That girl who had no ABC ballad, no history, who'd looked at him without hiding anything she felt...

"You're an important man on the waterfront..." Rosa Palmeirão said. "Ever since the *Canavieiras* job ..."

The girl must have known that he was Guma, the one who, all alone on his sloop, had saved a ship full of people on a stormy night. And he smiled.

Rosa Palmeirão smiled too. She would go away and never love again. Now all she wanted was to raise hell in what was left of her life. The dagger from her breast, the razor from her skirt would flash, her well-made body would disappear. And if she came back to her port, weary of riots and fights, maybe she could arrange for a child, some woman's abandoned son, and she would tell him stories of the lives of those men and she would teach him to be valiant, as a sailor should be. She would raise him as a son, as she would have raised that son of hers who'd been born dead, the son of her first man, the mulatto Rosalvo. She'd gone off with him quite young, because love knows no age. She'd gone off into the world with the curse of her old mother. He was a vagrant, a guitar player, traveling free on sloops, playing at festivals in all the towns around the bay. Rosa Palmeirão loved him very much, and she was only fifteen years old when she met him. She suffered from hunger, money was something he didn't have, she suffered beatings on Rosalvo's cane-liquor days, she even suffered when he went with other women. But when she found out that the baby had been born dead because he'd given her that bitter potion, that he didn't want it to live, then she became a different person, she became the Rosa Palmeirão of dagger and razor and left him dead beside his guitar. Everything had been false with him, his love songs, his looks, his soft way of speaking. He was only surprised when she stabbed him in bed. It was to pay for the child he'd killed. Then the months in jail, the trial, the man who said she'd been drunk. She was acquitted. And she became valiant, because there was no other way for her, that reputation had clung to her. Many years had passed, many men too. And only with Guma had she come back to the wish of having another son, a child who would wave his little arms and call her Mama. That's why she loved Guma so much, the one who no longer loves her because she's grown old. He hadn't given her a son either, but it was her fault, because she's grown old and useless. So she would go away, since he didn't love her any-more.

They left the Beacon of the Stars. A fine rain was falling. He held her around the waist and thought she deserved a night of love because of all the goodness she'd shown him. A farewell night, a last night under the cloudy sky, on the sea curled by the rain. They walked toward the *Valiant*. He helped her up, lay down beside her. And he reached over to make love. But Rosa Palmeirão stopped him (Would she pull out the razor from under her skirt? Or the dagger from her breast?) and she spoke:

"I'm going away, Guma…"

The rain was slowly wetting them and no music was coming from the sea.

"You'll get married one of these days, a bride will come for you… Pretty, like you deserve… But I want you to give me one thing…"

"What's that?"

"I want a son, but I'm too old now…"

"Come on…"

The rain was heavier now.

"I'm too old, your son won't stick in me anymore… But you're going to get married, and when you're married and have a son I'm coming back here. I'm an old woman with white hair, I'm too old now, Guma, I swear I won't fight with anyone anymore, I won't use any weapons, I won't raise hell.''

Guma looks at her as she seems to be someone else, pleading with her deep-sea eyes fastened on him, the loving eyes of a mother:

"I won't fight anymore... I want you to arrange a place for this old woman in your wife's house... She won't know anything about the two of us. I don't want anything else either, I won't fight with her. I want to help bring up your son, as if I'd had you... I'm old enough to be your mother... Will you let me?''

The stars are shining in the sky now, the moon has appeared too and soft music is coming from the sea. Rosa Palmeirão caresses the face of her son. That was the night of the feast of Iemanjá, she of the five names.

# A SHIP DROPPED ANCHOR IN PORT

A ship dropped anchor in port and Rosa Palmeirão went off on it. Guma watched the woman as she waved a handkerchief from third class. She was going off to the adventures that would be her last. When she came back she would find a child to care for, someone whose grandmother she would be. When she was already far off she was still waving her handkerchief, and the men on the pier answered with their farewells. Someone behind Guma spoke:

"A crazy doll, that one... All she does is wander around..."

Guma walked along the shore. Night would soon be falling and a cargo of merchandise was waiting for him to carry to Cachoeira, but he had no great urge to leave the docks, cross the bay. It had been several days since the feast of Iemanjá, and all he could think about was finding the girl who'd looked at him. He hadn't been able to find anything out about her, because there'd been a lot of people at Pai Anselmo's festival that night, people who'd come from far away, as far away as the farms in Conceição da Feira. He went through the streets near the waterfront, examining every house, and he couldn't find her. No one knew where she'd come from, who she was, what she did. She certainly didn't live on the waterfront, because everybody knows everybody else there. Black Rufino couldn't find out anything about her either. But Guma doesn't lose heart. He knows that he'll find her.

A cargo of merchandise is waiting for him. After it's been stowed on the sloop, he'll leave for Cachoeira. He'll go up the river again. Risky as the life of a sloop master may be, going up and down the river, crossing the bay no longer seems adventurous. It's an everyday thing, something that doesn't scare anybody. So Guma isn't even thinking about the trip. He's thinking that he'd give anything to find the woman from Iemanjá's feast again. Now that Rosa had gone away he was free to love. He goes along the shore whistling softly. In the market they're singing. It's a group of sailors and stevedores. A mulatto is in the middle, dancing and singing:

> "*I'm mulatto and I don't deny it*
> *Oh, Lord, give me pity today!*
> *Even if I wanted to deny it,*
> *My hair would give me away.*"

The others are clapping their hands. Their lips are open in smiles, their bodies move in the rhythm of an *embolada*. The mulatto sings:

> "*Even if I tried to be white*
> *my hair would incriminate me…*"

Guma goes over to the group. The first person to see him was Rodolfo, all elegant in navy-blue broadcloth, who hadn't been around for months. Rodolfo was sitting on a crate and laughing at the mulatto who was singing. In the group were Xavier, Maneca One-Hand, Jacques, Severiano. Old Francisco, sitting in the rear, was sucking on his pipe.

Rodolfo, as soon as he saw Guma, waved his hand:

"I've got to talk to you about something…"

"Fine…"

The mulatto had finished singing now and was smiling at the group. He was panting from his dance but he had a look of triumph on his face. It was Jesuíno, a canoeman from the *Sea Siren*, a punt that went between Bahia and Santo Amaro. He gave Guma a laugh:

"Hi there, brother…"

Maneca One-Hand saw the greeting, snorted:

"It's no use talking to Guma, Jesu... The kid's off course..."

"He's what?"

"He doesn't know where he's going. He's seen a vision..."

The others laughed. Maneca went on:

"They say that when a man's nuts about a woman he's as good as shipwrecked. Do you know that he almost put the *Valiant* on top of the big reef?"

Guma was getting angry. He never liked teasing, but this time, he didn't know why, he was full of anger. If Maneca One-Hand hadn't been crippled... But Severiano and Jacques intervened:

"What's eating you?" Jacques asked.

"Some old bag with no future who's shedding her shell..." Severiano answered with that loud laugh of his.

Rufino saw that Guma was going to fight and said:

"Let's cut this out right now, you guys. Let everybody mind his own business."

"Are you the woman's partner, man?" Severiano laughed even more. They laughed all around. But they didn't laugh much, because Guma was already on top of Severiano. Jacques went to separate them, but Rufino grabbed him:

"Let it be man to man..."

"Come off it, you're no man... You canoe fairy..."

And he charged the black man. Rufino leaped back and sang:

> "*Sissies who want to be men*
> *Should stop acting like a hen...*"

He avoided Jacques' blow, spun his legs, and the boy was laid out on the ground. Guma was hitting Severiano. The others were looking on and not understanding completely. Severiano got free and pulled his knife. Old Francisco shouted:

"He's going to kill Guma..."

Severiano backed up against the wall of the Market, knife in hand, and shouted to Guma:

"Send Rosa to fight me, you're not man enough."

Guma leaped, but Severiano's foot caught him in the pit of the stomach. He fell curled up. And the other one leaped on top of him with the knife. That was when Rodolfo, who'd been whistling the *embolada* the black man had been singing a moment before, intervened, grabbed the canoeman by the wrist until he dropped the knife. Guma had already got up. He punched Severiano until he laid him out:

"He's only a man when he's got a piece of steel in his hand..."

Now Rufino was singing in triumph:

> *"Fat-mouthed yellow halfbreed*
> *Face made of manioc mush*
> *Put shame where your mouth ought to be,*
> *Shout my name in the wild underbrush."*

The group broke up slowly. Some men carried Severiano to his canoe, Jacques went home swearing revenge. Guma and Rufino went to the sloop. Guma had already jumped on board the boat when he heard Rodolfo's shout:

"Where are you going?"

He turned:

"If it hadn't been for you I would have been a dead man..."

"Knock it off..."

Rodolfo remembered:

"It was even like that time we mixed it up when we were kids. Except this time I was on your side..."

He took off his polished shoes, went into the mud by the sloop moorings: "I want a couple of words with you..."

"What is it?"

"You're not busy now?"

"No..." Guma was sure he wanted money.

"Sit down, then, while I talk."

"So long, then," and Rufino went away.

Rodolfo ran his hand over his smoothed-down head. He smelled of cheap hair lotion. Guma was thinking about where he could have spent those last few months. In some other city? In jail for some robbery? He wasn't a good sort, they all said. He cheated at cards, swindled, once in Pitangueiras he'd stuck a knife in the chest of a man when he was asking for money. It was his first arrest. But this time Rodolfo wasn't broke, he hadn't come to borrow any money.

"Are you going out today?"

"I'm carrying to Cachoeira..."

"Much of a hurry?"

"Yes, I am. Some merchandise Mr. Rangel had in his warehouse. He wants it there in time for carnival..."

"This is going to be a wild carnival..."

Guma was stowing the bundles in the hold:

"Keep on talking, I can hear you."

Rodolfo found it even better like that, it was easier. That way he didn't have to look at Guma and could speak right out.

"It's a long story. I better start from the beginning..."

"Well, keep on talking..."

"Do you remember my father?"

"Old Concôrdia? Sure I remember... He had a stand in the Market."

"That's right. But you don't remember my mother. She died when I was born."

He stood looking into the water. He saw Guma's shape moving about in the hold.

"I'm listening."

"Well, let me tell you: old Concôrdia was never married to her..."

Guma looked up with surprise. He saw Rodolfo looking out over the water with thoughtful eyes. Why had he come to tell him that?"

"His real wife lived in the upper city, on a street up there. When he was dying he told me... You can see I didn't do anything, I didn't go to see his wife since I had no business there. I stayed here with that shell of a sloop the old man left me, then I went off to a different life, I don't like the one here on the docks.''

Guma came up after having stowed the cargo of merchandise. He sat down across from Rodolfo:

"It really is a rotten life... But what can you do?"

"That's right... I left and I fell in up there, rolling from one side to the other."

He lowered his head:

"You know very well that I've done time... Well, the other day I was calmly going through life, I'd picked up some change, a favor for a colonel from Bonfim... That was when I ran into my sister..."

"You had a sister?"

"I didn't know about it either. The old man forgot to talk about a daughter. He only told me to look up his wife, that she already knew and would raise me like she'd had me herself."

"And she had a daughter..."

"I ran into her that day. She'd already been looking all over for me, since she knew I existed. She'd been looking for me ever since her mother died a year ago."

"And where'd she been staying all that time?"

"She was with an aunt and uncle, relatives."

"Relatives of old Concôrdia?"

"No. Her mother's. A trick, how should I know."

Guma just didn't understand what all that had to do with him, the reason Rodolfo was telling him that whole story.

"Well, I'll tell you, friend. The girl won me over. She said she's going to keep tabs on me, talk to me a little. But I'll say one thing: God, she's as fine a girl as I've ever seen... She's younger than me, eighteen. Straighten me out, she won't straighten me out, I've lost any shame I had. When people fall into this kind of life they never get out..."

He paused, lighted a cigarette:

"They're not used to working anymore..."

Guma began to whistle softly. He felt sorry for Rodolfo now. They said such bad things about him on the waterfront. They said he wasn't good for anything, a bad apple, that he was a thief. He'd got into it and now he couldn't get out, not even with a good sister helping him.

"She's way above me, I can see, I feel sorry for her. She tells me I'm going to end up bad and she's right."

He made a broad gesture with his hands, as if pushing away all that conversation, and explained:

"Well, my sister wants me to take you there..."

"Wants me to come there?" Guma was startled.

"That's it... Those relatives of hers came in on the *Canavieiras* the day you went out to get the bugger. That was a real man thing you did. They were traveling to see if they could set something up in Ilhéus. They couldn't do anything and they came back here. They've got a store on the Rua Rui Barbosa. She came all the way in third class, she thought it was all over. She wants to thank you..."

"That's foolish. Anybody would have done it. I was lucky the sea wasn't too rough..."

"She saw you the other day, she came only to see you. On the feast day of Janaína. She was at old Anselmo's *candomblé.*"

"A dark girl with straight hair?"

"That's the one..."

Guma didn't know what to say. Startled, he looked around at Rodolfo, at the sloop, at the sea. His urge was to sing, shout, jump for joy. Rodolfo asked:

"What's got into you?"

"Nothing. Now I know who she is..."

"That's right. Be ready to go there when you get back. I'll tell her that you've promised to come."

Guma was looking angrily at the sloop, the cargo of goods. He would have liked to go that very night:

"O.K., I'll come."

"So long, then. Take it easy..."

Rodolfo jumped down, carrying his shoes in his hand. Guma shouted:

"What's her name?"

"Lívia!"

* * *

Guma spread the sails of the sloop, weighed anchor, and took advantage of the wind. Master Manuel in his *Sailor Without a Port* was passing by the breakwater. Nobody in those days could go faster in a sloop than Master Manuel. Guma looked at the *Sailor Without a Port*. It was going fast, its sail open in the wind. Night had fallen completely. Guma lighted his pipe, lighted the lantern on the *Valiant*, and the sloop slipped through the water.

Near Itaparica he caught up with Master Manuel's sloop:

"Do you want to race, Manuel?"

"Where are you headed?"

"Maragogipe first, from there to Cachoeira."

"Then we can race as far as Maragogipe."

"I'll go for five..."

"And ten more if you'll take it," shouted black Antônio Balduíno, who was riding in Manuel's sloop.

"You're on."

And the sloops left together, cutting the calm water. On the *Sailor Without a Port*, Maria Clara was singing. Right there Guma realized he would lose the bet. There's no wind that can resist a song when it's beautiful. And the one Maria Clara is singing is most beautiful. Master Manuel's sloop comes close. The *Valiant* goes along listlessly because Guma is all caught up in the song. The lights of Maragogipe are visible on the river bank. The *Sailor Without a Port* passes him, Guma tosses the fifteen *milreis* over, Master Manuel shouts:

"Have a good trip."

He goes along happily, because he's won another race and his fame is established once more. Guma, too, is famous on the waterfront. He's a good sloop master, a firm hand on the tiller, and courageous like no other. On the night of the *Canavieiras* nobody wanted to go out, only he had the courage. Not even Master Manuel wanted to go out. Nor Xavier, who'd had a disappointment in life. Only he went. From then on his fame has run up and down the waterfront. He's one of those people who will leave a story behind, things that other people will reflect on.

The sloop runs through the soft night of the river. It goes into the great bend by Maragogipe. Guma is happy. Her name is Lívia. He never knew a woman with that name. When she's with him Master Manuel will lose all their races, because like Maria Clara she'll sing those old waterfront songs. Iemanjá had heard him, she'd sent him his woman.

There's a song on the docks that tells how unhappy the life of a sailor's wife is. It also says a sailor's heart is as change-able as the wind, like ships that don't stay in the same port. But all ships have the name of their port on their stern. They may go to others, they may travel for years, but they never forget their port, they'll come back to it someday. The same with the heart of sailors. They never forget the woman who is theirs alone. Xavier, who's had so many women off the streets, never forgot the one who called him Black Owl and ran away pregnant one night. Guma, too, will never forget Lívia, that Lívia whom he has scarcely seen. He reaches Maragogipe.

The man is already waiting for him on the bridge. They settle over the cargo of cigars that the sloop is to pick up on the way back. Guma has a drink in the bar next door and sails off with the *Valiant* again.

He has to travel fast here. This is where the white horse appears. For so many years that everybody lost count, the white horse has run without stopping. Nobody knows why he runs like that through those woods alongside the river. The ruins of old feudal castles, ruined plantations, belong to the white horse today, the frightened horse who runs. Any-one who sees him won't be able to leave the place. It's true that by preference he appears during the month of May, which is the month for his running. Guma goes along with his sloop, and even though he doesn't want to, he peers into those woods where the specter reigns.

They say it's a soul in torment, an evil plantation owner who killed men, worked his animals until they fell dead. Now he's become a white horse and he runs like that along the river bank paying for what he did. He carries a heavy

load the way his horses did. And the straps of the load creak
as it rides through the woods. When he passes even the
ground trembles, even the flesh of a tortoise. Those who see
him can't leave the place. And he will only cease running
through those lands that had been his plantation when someone feels pity for him and takes the load off his back, ham-
pers full of stones for the construction of his castle. He's
been running like that for many years.

The noise that Guma hears is the noise of the white horse.
Today Guma would like to go into the woods and free the
master from his slavery. Guma is happy. The sloop runs
along the river. It goes swiftly, pursued by the sound made
by the hooves of the frightened horse. It goes swiftly too because he wants to return tomorrow, he wants to return to his
port to see Lívia.

The trip never seemed so long. He still has a lot to do,
however. Drop his cargo in Cachoeira, come back to load
up in Maragogipe, go down to Bahia. A long trip for someone anxious to return. It won't be long before she'll be on
the sloop with him and will sing so he can make the *Valiant*
win all its races. For that very reason he has to go faster, because the trip takes a long time, two days.


They greet Guma on all sides. The bar is overflowing
with people. The docks of Cachoeira are always full of people, boats come from everywhere, today there's a Baiana
Line ship moored to the bridge. It will leave around three in
the morning, and that's why the crew isn't sleeping, they're
all in the bar, drinking cane liquor, kissing women. Guma
sits down with a group and orders a drink. A blind man is
playing the guitar by the door. The women laugh a lot, they
laugh even when there's no reason to, just to please. One,
however, is complaining about a sailor's life:

"It's all so rotten... Miserable. They don't make nothing. Not even enough to eat on."

They tell Guma about the brawl there was the night before
between some canoemen and some town boys. It was in a
whorehouse. The boys were drunk, one of them wanted to

go into the room of a woman who was with Traíra, a canoe-man on the Maria da Graça. He began to put his foot in the door. Traíra got up, opened the door suddenly, and the guy fell inside. Then he got up, began to call names, and shouted that the woman was his, that that "dirty nigger" should get out if he didn't want his face cut in two. There were more than six boys, they laughed and hollered for Traíra to get out right there, if not they'd beat him up. The blood was rising to Traíra's head, he tangled with the guy:

"He was one against six... He couldn't have won except for a miracle from heaven," explained Josué, a fat black man. "He fought like a man, he came out of it beaten up but with honor. That's when the folks got together, a handful of men, and went over there, a real mess... The kids ran like mad. One even hid under a woman's bed..."

They laughed merrily. Guma laughed too:

"Good job... To teach them to behave themselves."

"You don't know the best of it. They all work in the different businesses. Today there was a hellish buzz-buzz. There was talk in corners like nothing you ever heard. Like females, a hellish whispering. All tangled up, and since they all belong to a military academy they have around here, there's talk that today after drill at the school, they're going to wait for the folks at the whorehouse."

"They're looking for a fight..."

"They think that putting on a uniform makes a man out of you," an albino laughed loudly.

"We'll be going to the house in a while. You come with all the people."

Guma made a negative sign with his head. On any other occasion he would have been the first to go, he would have been glad to go, because he never turned down a brawl. But now he wanted to be on the sloop, listening to any song at all that might be coming from the sea, thinking about Lívia.

"What? You're not coming?" Josué was surprised. "Well, I didn't think that of you. A brave buddy."

"It's not my kettle of fish," Guma tried to explain.

"Who said that? You're not a sailor, then?"

Guma saw there was no way out. If he didn't go, nobody would ever shake his hand again on the waterfront:

"The one who said that isn't around anymore. I'm in."

"Just now I was wondering..."

In a while Traíra arrived, already a touch drunk. He was greeted with shouts.

"Hey, Traíra! A real man!"

Traíra bowed:

"A good evening to all. And long live sailoring..."

Guma only knew him vaguely. He almost never went to Bahia, he went to the ports around the bay more often, carrying tobacco from one place to another. A reddish mulatto, ant-colored, he had a well-kept little mustache and a shaved head. Josué introduced him to Guma:

"This here is Guma, a real brave black man."

"We've already met," Traíra said.

He was smiling with his mouth open, a toothpick in one corner. He was wearing a striped shirt and bending over in a comical way:

"I already heard tell of you... Wasn't it you?"

"It was him, yes. He got into a little boat, he cast off in a storm like the end of the world, and he brought in the *Canavieiras.*"

"Well, today we've got a little game for a brave man."

"Josué was telling me about it..."

"First it was just me. They broke me, they almost ran me on the rocks. Then the winds changed."

"They left them like that..." And Josué made a mysterious gesture with his hand, opening and closing it, then dropping the closed fist on the table. It meant they'd crushed the boys.

"Now they're going around looking to stir things up. They say they're all going there..."

A noise of rhythmic steps came from the street. It was the squadron passing. They heard:

"By the left flank, march!"

And the noise of the feet scraping the ground. Josué ordered more cane liquor.

Traíra suggested:

"Shall we be on our way, people? If not, we'll be late, they say people were running." They tossed some coins onto the table and left. There were around twelve of them. The sailors from the Baiana Line ship didn't go because they had to be back on board, the ship sailed at dawn. One of them was regretful:

"Damn it, missing something like that. And me who's itching for a good fight... Rotten luck..."

Chatting, they left for the street of women. They were talking about different things, it was as if they'd already forgotten about the brawl. They were telling stories about seafood dishes, a skinny fellow was telling an endless tale about a *muqueca* he'd eaten at a friend's house in São Félix. Traíra was listening to everything all hunched over, the shell of his shaved head gleaming as they passed under a street light. But when they got to the street of women they began to shout:

"Here we come."

The people who passed looked at them startled. It was a strange group. From a distance it could be seen that they were sea people, for they were coming with that long, unsteady step of people who live on board ships. Their bodies wavered as if they were catching a strong wind. A young boy, sixteen maybe, said to his older companion:

"Here come some sailors. Let's get out of here."

The other one put on a pose, blew out some cigarette smoke:

"What's the matter with you? Aren't sailors just people? I'm not afraid, I'm not."

They stayed, watching. An old man passed mumbling:

"Where are the police?... A bunch of bums. An honest man's not safe anymore," and he looked with nostalgia at the women leaning out the windows.

The group passed by the boys. The one who was making a pose blew smoke that went right into Josué's face:

"Was that on purpose, you scum?"

It hadn't been. The boy explained in a quavering voice.

His companion backed him up. Josué glared at them. The group stopped farther along.

"You're not lookouts for the others?"

"Your people are leaving you behind. We haven't got anything to do with this, boss."

"I'm nobody's boss. Don't get fresh."

Traíra shouted to Josué:

"Hurry up and whack him and let's go, for God's sake. We're late."

With that the boy begged:

"Don't hit me, please, for the love of God. I didn't do anything."

Josué lowered his hand:

"Then beat it out of my sight."

The boys took off. Guma asked Josué:

"What was the matter?"

"Nothing. The kids were almost scared to death..."

They went up to one of the houses. From inside came a fat mulatto woman, hips swinging:

"What is it you want?"

Josué took her by the chin:

"How goes it, little mama?"

"The devil's mama, not yours. What did you all come here to do? Brawl like yesterday? The one who had to deal with the police afterwards was me. Go get on your way..."

"Come off it, Tibéria. The folks only came to kid around a little with the girls. Can't people come into a woman's house?"

The madam looked at them suspiciously:

"I know what you want. You only know how to raise hell. You think people's lives are going too good, so you want to arrange a rash for them to scratch..."

"The folks want to have a few beers, Tibéria."

They were entering. In the living room the women around the table were staring, frightened. One of the group said, turning to Guma:

"Do they think we're monsters? Or souls from the other world?"

A blond woman, showing her age, spoke to Traíra:

"Are you coming back to raise some more hell, you bum? May the Dirty One carry you off. Today I had to go to the police station…"

"I only came to finish yesterday's lovemaking, Lulu."

They sat down at the table. The beer came out. There were only five women. Tibéria warned:

"There aren't enough women for all of you. Only enough for five…"

"The rest can go to other houses," Traíra proposed.

"But first we're going to have a beer together," and Josué pounded on the table, urgently calling for beer. Then some of them went to other houses. They would come out as soon as they heard the soldiers from the military academy and would surround Tibéria's house, waiting for the riot to begin. Of the twelve the only ones left around the table were Traíra, Josué, the skinny mulatto, a guy who had a scar on his lip, and Guma, with whom Josué, now completely drunk, was huddling:

"You don't know what a good friend I am… On the waterfront nobody says anything bad about you in front of me."

The one with the cut on his lip said:

"I knew your father. They say he knocked off a…"

Guma didn't answer. A woman brought in a phonograph. Josué dragged a little mulatto girl off to her room. Traíra went with the old blond. Tibéria counted the bottles of beer that had been drunk. The one with the scar dropped his head on the table. A woman came over to him:

"What about me? Don't I get a man?"

The one with the scar was almost out. The skinny mulatto said:

"I came for the fight. But now that I'm here…" And he went off with the other woman.

The one that fell to Guma was a dark young girl. She couldn't have been in the business very long. In the room she began to get undressed right away:

"Will you buy me a cognac, sweety?"

"O.K...."

"Tibéria! Bring a cognac."

But she was already in her slip when she took in a glass at the door that she opened a little. She drank it in one swallow:

"Want one?"

He moved his lips in a "No, thanks." She lay down on her back:

"What are you waiting for there?" (Guma was sitting at the foot of the bed.) "Don't you want to?"

Guma took off his shoes and jacket. She spoke:

"I've got the feeling that you people came here for something else."

"No, this is what we came for."

A candle lighted the room. She explained that the bulb had burned out, "the electrical service in Cachoeira is miserable..." Guma, stretched out on the bed, was looking at the woman who was speaking. She was still quite young, but it wouldn't be long before she was old. His mother had lived a life like that. It's an awful lot, this. He asked the woman:

"What's your name?"

"Rita," she turned toward him. "Rita Maria da Encarnação."

"Pretty. A long name. But you don't come from here, do you?"

Rita made a face:

"No way... I'm here because..." She finished the sentence with a vague gesture and a sad look. "I'm from the Capital."

"Bahia, eh?"

"Where else? Or do you think I'm a greenhorn?"

"I'm thinking you're pretty young to be tied up in this life..."

"Bad luck doesn't have any age."

"How old are you?"

The shadows from the candle were sketching phantoms in

the room with adobe walls. The woman stretched out a leg, looked at Guma:

"Sixteen. Why, if I might ask?"

"You're so young and here you are mixed up in this. Look: I knew a woman once" (he was remembering his mother) "who got old very fast."

"Did you come to give me advice? Are you a sailor or a priest?"

Guma smiled:

"Just talking... I feel sorry, that's all."

The woman sat up on the bed. Her hands were shaking:

"I don't need your charity. What did you come here for?"

And (who knows why?) she covered herself with the sheet, with sudden shame. Guma was sad now and he didn't care if she insulted him. He found her pretty, young for her sixteen years, and he was thinking his mother had been like that once. He was sorry for her, and what she was telling him made him even sadder. He put his hand on her shoulder, and it was with such softness that she looked at him again:

"I'm sorry..."

"Do you know who the woman I knew was? She was my mother. When I saw her she was still young, but she was more worn out than the hull of an old sloop... You're pretty, you're a young girl. What are you doing here?" he shouted, and didn't know why. "You've got no business here. A person can see right away that you don't belong here."

She covered herself even more with the sheet. She was shivering as if she were cold, as if her body had been whipped. Guma was sorry he'd raised his voice.

"You've got no business here. Why don't you leave?" (His voice was loving, like that of a son talking to his mother. He was telling her everything he'd wanted to say to his mother.)

"Where to? People fall into here and it's like sinking into a bog. There's no tree to grab onto. Only reeds..."

She looked as if she were going to cry:

"Why did you come here to talk about this? I was getting

along fine. You came to hurt me. You don't get anything out of this.''

The light of the candle was dying and reviving with every movement:

''I'm not from Bahia, no. I never set foot there. I'm from Alagoinhas, I'm here out of shame. It was a traveling sales- man. I left my town in shame. My little son died...''

He laid his hands on Rita's head. She was sobbing softly, he held her head against his chest:

''Tell me what I'm supposed to do?''

They were pounding on the door. Guma heard Josué's voice:

''Guma!''

''What is it?''

''It's the people from the academy. There's to be a brawl.'' And he made a move to jump up from the bed.

She held him back with both arms, her face fearful, her eyes still full of tears. She held him the way one holds onto a last hope, a tree on the edge of the abyss:

''You're not going, no...''

He stroked her:

''It won't be anything. Let go...''

She was looking at him without understanding:

''And what's going to happen to me? What about me? You're not going, I won't let you... You're mine, you can't go off and die now... If you die I'll kill myself...''

He ran out of the room, and in the hallway, in spite of the uproar the boys were making, roaring in, he could still hear her, her sobs and her voice that asked:

''What about me? I'll kill myself too...''

There were close to seventy boys from the military acad- emy, excluding the married ones, who hadn't come. It was only because of that that the riot ended that way. They in- vaded the rooms, attacking men and women, the sailors re- acted. No one knows whether it was Traíra who pulled the knife first or the boy who shot him. When the police arrived the sailors had fled out the back way, leaping over the wall and disappearing toward the docks, a dangerous place to go looking for a sailor. The boy with the knife wound had just died. The other's wound was small, a stab in the arm. The trail of blood attested to the fact that Traíra had been shot, and the sergeant of the military group said it had been in the chest, he'd seen it when the boy fired:

"Even so, the mulatto stuck in his knife. Then he went out all bent over like an old man. The bullet was in his chest, I'm sure of it. He won't be able to make it to the docks..."

The woman had been killed too. She'd got between Guma and the bullet the sergeant fired, but nobody worried about Rita, because a prostitute was of no importance. The boy was, he came from a good family, highly regarded in the town, the son of a lawyer. The inspector scratched his head (he'd been sleeping when they called him), looked at Rita's corpse, pushed it with his foot:

"What about this one? Why her?"

The blond was surprised too:

"Something came over her. She came out of her room, she looked crazy, she grabbed the guy who'd been with her, tried to bring him into the room. It was when the shooting started, she got in front of him, she got the leftovers..."

"Was she his mistress?"

"Can't you see she'd only met him tonight?" She shook her head. "Something came over her..."

The other women didn't understand either. Nobody understood. Nobody knew that she had only been purified, had left that life for which she hadn't been born. And she'd left it through her love. Then Tibéria, the madam, with frightened eyes, repeated:

"Something came over her..."

Guma had jumped into the water a good distance away from the *Valiant*. He swam to the sloop, climbed on board. A shape appeared in front of him, speaking softly:

"Guma?"

It was Josué. He was naked from the waist up. The river was rising, the sloop was a good distance from shore:

"It was devilish... Traíra's here. I swam him over. My heart was in my mouth."

"Why him here?"

"He's in bad shape, Guma. He's got to get to Bahia. If they grab him here they'll finish the poor guy off. And with a bullet in the belly on top of it all..."

The docks were deserted. The illuminated Baiana Line ship had a few passengers boarding. The canoes had left. Josué explained:

"When I got here with him the people had sailed off. Only the *Valiant* was left. If I'd had a sloop I'd have taken him. But I couldn't get him there in my canoe."

"Where'd you leave him?"

"He's in the hold. I already fixed the place where he was wounded, he seems to be sleeping..."

"What am I supposed to do with him?"

"Take him to Dr. Rodrigo, he's a good man, he'll take care of him. Then he can lay low."

"O.K."

Guma took the lantern and looked at Traíra lying in the hold. The blood wasn't flowing from his wound anymore. Traíra looked dead. Only his breathing showed that he was alive. He was pale, the lantern lighted up his shaved head. Josué spoke:

"I have to warn you, boy, the police will be here any minute."

He helped Guma with his maneuvers. When the sloop was under way he dove into the water. He waved goodbye:

"So long... You can count on this black man here."

As he left port Guma could see unusual activity on the Baiana ship. Several men were going on board, talking in loud voices. The police, without doubt. Guma was at the tiller, the sloop was running at full speed. He'd put out the lantern, and he was going along carefully because there were a lot of shoals in the river and the night was dark. He heard the first call from the Baiana. "I've still got an hour," he thought. An hour's head start to avoid a search of the sloop. He had to hide in some corner of the river until the ship passed. If they made a search, if they found Traíra dying in the sloop, then his race would be over. There might not be any jail. It wasn't customary in cases like that. He might be found floating in the water with a knife in his side, as an example. It wouldn't do any good to take it out on Traíra, who was already dying, but they had to get their revenge on someone. The boy was from a good family, important people... Guma looked around, the sea was calm, the wind was blowing, a good breeze was carrying the sloop along. The sea helped its men. The sea is a friend, a sweet friend. The sloop slips along over the blue water. Guma avoids a reef. Now he's running in a narrow channel. He keeps his eyes alert and his hand firm on the tiller. Traíra moans in the hold. Guma speaks:

"Traíra... Can you hear me, Traíra?"

The moans increase, in reply. Guma can't leave the tiller now. It's too dangerous to turn the sloop loose in that channel:

"I'll be right there... Hold on a minute."

The moans become more frequent and mournful. Guma thinks that Traíra is going to die. He'll die on his sloop and the police will find him there. They'll take their revenge out on Guma then. That doesn't frighten him. He doesn't want to be left alone with the corpse of Traíra, who died because of foolishness. Traíra shouldn't have pulled out his knife. Since there were so many others it wouldn't have been cowardly to leave the field. But Guma reflects. Who wouldn't have done the same thing, who among them wouldn't have pulled a knife? Traíra is dying, it's no use arguing. He has to avoid a search so he can get the body to port, where he can turn it over to the people who will mourn him.

They went through the channel. Guma lights the lantern and goes over to the hold. Traíra has managed to turn and is lying on his side. A thread of blood is coming from the wound. Guma speaks:

"Do you want something, buddy? We're heading for Bahia."

Traíra's dull eyes turn toward him:

"Water..."

Guma brings the gourd, goes down, puts the spout to the wounded man's mouth. Traíra has difficulty drinking. Then he turns again and lies belly up. He stares at Guma:

"Is that you, Guma?"

"The very same."

"The other guy was killed, right?"

"Right..."

"I never killed a man... People bring on their own trouble..."

"It had to be."

"What's going to become of my wife now?"

"Are you married?"

"I've got a wife in Santo Amaro, I've got three little girls. What's going to become of them?"

"Nothing's going to happen. You're going to be O.K., you'll be back with them."

"Are the police after us?"

"We'll give them the slip."

"Then you better get back to the rudder."

Guma goes back up. He's thinking, because Traíra has a wife and three girls, Who's going to feed so many people? Old Francisco was right in saying that sailors shouldn't get married. One day trouble comes, tempts people, the children are left starving. But he wants to get married. He wants to bring Lívia to his sloop, have a son. Traíra's dull voice calls again:

"Guma!"

He goes below. Traíra is trying to lift his head.

"Did you hear the ship's whistle?"

"No."

"I heard it. It's leaving now. It's no use. They're coming on it, aren't they?"

Guma knows that he means the police. He doesn't deny it. Traíra goes on:

"They'll catch us. Kill us right here."

They remain silent. The lantern lights up Traíra's face, which is tight in a grimace of pain.

"There's only one thing to do. I'm going to die anyway. Help me up on deck, I'll jump overboard. When they get here they won't find me."

"You're crazy, man. I still know how to sail a sloop."

"Give me some water."

Guma goes back on deck after giving him the water. Now the ship does whistle. Now they will leave port and come after him. When they lower the boat with the men in it, it will all be over. The ship will continue on and the armed men will put an end to them. Later on they'll say they resisted. Guma can't even resist. A knife is only good when it's man to man. When they jump on board the sloop it will be pistol in hand, rifles shooting. They'll go to see Janaína that night. He'll never see Lívia again, he'll never see old Francisco again. The sloop runs with the wind. The *Valiant* is giving it all it's got, but this is its last run. It will be riddled with bullets, it might sink with its owner. Its lantern won't shine in that bay anymore, it won't go up that river anymore, it won't race with Master Manuel. The boy had been stretched out in the parlor, the woman was there too. Only now does Guma remember her. She died to save him, she was young and pretty. She'd left that life she hadn't been born for. If she hadn't died she wouldn't have been able to put aside that drink of cane liquor anymore and she would have got old before her time. She died as a sailor's wife. It wasn't a prostitute who died with a bullet in her breast. It was Guma's wife, Iemanjá knows that, she'll walk with her through the lands of Aiocá, she'll make her her slave girl in the stone by the Dike. She was young and beautiful. She died for a man of the sea, her body will go to the cemetery, but Iemanjá will surely come to get her to be her slave girl. Guma will tell Lívia the story. And if a daughter is born to him he'll name her Rita. He hears the ship's whistle. It's coming through the channel. It won't be long before it approaches them, lowers its boat, and disappears in the darkness. Then it will be all over. The *Valiant* is racing as fast as it can. It's racing to its death because its day has come. They'll sail to the lands of Aiocá, which are more beautiful. Rita will be there waiting.

Guma hears a sound. As if someone were crawling across the sloop. Someone's there, yes. Someone coming very quietly on board the sloop. He lets go of the tiller and goes to have a look. It's Traíra, who's going to jump into the water. He leaps on top of him and he still struggles, he wants to get it over with once and for all, he doesn't want Guma to be sacrificed because of him. The shaved head gleams in the light of the lantern. Guma drags him down into the hold. He looks at him with thanks and pride. He, too, knows that it's the law of the docks and that Guma knows how to obey it. The two of them will die, then. He asks Guma:

"Have you got an extra knife?"

"I have. Why?"

"Give it to me. I want to die like a man. I'm still capable of taking one of them with me..." He smiles with difficulty.

Guma gives him the knife and goes up on deck. He will defend himself too. He won't let himself be killed like a fish taken alive. He'll only give up the knife when he's already fallen. He won't see Lívia again, she'll marry somebody else, she'll have somebody else's children. Yet it will be Lívia's name that he will say when he falls. Too bad he doesn't have Rufino beside him. If the black man were there he could tattoo Lívia's name on his arm.

He catches sight of the lantern of a sloop. Who can be coming? He'll know in a little while. If it's a friend maybe everything can be saved. The sloop approaches. It's Jacques' sloop. Just that morning they'd had a fight on the waterfront. But Guma knows he can go to him for help. Because that's what the law of the docks says.

At a signal from Guma's lantern Jacques' sloop stops. Jacques is startled. He'd been waiting for the moment to get his revenge on Guma. But the latter explains what had happened, the chase, Traíra lying there. Jacques doesn't argue. They transfer Traíra to his sloop. He heaves, he's close to death. Guma advises:

"I'll wait in Maragogipe."

"O.K."

"Have a good trip."

The sloops part. Nothing will happen now. No one will suspect Jacques, who's going to Cachoeira. And they won't find anything on the *Valiant*. No one will even be able to say that Guma was mixed up in the brawl except the women, at moments like that a man is faceless. He'll be free.

He was searched (he'd washed off the bloodstains in the hold), they left him alone. Jacques wasn't long in coming back, Guma was carrying cigars. Then the sloops left together. Jacques had already lost his trip, now he would go with him to the end. Traíra hadn't died. He was moaning in the bottom of Jacques' sloop. It was a clear morning when they got to Bahia. The Baiana ship had docked a long time before. On the waterfront they already knew about the brawl. Jacques stayed on the sloop, Guma went to get Dr. Rodrigo. Traíra was moaning on the sloop and talking about his wife, his family, his three girls. In his delirium he saw a big ship, an ocean liner, anchored at the pier. It had come to take him to the bottom of the sea, it wasn't a ship anymore, it was a black storm cloud that had dropped anchor by the pier. A cloud had dropped anchor by the pier. The storm came to take away Traíra, who had killed somebody. Where is his wife, where are his daughters to say goodbye to him? He's getting on board the ship, he's getting on board the cloud. No, he's not going because his wife isn't there, his daughters aren't there for the last farewell. Traíra already on board the ship, already on board the cloud, in the center of the storm, is still talking about his wife, his family, his three little girls: Marta, Margarida, Raquel.

# MARTA, MARGARIDA, RAQUEL

If there's one thing certain on the waterfront, absolutely certain, unshakable, it's that Dr. Rodrigo comes from a family of sailors; his father, his grandfather, or others even older, had crossed the seas on ships, made that their way of life. Because that was the only explanation for why a doctor with a framed diploma would leave behind the nice streets of the city and come to die on the waterfront in a crude house, along with books, a cat, and liquor bottles. It wasn't lovesickness. Dr. Rodrigo was still too young to have suffered an incurable disease in his breast. Most certainly—the canoemen would repeat—he came from a family of sailors, had returned to the sea. And since he was thin and weak, incapable of taking a sloop over the waters or lifting a full sack, he took care of the ailments of the sailors, gave life to those who came in almost dead from the storms. And he was usually the one who gave money for the burial of the poorest, the one who helped widows. He got the ones who got drunk and were arrested out of jail. He did a lot for them and was highly thought of on the docks, his fame had even spread to places reached only by the fame of the most valiant sailors. He did other things, but the sailors had no knowledge of that. Dona Dulce may have been the only one who knew that he wrote poems about the sea, because he found his poetry too weak for the subject. Dona Dulce didn't understand why he was living there either, being rich and respected in the upper city. He wore threadbare clothes, no tie, and when he wasn't visiting his patients (he had a lot who didn't pay him anything), he would smoke a pipe and look at the ever-new panorama of the sea.

He had a radio set, and a lot of people came at night to hear music from other countries. They would come in without mistrust now, looking on the thick and pretty books as friends (at first they were fearful of those books that separated them from Dr. Rodrigo) and they almost always ended up turning off the radio and singing the songs of the waterfront for the doctor to hear.

His living on the waterfront, his life among them, completely for them, wasn't a secret for old Francisco, the only one, who once asked him:

"Your father was a sailor, wasn't he, Dr. Rodrigo?"

"Not that I know of, Francisco."

"But your grandfather..."

"I didn't know him and my father didn't have time to talk about his life..." Rodrigo smiled.

"Well, he was a sailor," Francisco affirmed. "I knew him. He was the captain of a ship. A good man. Loved around here."

And Francisco was almost certain of having known Rodrigo's grandfather in spite of having invented the lie at that moment. From that came the certainty on the docks. And they all hope that Dr. Rodrigo will marry Dona Dulce one day. They meet, take walks, chat. But they never talk about getting married. For a long time on the docks they talk about the festival on that day. The more intimate even make allusions from time to time, and Dr. Rodrigo smiles, as if hiding even deeper in his shabby clothes, and changes the subject. He goes back to his books, his patients (he has a tubercular boy who takes up almost all his time), to the contemplation of the sea.

At first Dr. Rodrigo went up to the city a lot. He went up to propose sanitary reforms for the houses on the waterfront. They were never made. He stopped going. Dona Dulce talks about the miracle she's waiting for. Then everything will be beautiful on the waterfront. Maybe then Dr. Rodrigo will be able to write his beautiful poetry, as beautiful as the sea.

* * *

Guma goes into the room that serves as a doctor's office. A fat woman is listening to the mother of the tubercular boy, who is being held by the hand. The boy is all skin and bones, he coughs from time to time, and when he coughs he does it so strongly that it makes him cry. A young girl in the corner looks on in horror and covers her mouth with a handkerchief. The mother is saying:

"Sometimes I even think, God forgive me," and she puts her hand over her mouth, "that it would be better if the Lord called him... It's suffering like no other, suffering for everybody. It's endless coughing, all night long... What fun can he have out of life, poor little thing, if he can't even play? Sometimes I think God would be doing me a favor if he took him." She rubs her sleeve against her eyes and hugs the little one, who coughs and seems so far away from it all.

The fat woman agrees with a nod. The girl asks from the corner:

"Where did he catch it?"

"It was a cold, it got worse, it got awful, it turned into the disease..."

The fat woman advised:

"Have you taken him to Pai Anselmo yet? They say..."

"It didn't do any good... Dr. Rodrigo has been a father to us too..."

"Iemanjá is calling him," the fat woman finished.

Guma asked:

"Is Dr. Rodrigo going to be long, Dona Francisca?"

"I don't know, Mr. Guma. He's with Tibúrcio in there, the one who hurt his leg... Are you sick?"

"No. It's something else..."

The boy coughed. The fat woman spoke:

"Then there's Mariana, you know her, don't you? Zé Pedrinho's wife..."

"Oh, yes!"

"Well, she was like that. She got as skinny as a dried codfish. She coughed up a whole lot of blood, it looked like she'd cough up her heart someday. Well, Pai Anselmo gave her something to drink, it was tree bark.''

"With Mundinho it didn't do any good. He was the one who sent us to Dr. Rodrigo. And it still hasn't turned around. He's done everything..."

The door opened, Tibúrcio hobbled out. Dr. Rodrigo appeared in the door, his face thin, bony. He greeted Guma:

"Sick, Guma?"

"I wanted to talk to you. Urgent business."

"Come in." He turned to the women. "Please wait a bit."

Then the two of them came out, Dr. Rodrigo wearing his jacket, his bag in his hand. He told the women:

"I'll be back in a couple of hours. It's an emergency."

From the door he advised:

"Don't forget the boy's medicine, Dona Francisca. Before lunch..."

They were already on their way to the docks when Rodrigo asked:

"Now tell me what happened."

Guma told him. He knew he could trust Rodrigo completely. He was one of them, it was as if he were a sailor. He told him everything about the brawl, Rita's death, Traíra's wound:

"The boy died. And Traíra's in bad shape..."

They entered the mud by the waterfront, climbed onto Jacques' sloop. Dr. Rodrigo then dropped down into the hold. Traíra was delirious and talking about his daughters, calling for *Marta, Margarida, Raquel...* And they all learned that Marta was already a young lady, she was eighteen beautiful years old, Margarida leaped on the rocks, swam in the river, she was fourteen and long-haired, just coming into youth, but the one he missed most was Raquel, who was only four and still had trouble talking, unable to pronounce words the right way. Jacques said:

"He's rambling..."

*Marta, Margarida, Raquel,* he called with insistence. Marta sewed clothes, was preparing a trousseau for the fiancé who might come at any moment, Margarida was leaping on the rocks, playing on the river bank, swimming like a fish, Raquel was curling up her tongue, talking to her old doll, the only person who understood her. Raquel was called most insistently, it was Raquel whom he wanted most. Raquel was talking to her old doll, telling her she was going to have to stay in the corner, that her father was going to bring a blond doll on that trip. And the dying father was calling to Raquel, calling for Marta and Margarida too, even calling for his old woman who would be waiting for him with a fish stew.

Rodrigo examined the wound. The patient couldn't hear anything anymore, he didn't perceive their presence. He only saw his three daughters, dancing around, leaping with a smile, laughing merrily. *Marta, Margarida, Raquel.* It's a new doll that Raquel has in her arms, a new doll that's talking to her, a doll that he brought on that trip. He's going away on a ship, he's going away on a cloud, and Marta and Margarida and Raquel are dancing on the pier, the three are dancing holding hands as on happy days when Traíra came back from long trips and laid the presents he'd brought on the table. Marta puts on the newest pieces from her trousseau, Margarida dances on the rocks that she saw on the bank of the river, Raquel hugs a doll to her chest.

"Only by operating."

"What, doctor?"

"Only by removing the bullet... That way... We've got to get the man to my house. And he has a family, doesn't he?"

Traíra was talking:

"Marta, Margarida, Raquel."

"How are we going to get him there?" Jacques asked.

But they found a way. It was with a hammock. First the sloop sailed over to the end of the docks, where it was almost deserted, they put Traíra in the hammock, put a pole through, and carried him on their shoulders. At the house Rodrigo had the instruments prepared already and the operation started immediately. Guma and Jacques assisted and they saw the flesh opened, the bullet extracted, the flesh sewed up again. It was as if they'd been watching a fish being cleaned. Now Traíra was sleeping, not talking about his daughters anymore, not calling for the three.

When it was all over, Guma asked:

"He'll be all right, won't he doctor?"

"I don't think he'll make it, Guma. It was awfully late." Rodrigo was washing his hands.

Guma and Jacques stood looking at their comrade. The pale face, the shaved head, the huge body, the wounded belly, he seemed to have gone already, no longer of this world. Guma said:

"He's got a family. A wife and three children. A sailor shouldn't get married."

Jacques lowered his head, because he was going to get married in a month. Dr. Rodrigo asked:

"Where's his family from?"

"He roosted up there around Santo Amaro..."

"They've got to be told..."

"They must know already... Bad news travels fast."

"The police must have stopped by there already."

Dr. Rodrigo said:

"You two go about your business, I'll take care of him."

They left. Guma took another look at the man, who was snoring heavily. Dr. Rodrigo, when he saw himself alone, looked at the sea out the window. A hard life, that of a sailor. Guma said they shouldn't get married. There's always a day when the family will be left in misery, there are always Martas, Margaridas, and Raquels to go hungry. Dona Dulce was waiting for a miracle. Rodrigo wanted to go back to his poetry, but the man who was dying was a protest against descriptive poetry about the sea. And for the first time Rodrigo thought about writing a poem that would talk about the suffering and the misery of life on the waterfront.

Then death came calmly. Traíra was no longer going on board the ship now. Rodrigo had called Guma and Jacques. Traíra saw the three of them at his bedside. He wasn't moaning anymore. He held out his hand, and it wasn't the doctor and the friends he was seeing. He saw the three daughters around his bed, the three daughters who were waking him because it was already well into the morning (the sun was coming into the room) and he had to go out in his canoe. He held out his hand, smiled lovingly (Rodrigo was wringing his hands), murmured the names *Marta, Margarida, Raquel*, repeated *Raquel*, and went off in his canoe.

Went off in his canoe.

# VISCOUNTS, COUNTS, MARQUISES, AND BEETLE

That town of Santo Amaro where Guma is with his sloop was the homeland of all sorts of barons of the Empire, viscounts, counts, marquises, but, people of the waterfront, it was also the homeland of Beetle. For that reason, for that reason alone, not because it produces sugar, counts, viscounts, barons, marquises, cane liquor, Santo Amaro is a town beloved by waterfront people. It is where Beetle was born, ran in the streets, shed blood, fought with his knife, with a gun, with *capoeira* foot-fighting, sang sambas. It was there, nearby, in Maracangalha, that they chopped him up with machetes, it was there that his blood flowed, and there that his star shines, large and clear, almost as large as Lucas da Feira's. He became a star because he was a brave black man.

Santo Amaro is Beetle's home town. That's what Guma is thinking at that moment, lying in his sloop. Three days ago Guma's thoughts had been different. On the day that Traíra died, he was ready to go see Lívia, who was all he thought about. But once more old Francisco's phrases, the song they sang on the sea, the daily example (*Unlucky the woman who marries a man of the sea, a sailor shouldn't marry*), the case of Traíra, leaving a wife and three daughters, came to upset him. A sailor should be free, old Francisco says, the song says, daily events say. Free not to love but to love more broadly. Free, however, to die, to have nuptials with Iemanjá, mistress of the sea. Free to die the death they live for, a death that is so close, as certain as it is unexpected, that they

*116*

don't even think about it. A sailor has no right to sacrifice a woman. Not because of the poverty of their lives, the misery of their houses, the fish every day, the eternal lack of money. Any one of them could stand that, because they are generally used to it or are from the waterfront itself or are the daughters of workingmen, laborers who are also miserable. They're used to poverty, often to things worse than poverty. But what they're not used to is sudden death, suddenly to be left without a man, without a roof, without protection, without food, to be swallowed up then by a factory or, when they're younger, by prostitution. Guma is horrified just thinking about Lívia, prettier than all the women on the waterfront, giving herself to other men, calling from a window, in order to support a son who will be a sailor too someday and will bring misfortune to another woman. Behind a barred window (like those of prisoners, condemned men), she would show her open face, her face that had no anguish, and call out to the passing men. The son, Guma's son, a son of the sea, might hide to avoid weeping, to avoid weeping for his mother. And she would open her body for her son's food, and tomorrow he would also leave a woman (it's the fate of them all...) when he went with Iemanjá to the Lands of the Endless Way of Aiocá. Land of Aiocá, homeland of sailors and of the only woman they really should possess: Janaína, mysterious woman with five names, Janaína, who is mother, who is wife, and for that very reason is fearsome. No one knows of any married man on the docks who grew old in his sloop or canoe. Iemanjá is jealous and then she is Inaê and unleashes storms. It does no good to bring her gifts, no good to offer her daughters as slave girls, because she wants their husbands, her sons and her mates.

It was for that reason, for not wanting to make misfortune Lívia's lot, that Guma fled the waterfront that night with a small cargo for Santo Amaro and the promise of a return trip carrying bottles of cane liquor. He fled so as not to go with Rodolfo to see Lívia, to look into her light eyes, even more to desire her. That's why he's lying in his sloop now by the docks of Santo Amaro, the town of counts, viscounts, barons, marquises, and Beetle's town.

People of other waterfronts of the world, here Beetle was born! Guma looks up to the sky where he is shining. Even though the moon is larger and brighter and it's there that the eyes first turn, what they seek immediately after is the star of Beetle, the bravest of all blacks on the waterfront. The sky is full of brave men: Zumbi, Lucas da Feira, Zé Ninck, Beetle. There between the moon and Lucas is a place for Virgulino Ferreira Lampião, who isn't to die so young.

But none of them was a man of the docks, the son of a sailor who traveled in swift sloops. Only Beetle. He was a man of the sea, he knew how to handle a rudder, bring a canoe in, run with the wind and with music. Of all these only he knows where the lands of Aiocá are located, which is the end of the world itself. That's why he's the one most loved by the men of the docks. And it was here, in Santo Amaro, oh! sailors of all the world, loaders, stevedores, dockmen, canoemen, Dr. Rodrigo, Dona Dulce, all who work on the sea, that he was born. And very nearby, in Maracangalha, they chopped him up with machetes, made mincemeat out of him, but, note well, oh! sailors of all the world, it was through treachery, it was while he was sleeping in a hammock, which, more than anything else in the world, is like a sloop, swaying as if it were on the waves.

He was born here. Brave watermen are born all around the bay. In Bahia, the capital, the city of the seven doors, the most beautiful women of the waterfront are born. Lívia was born there. If Beetle had seen her—Guma thinks, whistling on the *Valiant*—he would have gone mad over her, he would have cut down three or four of them for her cause. He was a brave man, Beetle the sailor. And on the waterfront there was no woman prettier than Lívia, Lívia who had come to the feast of Iemanjá only to see Guma, who is also brave, who's been through adventures too, who thinks about traveling to strange lands on great ships one day. He desires her, she's the woman he's been waiting for so long, and she loves him too, she came to invite him with her open eyes, her eyes where there is nothing false. And, besides, Guma has an agreement with Rosa Palmeirão. To have a son with Lívia so Rosa can help rear him, play with him, forget about a life of brawling, fighting, killing. It's true that Beetle never married. But Beetle didn't know Lívia either, he was already dead when she was born. For a woman like Lívia a sailor forgets everything, can even forget that he might leave her in misery with a son or with three daughters like Traíra, who left Marta, Margarida, Raquel.

Guma doesn't even hear the music that's coming from the docks. He only senses her, she dominates his thoughts and it's that old song that says night is for love. Nights for Beetle were not always for love. Many times they were for fights, for crimes. Others were for dangerous flights, as when after downing four policemen and wounding several others he went into the woods with two bullets in his jaw and one in his arm. It was a dark night and they followed him, surrounded the woods. He jumped into the water and, wounded like that, swam like the good sailor he was until a canoe picked him up and a *pai-de-santo* took care of him. But no doubt there were nights for love. On nights with a moon, on nights with music, when the water of the river is blue, on those nights he loved, sometimes Maria José, sometimes Josefa da Fonte, sometimes Alípia, or others that he found. But he never had one single woman, one who would be joined to his lot, who would suffer a terrible life because of his death. Many women wept for him, but all the people of the sea wept for him too, his funeral was like that of any baron, count, viscount, marquis of Santo Amaro. They wept, saying that he was good, open-handed with the poor, with a dagger ready to defend the rights of a sailor. But no woman wept for him without thinking about his bravery, his goodness, his deeds, no one wept for him as her man, her helpmeet, her happiness. Because old people say, the song says, men of the docks shouldn't get married. Guma moves restlessly. Night is for love, but casual love, love found by chance, on the sands of the waterfront, on river banks, in the Market, any old mulatto girl.

Night is for love, sings a black man on the waters of Santo Amaro. Another song (the history of the waterfront is all in verse: ABC's, sambas, songs, *emboladas*) states that the fate of sailors' women is misfortune. Waiting on the docks for a sail, weeping on stormy nights for the arrival of a body. Beetle never married, in addition to being a sailor he was an outlaw, in addition to his oar he had a rifle, in addition to a sailor's knife he had a switchblade. Rosa Palmeirão too, a woman of the docks who was worth two men, never got to have a son. Jacques, who that month was going to marry Judith, a little mulatto girl orphaned on her father's side, was uncertain after Traíra's death. He ran away too, went to Cachoeira, to think like that, the same way that Guma is thinking, lying in his sloop, sucking on a pipe, listening to the music. Lívia has no mystery, her eyes expect nothing evil from life. Joining her life to a sailor would be destroying her lot, the songs say so clearly. Guma is angry, he feels like shouting, diving into the water, because it's sweet to die in the sea, fighting with a lot of men the way Beetle did.

Beetle's star twinkles in the sky. It's bright and large. The women say he's watching the evil deeds of the men (barons, counts, viscounts, marquises) of Santo Amaro. He's watching all the injustices that sailors suffer. One day he'll come back for vengeance.

He'll come back as someone else, no one will know it's Beetle. His star will disappear from the sky and he will shine on earth. Maybe that's the miracle that Dona Dulce has been waiting for, the day Dr. Rodrigo's poetry talks about. Maybe sailors will be able to get married on that day, give a better life to their women and guarantee that they won't starve after their deaths or won't have to prostitute themselves. When will that day come?—Guma asks the moon and the stars.

Beetle was brave and he was only killed by stealth, they cut his body to pieces, they had to look for the pieces for the funeral. He fought against the barons, counts, viscounts, and marquises who were the owners of the plantations, the green cane fields, and who set the freight rates for sloops and canoes, he invaded plantations, took a little of what belonged to them and divided it among the widows and children whose fathers had died at sea. The barons, viscounts, marquises, and counts made speeches in Parliament, chatted with Dom Pedro II, drank expensive wines, deflowered slave girls, whipped blacks, treated the sloop- and canoemen like servants. But they were afraid of Beetle, he was the Devil for them, a name they didn't like to hear. They sent police, they sent men and more men out against him. And they couldn't get Beetle, because there wasn't a woman on the waterfront, on the river, in the towns around the bay who wasn't asking protection for him from Iemanjá. And there was no sloop, no canoe or punt that wouldn't give him a hiding place. The barons trembled, the viscounts of Santo Amaro trembled, they pleaded with God about Beetle, for their lands to be spared and in that way some black men and women, some sailors were spared. Because the masters were afraid of Beetle.

Beetle will return one day. Guma must be waiting for that day to get married. No one knows how Beetle will return. Maybe he will even return as many men, with the whole waterfront rising up, asking for different rates, different laws, protection for widows and orphans.

Lívia is waiting for him, he knows. The night is for love and she's waiting for him. Rodolfo must have been annoyed at not finding Guma. He doesn't know that Guma ran away, didn't want to ruin Lívia's lot. But now a temptation to go back comes over him, an urge to see her again, stand before her. Lívia will come with him, will sleep on that sloop many nights. And if he dies she will have to be brave in order not to prostitute herself. The night is for love and love for Guma is Lívia. He doesn't want casual love, love found by chance, any old mulatto girl. It was Lívia that Iemanjá sent to him, he can't go against Iemanjá's orders. Canoemen, fishermen, sloop masters are afraid of love. What can it be that made Jacques decide to go to Cachoeira to think? Guma doesn't want to ruin Lívia's lot, but he can't help himself. Fate is something that's done, nobody can erase it. Lívia's lot is the unhappy lot of waterfront women. Not she, not Guma, not Beetle who became a star himself can erase it. Guma will go get her, he shouldn't have run away, because with a beautiful moon and so many stars, that night was made for love. On a night like that no one thinks about storms, riots, winds, death. Guma thinks that Lívia is beautiful and he wants her.

Santo Amaro is Beetle's land. It doesn't matter if noblemen of the Empire had been born here, the masters of innumerable slaves. It doesn't matter, oh! sailors. Beetle was born here, the bravest seaman who ever sailed these waters. Barons, counts, viscounts, marquises sleep beside the ruins of their feudal castles in closed tombs that time is eating away. But Beetle glows in the sky, he's a star, he spreads his light over Guma's sloop as it leaves swiftly in search of Lívia. Beetle will return one day, oh! sailors of all the world, and then all nights will be for love, there will be new songs on the waterfront and in the hearts of women.

# MELODY

The sea was sending him the swiftest winds, was sending him the northeaster that is driving the *Valiant* toward the Bahia waterfront. Canoes that pass, sloops that go by, rafts carrying fishermen, punts loaded with firewood, wish him a good trip.

"Have a good trip, Guma..."

A good trip taken to find Lívia. The moon lights his way, the sea is a broad, smooth highway. And the northeaster is blowing, the terrible northeaster of storms. But now it is blowing as a friend, helping him cover that arm of the river more rapidly. The northeaster brings songs from the riverbanks, the songs of washerwomen, the songs of fishermen. Sharks leap out of the waves at the harbor entrance. On the illuminated incoming ship they're dancing. A couple is chatting in the moonlight. "Have a good trip," Guma says and waves. They answer and comment, smiling, about the greeting from that unknown sailor.

He's going for Lívia, he's going to bring a pretty woman to offer the sea. Lívia's flesh won't have long to wait, it will have the taste of the ocean's salt water, her hair will be damp from the sea splash. And aboard the *Valiant* she will sing the songs of the waterfront. She will also learn the story of Beetle, the story of the enchanted horse, all the stories about castaways. She will be like a sloop, the shell of a canoe, a sail, a chanty, nothing but a thing of the sea.

The northeaster blows, fills the sails of the *Valiant*. Run, sloop, run, the lights of Bahia are already aglow.

The drumbeats of the *candomblés* can be heard now, the music of guitars, the sad moan of concertinas. Guma can almost hear Lívia's clear laughter. Run, sloop, run.

# THE ABDUCTION OF LÍVIA

Six months with an intense desire to have her, possess her. The *Valiant* was cutting the waters of the sea and the river. The *Valiant* came and went, but the desire never left Guma. He had seen her as soon as he arrived from Santo Amaro that day. He went with Rodolfo and she looked even more beautiful to him, timid, looking at him with her clear eyes. Her relatives, the aunt and uncle who ran a small shop and had put all their hopes in Lívia's beauty (She could make a good marriage...) didn't look upon Guma with good eyes, right after thanking him. They expected him to appear, receive their thanks, and go on his way without looking back. What could Lívia hope for from a sailor? And what could they hope for from someone who was even poorer than they?

Six months during which, in order to see her, exchange a handful of words (she did all the talking, he listened in silence), he had to pass under the eyes of the aunt and uncle. Looks of anger, antipathy, disdain. He'd saved their lives, but now he wanted to carry off the only hope for a better life they had left. But in spite of the looks, the words whispered loud enough so he would hear, Guma kept coming back, always wearing the only suit he owned, awkward in it, clumsy in his movements.

The very first week he had written a letter to Lívia. At first he had wanted to show it to Dona Dulce so she could correct the mistakes. But he was bashful and sent it just the way it was:

*My esteemed L... all pure in heart.*

*Greetings.*

*It is with a heavy hand and a mad and passionate heart for you that I write these clumsy lines.*

*Lívia, my love, I beg you, my child, to read this letter carefully so as to be able to answer me urgently, although I want a sincere answer that comes to me from your heart.*

*Lívia, did you know that love begins with a kiss and ends with a tear of sorrow? Yet, my child, I think that if you feel the same as I, ours will be quite the opposite, it was born of a look, it will grow with a kiss, and it will never end, is that not what my love is like? I beg of you to answer all the questions I ask. Will you? My child, I think your heart is a golden seashell where the word GOOD-NESS is enclosed.*

*Lívia, my love, I was born loving you already and I can't hide that secret no more and can't get rid of the great pain my heart feels I declare its true adorable angel, see?*

*Youll be my only hope, I give you my heart Ill follow what you want, I think you dont like me but my heart was always in your hands and always will be until my last days.*

*When I saw you, my angel, I was crazy for you and I felt I was just waiting to confess when the time came when you could hear my plea.*

*I wrote to you in order to open my heart, I dont love nobody but you, I respect you and I love you, for my eternal happiness.*

*I ask a big favor now for you not to show anyone this letter so they wont think its the chicanery of a heart in love but I might break the rudder of anybody who laughed at me. So as I have hopes of your answering me satisfactory I wont tell no one this secret that stays between the two of us.*

*I ask for an urgent answer so I can know if you feel the same as this loving heart, but I want a sincere answer that comes out of your heart for mine, see?*

*Your answer will soothe my painful heart, see?*

*Please excuse the mistakes and the writing.*

*Youll see a difference in writing because I changed pens, see? I wrote this letter all alone at home writing to you and thinking about you, see?*

*Without laying it on anymore a hug from your G... who loves you so much and respects you with all his heart, see?*

*Gumercindo———URGENT*

The truth is that this letter almost caused a row, a great fight. The fact is that the one who started writing it was *Doctor* Filadélfio. Almost no one called him Filadélfio, they all knew him as *the doctor*. He wrote stories in verse, ABC's of the docks, chanties. He was always half drunk, muttering his learning (he'd attended a religious school for a year), earning a few cents here and there by writing letters for families, sweethearts, wives, and eventual lovers. He made speeches at baptisms, marriages, the opening of all shops in the Market, and the launching of all sloops. He was admired on the waterfront, they all kept him in food and drink. A pen behind his ear, an inkwell wrapped up in his pocket, a yellow umbrella, a roll of paper, a book by Alan Kardec under his arm. He read that book ceaselessly and never got to the end, never even got beyond page 30, and he called himself a spiritualist. He had never gone to a session, however, because he had a frightful fear of souls from the other world. Every afternoon he would sit in front of the Market and there, on a crate, he was the intermediary in the love affairs of the waterfront, the dramatizer of illnesses and poverty for the families of canoemen, he also wrote letters to Iemanjá, knew about everybody's life. When Rufino came by he would laugh his thin chuckle, shrug his shoulders, and ask:

"Who's the new one?"

Rufino would give the name and he would write the same letter as always. And when he saw someone he knew he would advise him:

"Elisa's free. Rufino's let go of the critter."

And he wrote letters for other people. That was how he earned his living, money for drinks. Once, for ten cents from Jacques he created a masterpiece he was very proud of, an acrostic that Judith now carried in her bosom:

> G od, I love you madly,
> O h, how you've won my heart,
> O h, how my soul esteems you,
> D on't ever leave, I beg you,
> B e with me till the day I die.
> Y ou are my only love.

He entitled it *Goodby,* looked at Jacques with emotional eyes:

"I was meant to go into politics, son. This waterfront stuff isn't for me. But you can see that even Rui Barbosa couldn't make it in politics..."

He read the acrostic aloud, copied it out in his beautiful hand, collected the ten cents, and said:

"If this doesn't make her tumble quicker than a swamped canoe I'll reimburse you...

"Reimburse you... Give you back your ten cents... Because it's..."

When the time for festivals in Cachoeira and São Félix arrived, he would get into the sloop of a friendly master and go to write letters, acrostics, poetry, at markets and fairs in those towns where his fame had arrived a long time before.

He was everyone's obligatory confidant. Many times he would answer the letters he had written himself. Through his intervention many a child was born on the waterfront, many a girl married. He was also the one who wrote to far-off families, giving news of the death of sailors who hadn't returned to their ports. On those days he drank even more.

Guma had waited for a time when he wasn't at all busy in order to talk to him. The "doctor" didn't have many customers that afternoon and was picking his teeth, thinking about who would buy him dinner. Guma came over:

"Good afternoon, doctor."

"May fair winds go with you, my son." He liked to speak elegantly.

Guma was silent, not knowing how to bring up the subject. The doctor encouraged him:

"So, aren't you going to pick up someone to take Rosa's place? I'm writing a poem here that nobody can resist."

"That's why…"

"Who's the fish to be caught?"

"That's what I don't want to say…"

The doctor was offended:

"In all the twelve years I've been here, no one has ever mistrusted me. I've always been as quiet as a chest locked with seven keys."

"It's not mistrust, doctor. You'll find out later…"

"You'll be wanting a nice loving letter, is that it?"

"I was hoping you could scratch me out a letter saying certain things…"

"Well, let's see, what's the lady's status?"

"She's very pretty."

"I'm asking you" (he was annoyed because he'd meant to say "inquiring of you" and had forgotten at the last moment) "if she's a maiden, a lady of the streets, or a sailor's lass?" By *sailor's lass* he meant the little mulatto barmaids who came to make love to sailors out of pure love, not expecting any other recompense.

"She's a proper girl. I want to marry her."

"Then you have to get some orange blossoms to put in the envelope. And stationery with two linked hearts."

Guma went off to get the material. The doctor advised him:

"A letter like that costs two *cruzados*. But she'll be all set to be gobbled up."

When Guma returned the doctor began to write, reading aloud at the same time. In place of the name of the beloved he put "L…," as Guma had asked.

The fight began when he got to the part that said "My child, I think your heart is a golden seashell where the word GOODNESS is enclosed," because he had written that the heart was a golden *coffer*. Guma disagreed about coffer and proposed seashell. He thought there wasn't anything more beautiful than a seashell. A coffer is an ugly thing. Well, the doctor would allow no arguments. He said it would be coffer or nothing. He wouldn't write the *epistle*. Guma pulled the letter from his hands, grabbed the pen and inkwell too, and went off to his sloop. He scratched out *coffer* and wrote in *seashell*. Then by himself, with great joy, he wrote the rest of the letter. When he got to the end he gave that explanation about the two different letters and went back to the doctor:

"Here are your goods."

"Don't you want me to continue it?"

"No. But I'll pay you..." And he gave him the eight hundred *reis*.

The doctor put the money in his pocket, closed the inkwell, and squinted at Guma with a serious look:

"Have you ever seen a coffer?"

"I even carried a big green one to Maragogipe on my sloop..."

"But you never saw a golden one, eh?"

"No."

"That's why you say a shell is prettier. If you'd seen a golden coffer there'd be no argument."

And the letter went off as it was, with the seashell. Guma took it by night, and at the end of the visit he said to Lívia:

"I've got something to give you. But swear you'll only open it inside."

"I swear."

He gave her the letter and went out almost at a run. He only stopped when he got to the docks, and he spent a night of agony thinking about the answer she would give him.

She gave him the answer verbally when he returned:

"I'm getting my trousseau together."

Aunt and uncle, who expected everything from her marriage. The aunt and uncle, when they found out, fought with Guma, told him never to come to their house again. No one knew where Rodolfo was wandering, Guma had no means of appeal to anyone. When he wasn't making trips he would stay until quite late at night, spying on her house to see her quickly, exchange a few words, arrange a meeting. And desire was growing inside him. Finally he opened up with Rufino. The black man scratched on the ground with a piece of wood and said:

"I can only see one way out of the thing..."

"What's that?"

"You kidnap the girl."

"But..."

"There's nothing to it. You set it up with her, pick a night, put her on the sloop, sail off to Cachoeira. When you get back you'll have to get married."

"And who'll she stay with over there in Cachoeira?"

"With Jacques' wife's mother," Rufino said after thinking for an instant.

"Let's go see what Jacques says."

Jacques had got married a few months before. His mother-in-law lived in Cachoeira, Lívia could stay with her while Guma arranged the marriage with the relatives. Jacques agreed. Guma went to figure out a way to see Lívia.

He managed to get to talk with Lívia. She agreed, she desired him too. They set everything up for a week later, the following Saturday night when her aunt and uncle were going visiting. She would think of some way to stay home and then they would run away. On that night, in the Beacon of the Stars, Guma bought a round of cane liquor and agreed with "the doctor" that *coffer* was prettier than *seashell*. But only a golden coffer.

It was in June, a month of south winds and storms. In June, Iemanjá unleashes the south wind, which is a terrible wind. It's quite dangerous crossing the harbor mouth in that season, quite dangerous, and the storms are terrible. It's the worst month for fishermen and sloop masters. Even Baiana Line ships are in danger in the month of June, even the big packets.

On that June night the sky closed in with clouds, Iemanjá

came to see the moon in vain. The south wind ran cold and
damp through the waterfront, making men bend over and
take shelter under their oilskins. Guma had been on the corner of the Rua Rui Barbosa for a long time. Rufino was with
him and they didn't take their eyes off Lívia's house. They
watched the store being closed, they heard noises in the back
room, and quite a bit later Lívia's aunt and uncle came out.
Guma relaxed. She'd managed not to go. She accompanied
the old people to the streetcar. The old woman was smiling,
the old man reading a newspaper. Then Rufino went to get
Lívia. Guma stayed on the corner. When Rufino knocked on
the door a neighbor woman was calling Lívia:

"Didn't you want to go, Lívia? Then you can come over
and chat."

Lívia saw Rufino knocking, spoke to him in a low voice,
turned to the neighbor:

"Aunty forgot her purse... She sent word for me to bring
it."

She went in, picked up the purse and an umbrella, then
spoke to the neighbor:

"She's waiting at the streetcar stop. I'm taking the umbrella too, because it's going to rain."

The neighbor woman lowered her eyes:

"I could have sworn she was carrying an umbrella...
Yes, it does look like rain."

And Lívia left. They crossed the square, went down on
the elevator, and she found herself facing the docks and the
sea, her new homeland. Guma wrapped her up in his oilskin
cape, Rufino went ahead so they could avoid any acquaint-
ances. A fine rain had begun to fall. Alongside the sloop Rufino took his leave.

It was in June, and it was in the month of winds that Lívia
moved her home to the sea. The sloop sailed off into the
wind and was heeling over, the red lantern lighting the way
along the surface of the sea. A canoeman who was coming
in wished Guma a good trip. For the first time Lívia returned
the greeting of the sea:

"Have a good trip..."

The south wind was lifting her hair. Guma was bent over the tiller, an incomparable aroma was coming from the sea, and inside her a joy that made her sing to the ocean. Lívia greeted the sea with the most beautiful song she knew, so the sloop passed the breakwater and entered the harbor mouth, because the beautiful songs that women sing are what buy off the wind and the sea. Lívia was happy and Guma so happy that for the first time he didn't see the approaching storm. Lívia lay down by his feet and her hair fluttered in the wind. They went along in silence because she was no longer singing. Now only the south wind was whistling its song of death.

The storm came on quickly, as June storms usually do. The south wind shook the sails of the *Valiant*. The lantern lighted up the breakers at the harbor mouth. Guma had been through many storms during his years at sea. Some had been tragic for a lot of canoemen and sloop masters. One night he'd gone out alone, the storm was so strong that no one else had dared, to save a ship. And he'd never been afraid. He'd become used to death, to the idea of remaining at the bottom of the sea. Today the storm would be strong too. The breakers were piling up, one on top of the other, wagering as to which was the higher. But he'd already gone through worse storms and had never been afraid. Why is he afraid today, why is he afraid that the lantern will go out? For the first time his heart is pounding rapidly in the midst of the storm. Lívia is tired after a whole day of waiting, after the anxiety of everything's possibly going wrong at the last moment, if her aunt and uncle had insisted on her going with them, and she's come to lie down on the deck of the sloop by Guma's feet as he holds the tiller. He feels the brush of her hair. He desires her very much and maybe he will never possess her. Maybe the two of them will go on to the lands of Aiocá without their bodies having come together. The hour of death still hasn't come because they haven't possessed each other yet, they still preserve a desire in their bodies that quiver with pleasure when they touch one another, in spite of the storm, of the wild sea all around. Guma doesn't want to die without possessing her, because then he would have to keep coming back in search of that body.

Lívia, who knows nothing of life on the sea, asks with frightened eyes:

"Is it always like this, Guma?"

"If it was like this for a lifetime people wouldn't go out on a second trip."

Then she gets up and holds him closely:

"Might we die tonight?"

"Maybe not... The *Valiant*'s a good ship. And I know a little bit about this." And in spite of the storm he smiles.

She huddles closer on his shoulder. And she murmurs:

"When you see we're going to die, come to me right then. It's better."

That's Guma's desire too. In that way they'd die after having belonged to each other, their flesh having met, their desires having been satisfied. Then they could die in peace. But he knows that if he can manage to cross the harbor mouth and get into the river they'll be safe, because then he'll anchor the sloop by one of its banks. It's impossible to keep on sailing against the south wind that is dragging the ship away. The lantern is still lighted, salvation is still possible. The water whips Lívia's dress, drenches Guma's clothes, washes the deck of the sloop. The sails receive all the wind and the *Valiant* tilts, tries to go back, ends up going along on its side, farther and farther out to sea, to a sea that's no longer theirs, that belongs to ocean liners and black freighters. Guma grips the tiller with all his strength, steering his ship in spite of the fury of the wind and the waves. Lívia clings to his head, begs:

"If we're going to die, come be with me..."

"Maybe we can get out of it..."

There's not a star in the sky, that night isn't for love. So much so that there's no singing on the docks, only the wind whistling. But they want to make love on that night, which might be their last. Everything is quick and uncertain in life at sea. Even love is in a hurry. The waves bathe their bodies

and the sloop. They hadn't gone very far in all that time. All
Guma was able to manage was not going out to sea, not
being pulled beyond the mouth of the bay. A ship comes in.
A thousand lights illuminate it. The waves break on its hull
and are impotent against it. But they're not against Guma's
small sloop, which looks as if it will disappear under a wave
at times. Only Lívia fills him with courage, only the desire
of having her, of living for her, makes him continue on.
He'd never been afraid during a storm. Today is the first
time. Afraid of dying without having possessed her.

They succeeded in getting into the river. But even there
the storm is no better. The lantern on the *Valiant* goes out
with a gust of wind. Lívia tries to light it but uses up the
whole box of matches without being able to. Guma is looking for a small inlet where he can anchor the sloop. There
aren't many at that mouth of the river. Only at the place
where the specter of the white horse runs is there one. But
for a sailor it's better to stay in the middle of a storm than to
stop there, hear the gallop of the former plantation owner.
They're near. The hoofbeats of the strange gallop can already be heard clearly. The horse passes, returns, the ham-
pers bump against his sides, flashes of lightning outline his
shape.

Lívia, in a low voice, sings a song that is an invitation to
Guma. But the white horse is running, it's better to die in the
storm. But how good it would be to possess her, press his
body against Lívia's virgin body! She sees the inlet in the
flash of lightning that cuts through the night:

"Look, Guma... You can anchor the boat there."

Who cares about the white horse? He won't let her die
that night, which is their wedding night. The white horse
runs, but Lívia sings and isn't afraid of it. She's afraid of the
storm and the south wind, the thunder that's the angry voice
of Iemanjá, the lightning that's the flash of Iemanjá's eyes.

And Guma heads the sloop into the small inlet.

Many years later a man (an old man whose age no one can
remember anymore) told again how moonlight nights are

not the only ones made for love. Stormy nights too, nights of the wrath of Iemanjá, were good for love. The moans of love were the sweetest kind of music, the lightning flashes ceased in the sky and became stars, the waves became ripples when they arrived to break on the sand where someone was making love. Stormy nights are good for love too. Because in love there is music, stars, calm.

There was music in Lívia's moans of pain. There were stars in her eyes and the lightning ceased in the sky. The shout of pride from Guma quieted the thunder. The waves came to break softly on the sand of the small inlet, as soft as ripples. And they were so happy, it was so beautiful, that dark night, without moon and without stars, so full of love, that the enchanted horse felt his harness removed and his punishment ended. And never more did he trot along those roads beside the river, where sailors come to make love now.

# WEDDING MARCH

The aunt and uncle said they would kill, they would make things happen. Guma had left Lívia with Jacques' mother-in-law and returned to Bahia. Rodolfo, who had come out of nowhere as always, calmed the aunt and uncle, stopped them from going to the police. Guma had already met him by the boats. Rodolfo was trying hard to put on a stern face. He couldn't bring it off. He embraced Guma, advised him:

"I really and truly do love my sister. You know that I'm no good, but I want her to be happy. Be careful what you're up to..."

Guma spoke:

"What I want is to get married. If I did it this way it's the fault of the old people who didn't want—"

Rodolfo laughed:

"I know, yes. I'm patching everything up with them. Have you got any money to take care of the paperwork?"

Guma left everything in Rodolfo's hands, and the next day he was told that the wedding would take place twelve days later at the church of Monte Serrat and at the courthouse. The person who was all upset was old Francisco. He'd always believed that a sailor shouldn't get married. A woman would only mess up their lives. But he didn't say anything, because Guma was getting to be a man and he wasn't one to stick his nose into his business. But as for thinking it was fine, approving, no. Especially now that life was so hard, when the freight rates for sloops and canoes were so low... He told Guma he was going to move out:

"I'll find anchorage in some inlet out there..."

"You're crazy... You're going to stay right here."

"Your wife won't like it..."

"You're calling me a chicken. Who ran your house, you or aunty?"

Old Francisco muttered something. Guma went on:

"You're going to like her. She's really nice."

Old Francisco went on mending sails. He spoke about his own marriage:

"It was a feast to make your eyes pop out. People came from all over to eat fish that day. Even your father, who was a good-for-nothing that nobody ever heard from, showed up. The only thing bigger was her funeral."

He sat thinking, the needle for repairing the sail in his hand:

"It doesn't get people anywhere, marriage doesn't. It always ends up bad. There's never any telling, there isn't..."

Guma knew it was like that, knew that old Francisco was right. His aunt had died of joy on a stormy night when old Francisco returned. She'd died of joy, but most of them died of sadness for the husbands who hadn't come back.

That was why Dr. Rodrigo looked at him with surprise when he went to invite him to his wedding. Guma knew quite well what Dr. Rodrigo was thinking as he looked at him. He was no doubt remembering that day when Traíra had died, had gone off on a ship or on a cloud, calling for his daughters in the midst of his delirium. Raquel received a doll, it's true. But not from her father's hand, it wasn't on the return from one of his trips. Guma remembered, he remembered others too. They'd stayed behind in the sea, they'd stayed behind in a brawl, they were going to the Lands of the Endless Way. How can a woman live on the waterfront without a husband? Some wash clothes for families in the upper city, others become prostitutes and drink at the Beacon of the Stars. Both types are sad, sad are the washerwomen who weep, sad are the prostitutes who laugh amidst drinks and songs. Dr. Rodrigo put out his hand and smiled:

"I'll be there to give you a hug..." But his voice came

without enthusiasm, without joy. He was thinking about Traíra, about others who'd also passed through his office.

Only Dona Dulce smiled with joy and enthusiasm:

"I know that life for the both of you will be even more difficult. But you love her, don't you? It's good for you to get married. Life won't be like this forever. I get to thinking sometimes, Guma..." And there was a childlike hope in her voice. She was waiting for a miracle, Guma knew that, everybody on the waterfront knew that. And they loved her, loved her thin face with its glasses, her slim and aging body. And they gave her their children for five or six months. She searched avidly for the word she would have to teach them, the word that would bring on the miracle.

She shook Guma's hand and asked him:

"Bring her here, I'd like to meet her..."

"Doctor" Filadélfio stuck his fingers into his dirty stiff collar and laughed his thin chuckle:

"Let's have a drink to celebrate..."

He recalled:

"If you'd put in *coffer* it wouldn't have taken so long..."

In the Beacon of the Stars he drank to Guma and his fiancée. Everybody at the bar drank. Many were married already, others were ready. A good number, however, didn't have the courage to sacrifice a woman to their lives.

Lívia came to Dona Dulce's house. The aunt and uncle came to visit her, they were resigned now. They brought the trousseau and the reception was organized. Old Francisco was the one completely taken by Lívia. He was so happy that one would have thought he was the one to be married. On the waterfront all they talked about was Guma's wedding, which took place on a Saturday, first at the courthouse with only a few people (Rufino was best man and took half an hour to sign his name) and then at the church of Monte Serrat, all filled with flowers. All the people from the waterfront who had come to see Guma and his bride were there. They found her beautiful. Many of them looked at Guma with envy. In one group they were commenting:

"He's lucky, a great woman... If I only could have had her for myself."

They laughed:

"But it's too late now..."

Somebody in the group said:

"All you've got to do is wait a little while. It won't be long before she's a widow..."

No one laughed anymore. But an old sailor made a sign with his hand and said to the boys:

"Things like that are left unsaid."

The one who had spoken lowered his head, ashamed, and one of them who was married felt a chill run up his spine, as if it had been the south wind.

Lívia passed by in beauty and Guma laughed for all without really knowing why. The cold June evening was falling over the city. The waterfront was already aglow. They went down the hillside.

It was a damp and foggy evening. The men went along all wrapped in their capes as a fine, cutting rain fell. The ships, even though it was early, were lighted up. The sloops with their sails furled pointed their masts up to the leaden sky... The waters of the sea had come to a halt on that damp afternoon of Guma's wedding day. Old Francisco walked along and told Rufino the story of his own wedding, and the black man, half drunk already, listened and made scabrous comments. Filadélfio was thinking about the speech he would soon be giving at Guma's table and about the applause he would receive. The rain was falling on the wedding procession as the bells of Monte Serrat rang announcing the coming of night. The sand by the docks was streaked and the departure of a ship on that grayish afternoon was sad.

To the rear of the procession Dona Dulce was chatting with Dr. Rodrigo. They were arm in arm like newlyweds, but she was a little stooped now and had trouble seeing, even with her glasses. He was puffing on his pipe.

"Mundinho died..." he said.

"His poor mother..."

"I did everything. But there was no way to save him here. No sanitation at all, no cures..."

"He was in my school. He was a good student. He would have gone far..."

"In any case, he shouldn't have stayed around here."

"These people can't do anything else, doctor. They need their children to help them earn their living. A lot of them are so smart they make you jump for joy. Guma himself..."

"You've been here a long time, haven't you, Dona Dulce?"

She gave a little nod and replied:

"It's been a long time, yes. It's been very sad..."

Dr. Rodrigo didn't know whether she meant her own life or life on the waterfront. She was hunched over and the rain was turning her hair silver:

"Sometimes I get to thinking... I could have left here long ago, got a better position... But I feel sorry for these people. They love me so much. But I don't know what to tell them..."

"What do you mean?"

"Hasn't a woman ever come weeping to your place? Hasn't a new widow ever come? I've watched a lot of them get married like Lívia. And then they come weeping to my house because their husbands have been left behind in the sea. I don't know what to say..."

"A man died in my office not too long ago, if you can call that place an office... He died with a bullet in his belly. All he talked about were his daughters, he was a canoeman..."

"I don't know what to say to them... I had faith at first, I was still happy. I believed that God would take pity on these people someday. Today I've seen so much that I don't even believe anymore. But in those days at least I had some consolation..."

"When I came here, Dulce," (she looked at him when he addressed her simply as Dulce, but she understood that he was her brother) "I believed too. I had faith in science, I had come to help all these people..."

"Today..."

"I don't know what to tell them either. Talking about sanitation where there's nothing but misery, talking about comfort where there's only the danger of death... I think I've failed..."

"I'm hoping for a miracle. I don't know what kind, but I'm hoping."

Lívia was there in front, smiling at Dona Dulce. Dr. Rodrigo clutched the collar of his cape:

"Nothing but a miracle. That proves you still have faith in your God. That's something. I've lost my faith in my goddess by now."

They heard the sound of conversation, old Francisco's laughter as he listened to Rufino's comments, saw Guma's happy smile, the friendly signal from Lívia to come closer. Then Dona Dulce said:

"It's no longer a miracle from heaven that I'm hoping for. I've already prayed to the saints so much, and men and children have died just the same. Something tells me they're the ones who will bring on the miracle..."

Dr. Rodrigo looked at Dona Dulce. The teacher's eyes were kindly and smiling. The doctor thought about the failure of his poetry, the failure of his science. He was looking at the smiling people around him. Master Manuel leaped down from the *Sailor Without a Port* with Maria Clara and came running toward the bridal couple. He'd been delayed, and he laughed a lot as he excused himself. Dr. Rodrigo said:

"What miracle, Dulce? What miracle?"

She was transfigured, she looked like a saint. Her soft eyes stretched out over the sea. A child came to her and she rested her fleshless hand on its head:

"A miracle, yes."

The child was walking along with them now in the damp night that was coming on. Dulce went on speaking:

"Have you ever imagined this sea full of clean sloops, with well-fed sailors earning what they deserve, their wives with a guaranteed future, their children in school, not for six months but all the time, and those with talent going on to the university later? Have you ever thought of rescue stations along the rivers, at the mouth of the bay? Sometimes I can imagine the waterfront like that..."

The child was listening in silence and not understanding. The night was damp, the sea still. Everything was sad and without beauty. The voice of Dulce:

"A miracle from these men, Rodrigo... Just like the moon on this winter night. Lighting everything up, beautifying everything."

Rodrigo looked at the moon that was rising in the sky. It was full and it was lighting everything up, transfiguring the sea and the night. The stars had come out and a song was coming from the old fort, the men no longer walked hunched over, the wedding procession was beautiful. The dampness of the night had disappeared, dry cold remained. The moon lighted the night over the sea. Master Manuel had his arm around Maria Clara and Guma was smiling at Lívia. Dr. Rodrigo looked at the miracle of the night. The child smiled at the moon. Dr. Rodrigo then could see what Dulce was talking about. He picked up the child in his arms. It was true. One day those men would bring on a miracle like that. He said to Dulce softly:

"I believe."

The procession was going into Guma's house. Old Francisco was shouting:

"Come in everybody, this house belongs to all of you. It's poor but it has a good heart."

When Dr. Rodrigo and Dona Dulce passed he asked:

"Were you talking about the next wedding?"

Dr. Rodrigo answered:

"We were talking about a miracle."

"The time for miracles has passed..." Francisco laughed.

"Not quite yet," Dona Dulce put in. "But it'll be a different kind of miracle this time."

The moon was coming in through the window.

Jeremias had brought his guitar. Other people had brought concertinas, and Rufino his guitar too. Maria Clara was there with her voice. And they sang sea chanties, start-ing with the one that says the night is for love (and they all smiled at Guma and Lívia) and going on to the one that says it's sweet to die in the sea. And they danced too, they all wanted to dance with the bride, they drank cane liquor, they ate the sweets that Dona Dulce had sent and the black bean stew that old Francisco had prepared with Rufino's help. They laughed a lot, forgetting about the damp night, the south wind, the month of June. Soon it would be Saint John's Eve and the bonfires would crackle on the waterfront.

Guma was waiting for them to leave. He was like Lívia's aunt and uncle during the early days. Since that night when he had stolen her away and possessed her in the storm he hadn't had her in his arms again. And from that day on his desire had only grown. He looked at the eyes that were laughing, drink-ing, and chatting. They were certainly not going to leave so early. Master Manuel was telling a story about fights:

"It was a whack the likes of which you've never seen. The man spun around, went into a dance, and was out like a light..."

Then they asked Rufino for an *embolada*. Lívia rested her head on Guma's shoulder. Francisco called for silence. Ru-fino plucked his guitar, his voice echoed through the house:

> *"Money is what runs the world,*
> *The world is run by money."*

The *embolada* went on. The singer's voice was quick, like waves in a storm. The lines ran one on top of the other:

> *"Dig in the ground for a hole*
> *A hairpin of wood when you see her,*
> *So tie up and untie your hair,*
> *Tie up your hair, oh Maria."*

He was looking at the girls in the room and singing to them that he liked to vary his women and women liked to roll in the sand with him. On the docks they said he was such a good canoeman that "he would turn his canoe into the wind, hold tight to the paddle, and head it on through." And that was a sign of rare skill, driving a canoe prow first through the water. Something that only old canoemen could bring off.

> *"He was the one who taught me*
> *Love—I didn't know how before.*
> *A wildcat grabs onto the rigging,*
> *A snake grabs onto the pot.*
> *But a cowboy does it the right way,*
> *He draws his sweetheart by lot."*

They laughed in the room, mulatto girls rolled their eyes at Rufino. Master Manuel was keeping time to the music of the *embolada* by slapping his knees. Rufino sang:

> *"A person who's wounded moans,*
> *A person who moans is in pain.*
> *A blacksmith pounds with a hammer,*
> *A sexton pounds with his bells."*

He was plucking his guitar. Lívia liked it, but she would rather have a chanty, one of those old chanties sung on the docks. The *embolada* didn't tell her much. A chanty always has a lot to say. Rufino was finishing:

> *"I'm kind of like a toothache*
> *When it begins to stab around.*
> *I can make sauce without pepper,*
> *Soften a thistle barb.*
> *No sugar cane sprout am I,*
> *Dying and coming to life."*

After all that boasting he laid the guitar on the floor, winked:

"Let's dance, people, this is a happy day..."

They danced. The concertinas were desperate in their music, like waves coming and going. Master Manuel was telling Dr. Rodrigo:

"The weather's rough, doctor. People are kept busy on their trips. A lot of people are going to stay behind with Janaína this winter..."

The sound of the music spread out over the nearby waterfront. Mr. Babau came in bringing some bottles of things to drink, his present to the newlyweds. He'd closed the Beacon of the Stars, nobody had come in that night. And he immediately chose a woman and danced around the room. The samba grew stronger, the floor resounded with pounding feet. Then Maria Clara sang. Her voice penetrated the night, like the voice of the sea. Melodious and deep. She sang:

> *"The night he didn't come back*
> *Was a night of sadness for me..."*

Her voice was soft. It came out of the deepest part of the sea, it had a smell of the waterfront as its body, a smell of salted fish. Now the room was listening to it attentively. The song that she was singing was very much theirs, belonged to the sea.

> *"He stayed behind in the waves,*
> *Where he went under to drown."*

An old *moda* about the sea. Why do those songs talk only of death, sadness? The sea is beautiful, the water blue, and the moon yellow. But the songs, the sea *modas* are sad like that, they make you want to cry, they kill everybody's joy.

> *"I'm going to other lands*
> *Where my man has gone before*
> *In the deep green waves of the sea."*

In the deep green waves of the sea they all go one day. Maria Clara sings, she too has a man who lives on the water.

But she was born on the sea, she came from it and lives on it. That's why the song doesn't tell her anything new, doesn't make her heart shudder like Lívia's:

*"In the deep green waves of the sea."*

Why is Maria Clara singing like that on her wedding night?—Lívia thinks. She's like an enemy, her voice is like a storm. An old woman with her hair in a knot who lost her husband many years ago is weeping in the parlor. The waves of the sea carry everything off. The sea that gives them everything takes everything away from them. Maria Clara says:

*"I'm going to other lands..."*

It's to those lands that sailors go. The faraway lands of Aiocá. Guma smiles with his mouth half open. Lívia is resting on his shoulder and for the first time fears for the life of her man. And if he stays behind at sea someday, what will become of her? The song says that everybody will stay behind in the green waves of the sea. And nobody in the room disagrees, no one is even upset. Only Lívia, who sobs aloud, who wants to flee, take Guma far away from there, to the ends of the earth, to a place where they won't hear the call of the "deep green waves of the sea."

Lívia is barely breathing. The song has ended. But on the cold June night its voice goes out over the ships, the docks, the sloops. And it keeps on beating inside all hearts. And in order to forget they all start dancing. The ones who aren't dancing are drinking.

Maneca One-Hand holds out his thick mug and shouts:

"This damned booze. Even the drinks are heavy like lead."

The rain is falling outside. Clouds have covered the moon.

Her wedding march had been that song of misfortune. A song that summed up life on the waterfront. "He went under to drown." Any woman could say that when her husband went out. Hers was a sad fate. Her brother appeared and disappeared, nobody ever knew what he was up to. He hadn't come to her wedding, it had been days since she'd caught sight of him. He'd been the one who'd taken care of the paperwork, set the date, then he disappeared. Nobody knew anything about him, where he lived, where he ate, where he rested that handsome head of flowing hair. Her husband went out every day to drown in the deep green waves of the sea. One day, instead of him, his body would return, he would be sailing in the Lands of the Endless Way of Aiocá.

Lívia takes off her dress, dries her tears. Her body no longer has any wish for love now. She's not satisfied, however, because she'd only felt her man once. And they'd been married today, it's a day for making love and she's sad, the song had taken away the desire that had been in her body. She would think of Guma's corpse coming out of the waves when she embraced him. She would think about her husband going to drown. She could only feel desire, only love him completely if she could flee far away from the sea that night. Go to the rough soil of the backlands, flee from the fascination of the waves. The men there, the women there live with thoughts about the sea. They don't know that the sea is a brutal master who kills men. A song from the backlands says that the wife of Lampião, who is lord of all that, had wept because she couldn't have a dress made out of steamer smoke. A steamer comes from the sea and no one rules on the sea, not even a courageous *cangaceiro* bandit like Lampião. The sea is master of lives, the sea is terrible, mysterious. Everything that lives off the sea is surrounded by mystery. Lívia hides under the covers and weeps. Her days will be tragic from now on. She will help Guma go off every day to drown in the deep green waves of the sea.

And then she makes a sudden resolution. She will always go with him. She'll be a sailor too, sing sea chanties, she'll get to know the winds, the shoals in the river, the mysteries of the sea. Her voice, too, will calm the storms like Maria Clara's. She'll make bets on her sloop, she'll win with her music. And if he goes to the bottom of the waters one day she'll go with him and together they will take the trip to the unknown lands of Aiocá.

Outside the room Guma asks if he can come in yet. She dries her eyes and tells him to come in. The flame of the candle goes out, the moans of love grow in the early morning. He will go off to drown, will stay behind, sailing in the deep green waves of the sea. She sobs and loves, they possess each other madly, as if death were stalking about their bed, as if it were the last time.

Dawn breaks and Lívia swears her son won't be a sailor, won't sail in sloops, won't listen to that music, won't love the treacherous sea. At dawn a black man sings that the sea is a sweet friend. Lívia's son won't belong to the sea. He'll be a man of the land and will lead a peaceful life, his wife won't suffer what Lívia is suffering. He won't go off to drown in the deep green waves.

Dawn breaks and Guma thinks that his son will be a sailor who will handle a sloop that's better than Master Manuel's, will sail in a canoe better than Rufino's, and one day will travel on an enormous ship to lands farther away even than those where Chico Tristeza goes. The sea is a sweet friend, he will go to sea.

Dawn breaks and the moans of love rise up again.

# THE *FLYING PACKET*

# THE MAR GRANDE RUN

Bad months for the waterfront. The sloops weren't making many trips, freight rates were very low, a lot of them went fishing in order to scrape up enough money to keep them afloat. Guma was active, carrying any cargoes that appeared, taking any risk. Lívia almost always went with him. Faithful to what she'd promised herself, she always tried to be beside her husband. On one stormy night, however, Guma confessed to her that trips were becoming much harder with her by his side. He, who was never afraid, felt a real terror when the afternoon became cloudy and they were at sea. Her life brought on that terror, that fear of the winds and storms. She spaced out her trips more then, she only went with him when he was in a good mood. Sometimes he even invited her, sensing the desire in her eyes:

"Do you want to come with me, black girl?"

He called her "black girl" affectionately. She would go get ready, smiling, and if he asked her why she liked to go out with him, she would never say she was afraid for his life. She said she was jealous and was afraid he'd get involved with women in other ports. Guma would smile, blow out a puff of smoke from his pipe, say:

"You're silly, girl. I stay on board thinking about you."

When she didn't go, when she stayed at home alone with old Francisco, listening to old waterfront stories, hearing about shipwrecks, deaths, and drownings, terror came over her. She knew that her husband was at sea, aboard a fragile craft at the mercy of the winds. He might not come back or would come back a corpse, carried in a net by two strong men. Or he might come back with his body all covered with small crabs, rattling, like Mr. Andrade, whose story old Francisco tells while he mends sails, aided by Lívia.

She'd never been able to forget the song that Maria Clara had sung on their wedding day. "He went off to drown in the deep green waves of the sea." Now she watched, unable to make a gesture, unable to hold him back, her husband leave in the morning or at night to meet death. Other waterfront women looked indifferently at their husbands as they left. But they'd been born there, they'd witnessed the arrival of the body of a father, a brother, an uncle. They knew that was the way it was, the law of the docks. There's something on the docks that's even worse than the misery of factories, the misery of plantations: It's the certainty that the end will be death at sea unexpectedly some night, suddenly some night. They knew that, it was their age-old lot, it was a fate that had already been cast. No one revolted. They wept for their fathers, they tore their hair when their husbands were left behind, they threw themselves furiously into work or prostitution until their children were grown and then they went away in turn. They belonged to the waterfront, their hearts were already branded.

But Lívia didn't belong to the waterfront. She'd come there because of a man she loved. And she was afraid for him, she was looking for a way to save him, or if there was no other way, to die with him, not to have to weep for him. He was going to be drowned, she wanted to go too. Old Francisco only knows about things that happen on the sea. He tells stories all day long, but his stories are full of ship- wrecks, storms. He proudly narrates the brave death of sloop masters he has known, he spits when he mentions the name of Ito, who, in order to save himself, let four people on his sloop die. He spits with disgust. Because a sloopman never does that. That's what all the stories that old Francisco tells are like. They don't console Lívia's heart, they make it all the more bitter, many times they make her eyes fill with tears. And old Francisco always has new stories to tell, new misfortunes to announce. Many times Lívia weeps, many times she flees to her room so as not to hear any more. And old Francisco, who is getting senile now, goes on telling stories to himself, somber in his expression, somber in his words as well.

It was for that reason that Lívia was pleased when Esmeralda, Rufino's mistress, came to live next door. She was a pretty, busty mulatto girl, with rolling hips, a good chunk of womanhood. She talked a lot, laughed too much, had a wild laugh, didn't worry about what might happen to Rufino, who had a great affection for his mulatto girl. All she talked about were new dresses, pomades, sandals that she'd seen in shop windows, but she helped time pass for Lívia, got those thoughts of death out of her head. Maria Clara would come by too, but Maria Clara, who'd been born and had always lived on sloops, loved the sea above all things and Master Manuel even more than the sea. All she wanted was for him to keep on being the best sloop master in that region, give her a son, and go off bravely with Iemanjá when his time came.

When her classes were over, Dona Dulce would stop by for a chat, but the one who was most fun was Esmeralda, with her comical voice, her voluptuous body, her senseless conversation. She was always borrowing things too, coming right into the house (old Francisco would lick his lips, wink, and she would smile: "Look at that funny old ray fish..."), asking about everything. Rufino was going up and down the river, spending one night at home, a week away, it never bothered her. One day, when Lívia was weeping, she said:

"You're all mixed up. Giving a man all that importance... Let them have their women out there. Do what I do... I don't get too tied up."

"That's not it, Esmeralda. What I'm afraid of is that he'll be killed on one of his trips."

"Don't we all have to die? I'm not one to get worked up. If mine dies, I'll get another."

Lívia didn't understand. If Guma died she would die too, because besides missing him so much she wasn't a woman for hard work and she didn't intend to sell her body in order to make a living.

Esmeralda didn't agree. If Rufino died, she'd get herself another, she'd go on with her life. He wasn't the first one she'd had. One had stayed behind in the waves too, her husband had gone off to other lands on a freighter, the third one had taken off in a canoe with a girl friend. She paid no attention, went on living. How could she tell what Rufino would do someday, what his end would be? What she wanted was some pomade to straighten her hair, sandals to walk on the docks with, a pretty dress to cover her thighs. Lívia laughed, long and hard. Esmeralda amused her. It was still a piece of luck to have her there as a neighbor. If not, what would her days have been like, listening to sad stories from old Francisco, thinking about her husband who'd gone off to drown?

But when Rufino would arrive in his canoe, Esmeralda was a different woman. She would sit on the black man's lap, shout to Lívia:

"Neighbor, my darky's back. Dinner's going to taste better today..."

Rufino was mad about her, there were even people who said that she'd had a strong spell cast, had written notes to Dona Janaína. Rufino took her to the movies, to the circus when it was in town, sometimes they went dancing at the Oceano Soccer Club, which didn't have a soccer team but, as compensation, held dances on Saturdays and Sundays for waterfront people. They seemed happy, and many times Lívia envied Esmeralda. Even when Rufino drank and slapped her around at home. Esmeralda wasn't afraid for him. Her heart rested easy.

Sometimes she would expect Guma on a certain day and spend all her time on the docks watching for the *Valiant*'s sail among those coming in. When one like his appeared, her heart would leap with joy. She'd asked Rufino to tattoo the names of Guma and the *Valiant* on her chubby arm. She looked at the arm, she looked at the sea, until she saw that she was mistaken, it wasn't his sloop coming in. It was time to wait for another sail. Can that be his showing now? And hope filled her heart. It still wasn't. Sometimes she would spend the afternoon and part of the night waiting like that. And when he didn't come on the indicated day, delayed by one thing or another, she would return home with a bitter heart. It did no good for Esmeralda to say:

"If anything's wrong you find out right away. If anything's wrong you find out right away. If anything had happened people would already know..."

It wouldn't do any good either for old Francisco to search in his weary memory for cases where men had been delayed, where sometimes months had gone by without anyone's knowing where they were and one day they would show up. She couldn't sleep, she would walk back and forth in the bedroom, many times hearing (the houses were close together) Esmeralda's moans of love as she twisted in Rufino's arms. She couldn't sleep and she seemed to hear Maria Clara's voice singing in the voice of the wind:

> *"He stayed behind in the waves,*
> *He went off and was drowned.*
> *I'm going to other lands*
> *For my love has gone away*
> *In the deep green waves of the sea."*

And if sleep overcame her, if weariness threw her onto the bed, then her dreams were nightmares, full of visions of storms and the tinkle of crab-encrusted bodies.

She only rested when she heard his voice in the middle of the night or on clear mornings. He would come along shouting with childlike joy:

"Lívia! Lívia! Come see what I've brought you..."

But almost always the one he saw first was Esmeralda, who would appear in the doorway of her house, give Guma a strong hug, rubbing her breasts against his body and asking:

"Didn't you bring me anything?"

"Rufino's the one to bring you things..."

"That one? He doesn't even remember to bring a dry fishtail..."

Lívia would appear, her eyes dry now, and she couldn't believe it was he, so many, many times she'd seen him dead during the night before.

One Friday Guma invited her:

"Do you want to go out with me tomorrow, black girl? I'm taking some tiles to Mar Grande. Manuel's going too. And you'll give me the advantage..."

"What advantage?" Lívia asked, fearful of a fight.

"It's a bet we've got. Once I bet him on a race, he won. A long time back. Now we'll have another look-see. And you'll sing to make the *Valiant* run..."

"Singing helps?" She smiled.

"Didn't you know? The wind helps, singing even more. The only reason he won the last time was because Maria Clara was singing a good number. I didn't have anyone to sing for me."

He grasped the woman by the waist, looked into her eyes:

"Why do you cry when I'm not here?"

"That's a lie. Who told you that?"

"Esmeralda. Old Francisco had told me about it before too. Is everything all right with you?"

Her eyes held no mystery. Limpid and clear like water, the clear water of the river. Lívia ran her fingers through Guma's long hair:

"Me, if I had my way, I'd go out with you on the sloop every time..."

"Are you afraid for me? I know how to handle a ship..."

"But everybody ends up out there..."

"Up there too,"—he pointed toward the sky—"if they die. It's the same thing."

Lívia hugged him. He laid her on the bed, pressed against her lips with the haste he always had, the haste of men who don't know where they will be tomorrow. But Esmeralda was coming in, and her voice disturbed Guma's caresses.

Guma left, he went to load the sloop. Later in the afternoon Lívia put on her good clothes and took the elevator.

She was going to visit her aunt and uncle. She was content because she was going to sail with Guma the next day, would spend two days with him, half of the time on board the sloop, because from Mar Grande they would go to Maragogipe.

Guma returned at the end of the afternoon. He knew that Lívia had gone out, that was why he delayed all the more. He'd had a drink at the Beacon of the Stars (Mr. Babau was limping around, "Doctor" Filadélfio was writing a letter for Maneca One-Hand and downing one drink after another), and now he'd stopped to chat with Esmeralda, who, all prettied up, was boldly provocative in the window.

"Don't you want to come in, neighbor?"

"I'm fine right here, neighbor."

She invited him in with a smile:

"Come in. You can relax better sitting down."

He resisted. He was fine right there, he wouldn't take the time to go in, Lívia wouldn't be long. Esmeralda spoke:

"Are you afraid of her or of Rufino? Rufino's on a trip..."

Guma looked at her with surprise. It was true that she would hug him and rub her breasts against him, that she took liberties, but she'd never thrown herself at him like that. She was inviting him, no doubt about it. She was just another mulatto girl. But she was Rufino's girl, Rufino, such a good friend of his, and he couldn't betray either Rufino or Lívia. Guma decided to pretend he didn't understand, but it wasn't necessary. Lívia was coming up the hill. Esmeralda said:

"We'll leave it for another time..."

"O.K."

Now he wanted love, the love he hadn't been able to have that morning because Esmeralda had prevented it, love he couldn't have now because friendship had prevented it. Friendship or because Lívia was coming? Guma was thinking to himself. Esmeralda was a mulatto girl who made your mouth water. And she was giving herself to him, offering herself. She was Rufino's mistress, Rufino was Guma's friend, did him favors, the best man at his wedding. Besides, Guma has the prettiest woman on the waterfront, he doesn't need any other. He's got a woman who loves him. Why Esmeralda's wiggling body? Esmeralda's hips sway, her mulatto breasts throb under her dress. And she's got green eyes, she's a green-eyed mulatto. What would Rufino do if Esmeralda cheated on him with Guma? He'd kill them both, certainly, then he'd head out into the open sea, Lívia would take poison. Esmeralda's eyes are green. Lívia warns:

"The food's getting cold."

Let it get cold. He carries her into the bedroom:

"Show me something."

She quivers on the bed. He has the most beautiful woman on the waterfront. He will never betray a friend.

The morning is beautiful, full of sun. October is the most beautiful month on that waterfront. The sun isn't hot yet, the mornings are clear and cool, they're mornings without mysteries. From the nearby sloops comes a smell of ripe fruit that reaches the market. Mr. Babau is buying pineapples to sweeten his drinks for his customers at the Beacon of the Stars. A black woman passes with cans of manioc pap. Another is selling *mungunzá*, sweet corn cakes, to a group. Old Francisco buys two cents' worth of manioc. A sloop leaves with a full load. Boats are going out to fish, the fishermen naked from the waist up. The Market is beginning to become active, men are coming down on the elevator that joins the two cities, the upper and the lower.

Master Manuel is already on the docks. Maria Clara is wearing red calico, a ribbon in her hair. Old Francisco, who always rises early, comes over to them:

"Are you going out, skipper?"

"I'm waiting for Guma. He's a newlywed, he's late..."

"It's five months now..."

"It seems like only yesterday," Maria Clara said.

"They have a good life, that's what counts."

They were coming. Lívia with her eyes still puffy from a

sleepless night. Guma with weary arms, sure he would lose the race:

"The bet's lost. I'm washed out."

She chuckled, clutched her husband's arm:

"That's all right..."

Master Manuel greeted them:

"You don't seem to be in any hurry..."

Lívia was chatting with Maria Clara now, who was saying:

"You're putting on weight. Look at that business."

"No, it's not anything."

"Look, there's a sloop master on his way."

Lívia blushed:

"No sloopman and no canoeman. We're not thinking about that... We've barely got enough money for two."

Maria Clara confessed:

"That's it exactly. But I've got to say that as soon as Manuel wants to I'll want to too. I'm just afraid that it might be a girl..."

Master Manuel was already on board. Old Francisco walked over to a group by the Market. But first he advised Guma:

"Gain some ground on your way around the island. Maneuvers like that are Manuel's weak point."

"That's right." But Guma is sure he'll lose.

They were laying bets in the Market. A lot of them were betting on Master Manuel, but Guma, ever since he'd saved the *Canavieiras* and especially after the Traíra episode (that was known on the waterfront immediately), had his admirers.

The *Sailor Without a Port* was heading out. The wind was favorable, it took right off, heading for the breakwater. Guma had just weighed anchor on the *Valiant*. Lívia was holding onto the sails. From close to the breakwater came the voice of Maria Clara:

> *"Run, run my sloop,*
> *Run, run with the wind."*

At the breakwater the *Sailor Without a Port* was waiting.
That was where the race began. The *Valiant* was beginning
its first maneuvers. A group was watching on the dock.
Guma's sloop caught the wind, its sails filled, it soon came
alongside the *Sailor Without a Port*. And the two of them
took off. Master Manuel was leading a little, Maria Clara
was singing, Guma felt fatigue in his arms, in his body.
Lívia came and lay down beside him. The wind was carrying Maria Clara's voice:

> *"Run, run my sloop,*
> *Run, run with the wind."*

Lívia sang too. Only music can buy the wind and the sea.
And they were beautiful voices, voices offered by the
waterfront. Lívia sang:

> *"Run, run my sloop,*
> *Run more than the wind."*

She strokes the *Valiant*. The clear morning casts reflec-
tions on the blue water. Guma soon ceases to feel the fatigue
of a night of love and helps the sloop, helps the wind.
They're almost even now, and Master Manuel says:

"It's going to be rough, boy."

The island of Itaparica is a green blotch on the blue sea.
It's so shallow at a certain spot that the stones on the bottom
can be seen. There must be seashells too. Guma almost had
a fight with Filadélfio once over a seashell and a coffer. He
was infatuated with Lívia in those days, all he could think
about was possessing her. And can he be thinking about
anything else today? He's come out of a night of love, and in
that race he's not thinking about winning, he's thinking
about having her in his arms again, hugging her hard. Guma
calls her. Maria Clara's voice cuts across the mouth of the
bay.

"Come and lay down over here, Lívia."

"Only after you win."

She knows that if she lies down beside him he won't pay attention to his steering, to the race, to the good name of the sloop. He'll only be thinking about love.

The sloops are going along side by side in a straight line. The wind carries them, the men help. Who'll get there first? Nobody knows, Guma is giving it his all, Maria Clara is singing. Lívia sings again. And the *Valiant* takes a small lead. But Master Manuel leans over aboard the *Sailor Without a Port* and goes ahead.

Now it's time for the turn. Right about here there's a shoal. Master Manuel maneuvers to the right in order to get some distance for the turn. He's in the lead. But Guma does something unheard of, a close-in turn, right over the shoals that scrape against the hull of the ship. And when Master Manuel comes back in with his sloop, Guma's is already well ahead, and on the miserable docks of Mar Grande the fishermen wave to the hero of such a difficult feat. They'd never seen anything like that, they'd never seen a turn right over the shoal. But one old fisherman disagreed:

"He's won, but the other one's a better sailor. A sailor shouldn't risk his ship over shoals."

But the young men don't want to hear sensible words and they cheer Guma. The old man mutters and goes off. The sloop ties up. Master Manuel arrives shortly after and laughs:

"We're even. I won that other time. Now it's your turn. One of these days we'll get over being stubborn."

He puts his hand on Guma's shoulder:

"But always remember that a man can't do what you did today twice. The next time you'll go under."

But Guma's not listening:

"Easiest thing in the world..."

Lívia smiles, Maria Clara teases:

"Will the one who's on his way there ever have to do that?"

Lívia turns serious and thinks that her son will never do things like that. Yet, even without wanting to, she finds it beautiful, a lot worthy of a man.

* * *

Guma and Master Manuel remained behind unloading the sloops. Then they'll load them up again and leave for Maragogipe, from where they'll return with cigars and tobacco for Bahia. They took on that haul together, a good haul in those bad months when not very much was moving.

Maria Clara and Lívia go off along the Mar Grande shore, which is a beach. The houses are of straw. They pass men selling fish, their pant legs rolled up, their arms tattooed. Here in Mar Grande there are famous *candomblés*, respected *pai-de-santo* priests. There are some stone houses in the summer people's section. It's fisherman country. From here the boats go out to fish every morning and return in the afternoon, around four o'clock. In the old days they used to carry summer people from the city. Nowadays there's a ferry for that service.

It's October and there's still a southeast wind. But when summer comes "the breeze" will arrive, the gentle northeaster. The summer people, when they come, have to be carried in the arms of the fishermen over the reefs where the ferry can't come. Only sloops can pass through them. Nowhere are storms as strong as in this Mar Grande part of the bay.

Lívia is thinking about that as she crosses the beach, the only road here. Maria Clara goes along in silence, picking up a shell from the beach from time to time:

"It's to make a picture frame with," she explains.

Suddenly they come upon the Gypsy women. A man beating on pots had already passed them. He was a Gypsy. Now the women are approaching in a group of four. Dirty, speaking an unknown language, they seem to be arguing among themselves. Maria Clara asks:

"Shall we have our palms read?"

"What for?" wonders Lívia, who is afraid.

But the other one runs over to the Gypsies without hearing what Lívia says. And old woman takes Maria Clara's hand and tells her:

"Give me four hundred *reis* and I'll tell you everything, past, present, and future."

Another asks Lívia:

"Do you want me to read your fortune?"

"No."

Maria Clara encourages her:

"It's only one *cruzado*, silly, and you'll find out everything…"

Lívia gives her the coin and her hand. The old woman is telling Maria Clara:

"I see a trip. The lady is going to do a lot of traveling. She's going to have a lot of children…"

"May Janaína hear you…" Maria Clara laughs.

The other Gypsy woman, who is pregnant, with large earrings, warns Lívia:

"You're going through a very bad time for money, but it's going to get worse. Then your husband will be a lot better off, but it will be very dangerous."

Lívia is frightened. The Gypsy goes on:

"But if you give me ten pennies I'll conjure away the danger."

Lívia doesn't have any money, she asks Maria Clara. She gives it to the Gypsy, who mutters a strange prayer. And the group leaves, picking up the interrupted argument in that unknown language. Maria Clara laughs:

"She said that I'm going to have a dozen kids. Manuel's going to be wild. I'd just as soon. I'd put everything in the *Sailor* and go right on out there."

Lívia is hearing the Gypsy woman's words:

"It will be very dangerous…"

What is Guma going to get into that's so dangerous? It certainly must have something to do with his life on the waterfront. The beach at Mar Grande stretches out endlessly. They come back to the port. The sloops are unloaded already. Now they cook dinner, fry fish. Guma and Master Manuel laugh, smelling the breeze that brings the odor of fried fish. Then they go back to loading the sloops.

And at night they leave. The sea is still calm on the difficult Mar Grande run. And on the sloops they can hear the music and the strange language of the Gypsies' songs. It's pretty, but it's sad. Guma says to Lívia:

"It seems like that music is only predicting something bad..."

Lívia lowers her head and doesn't answer. There are more stars in the sky than can be counted.

That Mar Grande run is a hard one. That's why the sloops are so careful going through the reefs. A lot of people have been drowned there. And days later, on a stormy night, it's where Jacques and Raimundo, his father, were left behind. It was Guma who discovered the bodies on his way back from Cachoeira. The old man was hanging onto the son's shirt, doubtless trying to save him. And Judith became a widow that night. Lívia had been waiting for Guma on the docks. It was Rufino who brought the news that Jacques had died. It had been Jacques' mother-in-law who'd put her up when she ran away from home with Guma.

Now the reefs of Mar Grande had swallowed up Jacques and his father too. A hard run, the Mar Grande one, a run covered by dozens of vessels every day. The Gypsy woman had told Lívia that a dangerous chore was ahead. What new Mar Grande run would Guma have to go through? Lívia's life is already full of so much despair, so much anxiety. When he leaves for Mar Grande on the *Valiant* her heart can only think of misfortunes. Maria Clara had already told her that she foresaw something like that for Guma.

A hard run, the Mar Grande one, it had swallowed up so many bodies already! Someday Guma's turn will come, but first—the Gypsy said—he has more dangerous chores to do. Can it be that he'll end up sailing only to Mar Grande? Who knows what's going to happen to him? Not even the Gypsy women know, the Gypsy women who can hear the voice of the sea in a conch shell. Not even they know.

Lívia brought some shells from Mar Grande and she would frame Guma's picture with them, one that she'd taken in the park, beneath the elevator, leaning against a tree. The other one, the one that shows him and the *Valiant,* she'd sent to Janaína in an envelope, asking her not to take that one along, not the father of her child. Because Maria Clara is right. There is a creature in Lívia's womb, a being who someday—it's fated—will also make the Mar Grande run.

# ESMERALDA

Lívia first sought out Dr. Rodrigo. He strongly recommended that waterfront women who found themselves pregnant come to him. The treatment didn't cost anything and the births turned out easy. And they also said on the docks that he wouldn't refuse to "make angels." Many a woman had an abortion with Dr. Rodrigo's help. Once even Dona Dulce asked him if it were true:

"Yes, it is. Those poor women go through hell, starving, watching their husbands die. It's only right that a lot of them shouldn't want to have any more children. Sometimes they've got eight or ten and no means to bring them up. They come and ask me, what can I do? Let them get abortions from those folk-doctor quacks around here? That's worse..."

Dona Dulce wanted to say something in reply, but she was silent. He was really right. And she lowered her head. She knew quite well that it wasn't for evil reasons that the women on the waterfront had abortions. If they did it was so they wouldn't have to abandon their children later on in taverns along the docks, not have to see them working from the age of eight. There was never enough money. Dr. Rodrigo was right. Except that in Dona Dulce her failed instinct of motherhood was speaking. She thought about children's little arms waving, blond heads, babbling voices. Dr. Rodrigo said:

"We have to face reality for what it is. I don't expect any miracles..."

She smiled:

"You're always right. But it's such a pity…"

Nevertheless, Lívia didn't go there to have her child pulled out of her womb. She went to find out if it really was true, because it must have been recent, since her belly still hadn't swelled up. Dr. Rodrigo affirmed that it was almost certain. And he told her that he was ready to help in her treatment so the birth would be easy and the child strong. She certainly wouldn't want an abortion. Dr. Rodrigo knew perfectly well that they never aborted the first child.

Guma arrived at midnight. He tossed the things he was carrying to one side, showed Lívia the present he'd brought. He'd won a bet with a sailor from a Lloyd Brasileiro ship docked in port, a cut of fabric. The ship's engines had broken down and the sailor had taken advantage of it to go see his family in Cachoeira. He'd gone on Guma's sloop, which was going to leave (that was three days ago), and he'd bet him he wouldn't cut in front of the Bahia Line ship that was heading in the same direction. Guma won the bet:

"It was a risky pass, but I thought the cloth was pretty. He was taking it to a girl he knew—"

Lívia said:

"Don't you ever do that again."

"It wasn't anything—"

"Yes it was."

Only then did Guma notice that she was serious.

"What's come over you?"

"I've got a present for you too."

"What is it?"

"Pay me my finder's reward…"

He took two hundred *reis* out of his pocket:

"Paid in full."

Then she came close to him and told him:

"We're going to have a baby…"

Guma leaped up from the bed, he still hadn't got completely undressed. He dashed outdoors, Lívia asked:

"Where are you going?"

He pounded on Rufino's door, pounded hard. He heard the sound of people waking up and he was sorry he'd come to wake people up just to spread the news that Lívia was going to have a child. He heard Rufino ask:

"Who's there?"

"A friend. It's Guma."

Rufino opened the door. His eyes were puffy with sleep. Esmeralda appeared in the bedroom door wrapped in a sheet:

"Has something happened?"

Guma had lost his spirit. Foolish news to come give, to wake up people about. Rufino repeated:

"What is it, buddy?"

"Nothing. I just got in, I stopped by to see you people."

Rufino didn't understand:

"Well, if you don't feel like telling..."

"It's something foolish..."

Esmeralda didn't think so:

"Out with it, man. Loosen up your tongue."

"Lívia's going to have a baby..."

"Now?" Rufino asked.

Guma was angry:

"No. A while from now. But today she found out she's pregnant."

"Oh!"

Rufino looked out into the night. Esmeralda waved to Guma:

"Tomorrow I'm going to have a fight with that little faker. She was telling me she wasn't."

Rufino came out. He was walking in silence beside Guma:

"Let's go have a drink at the Beacon to celebrate."

They drank. Not one drink, a lot. There were quite a few people in the bar, sailors, canoemen, prostitutes, stevedores. When the night was over, completely drunk now, Rufino proposed:

"My good people, let us drink a toast here in honor of a happening that's going to happen to my chum Guma."

The others looked. They filled their glasses. A skinny woman came over to ask Guma:

"What is it?"

She wasn't drunk. Guma said:

"My wife's going to have a baby."

"How nice..." and she drank a little beer out of a shot glass. Then she went back to her corner and to the man who'd paid her for that night. Before leaving she smiled at Guma again and said:

"I hope she'll be happy."

With morning they went back home.

Guma carried the news to everybody he knew, and there were many of them scattered over different parts of the bay shore. Some gave presents for the child that was going to be born, most of them congratulated him. Esmeralda had also gone to his house, first thing in the morning the next day. She'd made a lot of fuss, told a lot of intimate stories, she was as happy as if it had been she, but when Lívia went into the kitchen to prepare some coffee, she ventured:

"I'm the only one who hasn't come up with a man who can give me a child. I'm sick and tired of it. My man doesn't give me a child..." She was revealing a portion of her thighs, her legs crossed.

Guma laughed:

"All you have to do is ask Rufino."

"Him? I don't want any black man's child. What I need is a child by someone whiter than me, to make the line better..."

She was looking at Guma, as if indicating that he was the one who could make her a child. Her green eyes were indicating that too, because she was staring at Guma in a strange way, calling. And her lips were half-open, her breasts heaving. Guma was in suspense for a moment, then he wanted her with everything he had. But he thought of Rufino, thought of Lívia:

"What about Rufino?"

Esmeralda leaped up. She shouted to Lívia:

"I'm leaving, neighbor. I've got a lot to do. I'll drop by later."

Her face was full of rage and shame. She stormed out, passed by Guma, spoke:

"Sucker..."

He remained seated with his head between his hands. Hellish woman, that one. She was trying to force him into something bad. And later on, what about Rufino? What he should do was tell everything to Rufino, tell the truth. But maybe he wouldn't believe, maybe he'd even fight with him, Rufino was mad about the mulatto girl. It wouldn't be good to say anything. But he wouldn't go with her either, betray a friend. The worst is that when she tempted him, when she looked at him with those green eyes, he didn't see anything else, he didn't think of Rufino doing him favors or Lívia's being pregnant, he only saw the mulatto woman's sexy body, the pointed breasts, the rolling hips, the body calling, the green eyes calling. A song of the sea talks about men who go off to drown in the deep green waves of the sea. That's what Esmeralda's eyes were like. It's as if he were drowning in her green eyes. She tempts him, she wants him. Her body danced before Guma's eyes. And she'd called him "sucker," she must have thought Guma was incapable of pulling her down, making her body moan with so much love. Oh! but Guma would show her. She would moan so much, she would bend so much that she'd have to confess that she'd been wrong. What did Rufino matter if she wanted him? When Lívia would never know. And Lívia coming in. She's bringing a mug of coffee and notices Guma's troubled face:

"Is something wrong?"

She's pregnant, her belly is getting rounder every day. Inside there she has a son of his, she doesn't deserve to be betrayed. What about poor Rufino, so good, always beside him, ever since childhood? He sees Esmeralda's green eyes in the cup of coffee. Her breasts are pointed like Rosa Palmeirão's. He has to write to Rosa Palmeirão, he thinks, to pass on the news of the kid's coming birth. But his thoughts won't leave him. Esmeralda's figure is before him. And Guma flees to the docks, where he agrees to go get a load of tobacco in Maragogipe, without even having anything to take out.

From Maragogipe he goes to Cachoeira. Lívia waited for him in vain. She stayed by the edge of the docks for a long time, all day and all night. Esmeralda waited for him too. She has a strong desire for him, a desire for that almost-white sailor who they say is so brave. And she has a desire for him mainly because Lívia is so happy, and so different from her, so concerned with the welfare of her husband, that she would like to wound her in the deepest part of her heart. She knows he'll come. She has to do everything to see to that. She has to tempt him in every way possible. Guma got in two days late.

Esmeralda was waiting for him at the window:

"You disappeared..."

"I was sailing. Carrying tobacco."

"Your wife even thought you'd run off..."

Guma laughed listlessly.

"I thought you were afraid..."

"Afraid of what?"

"Of seeing me."

"I don't know why."

"You don't remember the insult you gave me anymore?" The beginnings of her breasts appeared in the cut of her dress.

"You'll see someday..."

"What?"

But Guma ran away again. If not, he would have gone into her house right then and there and wouldn't have let her out of the room, it would have been right there. Lívia was waiting for him:

"You took a long time. Almost a week to go to Maragogipe..."

"Did you think I'd run away?"

"You're silly."

"That was the word I got."

"Who made that up?"

"Esmeralda told me."

"Now you stop to talk to the neighbors before coming home, is that it?"

The worst was that there was no anger in her voice. Only sadness. Suddenly, without knowing how, he found himself defending Esmeralda:

"She was fooling around. We said hello, she started saying nice things about you. She seems to be a good friend of yours. That's nice, because I like black Rufino."

"She's the one who doesn't like him one little bit."

"I've noticed that..." Guma said grudgingly. He wasn't remembering anymore that Esmeralda was close to becoming his lover. He was angry with her because the mulatto girl didn't return Rufino's affection. "I've noticed. The day Rufino catches on, she's in trouble..."

"Stop saying bad things about other people..." said old Francisco, coming in. He was drunk, which was unusual, and he was bringing Filadélfio to dinner. He'd run into "the doctor" at the Beacon of the Stars without a nickel and after they'd drunk up everything the old man had, the latter brought him to dinner:

"Can you feed another mouth? A good mouth."

Filadélfio shook Guma's hand:

"Whatever you've got is fine. You don't have to kill the fatted calf." And he laughed at his witticism. The others laughed too.

Lívia served dinner. The eternal fish as always, beans and dried meat. Filadélfio, halfway through dinner, told Lívia the story of the letter, about the fight over the seashell and the coffer. And he asked Lívia:

"Isn't coffer a lot prettier?"

She took Guma's side:

"I like seashell..."

Guma was downcast. Lívia hadn't known that the letter had been a joint effort. Filadélfio insisted:

"Remember, it's a golden coffer. Did you ever set eyes on a golden coffer?"

When they'd left, Guma started to explain the story of the letter. Lívia threw her arms around his neck:

"Be quiet, you good-for-nothing. You never liked me.,,"

He carried her into the bedroom. She protested:

"Not after dinner, no."

But in the middle of the night Lívia began to feel ill. Something was wrong, her stomach was rolling, she thought she was going to die. She tried to vomit, but she couldn't. She was rocking on the bed, she needed air, her stomach ached all over.

"Do you think I'm going to have the child?"

Guma ran out madly. He woke up Esmeralda (Rufino was on a trip), pounding on the door. She asked who it was:

"Guma."

She came, grabbed his hand, pulled him inside:

"Lívia's dying, Esmeralda. Something's happened to her. She's dying."

"What?" Esmeralda had already gone back in. "I'll be right there. Just let me get some clothes on."

"You stay with her, I'm going for Dr. Rodrigo."

"You can go, I'll stay."

From the corner he could see Esmeralda already crossing the small stretch of clay that separated the two houses.

Dr. Rodrigo, while he was getting dressed, asked him to tell him what they'd done. Then he calmed him:

"It's probably nothing... Just something to do with her pregnancy."

Guma managed to find old Francisco sitting at a table in the Beacon of the Stars, drinking with Filadélfio, telling stories to some sailors. In the bar a blind man was playing the guitar. Guma roused Francisco out of his drunkenness:

"Lívia's dying."

Old Francisco popped out his eyes and wanted to run out. Guma stopped him:

"No, the doctor's gone to see her. You go up above and get her aunt and uncle. Hurry up."

"I wanted to see her," old Francisco's voice was choked up.

"The doctor said maybe nothing's wrong."

Old Francisco left. Guma went back home. He went with fear. Sometimes he almost ran, other times he slowed his steps as if fearful that he would find her dead, she and the son both lost. He went into the house like a thief. The candlestick was in the bedroom, from where voices were coming. He saw Esmeralda rush out and go back in with a basin of water and a cloth. And he without the courage to approach. Then it was Dr. Rodrigo who came out. Guma caught up with him in the hallway:

"How is she, doctor?"

"It wasn't anything. It might have been if you hadn't called me right away. She could have had a miscarriage. What she needs now is rest. Come by my place tomorrow, I'll give you some medicine for her."

Guma was laughing with his mouth and with his eyes:

"So nothing's going to happen to her?"

"You can relax. What she needs is rest."

Guma went into the bedroom. Esmeralda put her finger to her mouth, calling for silence. She was stroking Lívia's head, sitting on the edge of the bed. Lívia turned her eyes, saw Guma, smiled:

"I figured I was going to die."

"The doctor says it's nothing. You've got to go to sleep."

Esmeralda made him leave. He went away, and he was feeling a different tenderness for Esmeralda now, a wanting to caress her without any desire of possession. She'd been good with Lívia.

He went into the dark parlor. He had a hammock stretched out from one side to the other, he lay down in it and began to puff on his pipe. He heard Esmeralda's soft steps as she came out of the bedroom with the candle. She was walking on tiptoes, he could have sworn. Her strong body was swaying like a sloop, because she never walked on tiptoes. Her buttocks were rolling like a sailor. A mulatto woman and so much a one. She put the candlestick down in the dining room. Now she goes over to where Guma is. He hears her steps, softly. And desire quickly begins to take him over. Lívia's still labored breathing reaches out to the parlor. But Esmeralda's steps come closer, cover the sound of Lívia's breathing with their sound.

"She's sleeping," she said.

She leans against the cords of the hammock:

"You had a bit of a fright, eh?"

"Are you tired? I woke you up..."

"I'd do it willingly for you."

She sat down in the hammock. Now her legs touch Guma's. And suddenly she throws herself on him and bites him on the mouth. They roll around in the hammock and he possesses her without even getting undressed, without thinking. The hammock creaks and Lívia wakes up:

"Guma!"

He shakes Esmeralda, who is up on his feet. He runs to the bedroom. Lívia asks:

"You there?"

"Yes."

He went over to stroke her hair, but his hand still held the warmth of Esmeralda's body and he held back the gesture. She calls:

"Come to bed with me..."

He stands there, not knowing what to say. In the other room Esmeralda is waiting for him to finish what they had started. But he remembers her aunt and uncle:

"You go to sleep. I'm waiting for your aunt and uncle. I sent old Francisco to get them..."

"You've given them a scare."

"I was afraid too."

Again he holds out his hand to caress her. Again he remembers Esmeralda and a knot forms in his throat. What about Rufino? Lívia turns over in bed, closes her eyes. He goes into the parlor. Esmeralda is stretched out in the hammock, she's opened her dress, her breasts throb. He remains standing like a booby. She stretches out her hand, calls him.

She pulls him down on top of her, presses against him. But he's so far away that she asks:

"Am I that sour for you?..."

And they start all over again. He's crazy now, he no longer knows what he's doing, doesn't think, doesn't remember anyone. Only the body that he tightens against his in a struggle that seems more like one to the death. And when they fall on top of each other Esmeralda speaks softly:

"If Rufino could only see this..."

Guma comes to. It's really Esmeralda who's there. It's Rufino's woman. And his own woman is sick and asleep in the next room. Esmeralda mentions Rufino again. Guma can't hear anything more. His eyes are bloodshot, his mouth is dry, his hands look for Esmeralda's neck. They begin to tighten. She says:

"Stop that fooling—"

It's not fooling. He'll kill her and then he'll go off to meet Janaína at the bottom of the sea. Esmeralda is already about to cry out when Guma hears the voices of Lívia's aunt and uncle talking to old Francisco. He leaps out of the hammock, Esmeralda is fixing herself up hurriedly, but Lívia's aunt is peeping into the parlor with startled eyes. Guma rubs his now useless hands:

"Lívia is better now."

# THERE WERE FIVE CHILDREN

As soon as Lívia was better he took a trip. He was running away from Esmeralda, who was pursuing him now, wanting to make dates at deserted spots on the sand of the waterfront, threatening to raise a row. But he was running away mainly from meeting Rufino, who would be coming in a few days later, bringing a load for the market at Água dos Meninos.

He'd taken a trip to Santo Amaro, had lingered. Contrary to his custom he'd gone to all the bars, practically not staying on the sloop to look at the moon and the stars in the sky. Then he would see Rufino, would see the face of horror he would put on if he found out. Guma saw his life of misfortunes. Ever since he was small a curse had been laid on him. One day his mother had come, he was expecting a woman of the streets, he'd felt desires for her. On that day he'd thought of jumping into the water, going with Iemanjá on the endless trip through the seas of Aiocá. It would have been better if he had killed himself that time. Nobody would have missed him, old Francisco might have been a little sad, but then he would console himself. He would have Guma's name tattooed on his arm beside those of the four sloops he'd owned and would add the child's tale to the many he knew:

"I had a nephew that Janaína wanted. And one full-moon night she carried him off to be with her. He was still only a child but he knew how to sail a sloop and could lift a sack of flour. Janaína wanted him..."

That's how old Francisco would have told the story. Now

it would be different. He couldn't even kill himself, couldn't leave Lívia in poverty with a child in her belly. And what story would he leave for old Francisco to tell? He'd betrayed a friend, he'd had the woman of somebody who'd done him favors. And then he'd jumped into the water, afraid of what the friend would do, leaving his wife starving with a child in her belly. Old Francisco would add that it all came from his mother's blood, a woman of the streets. And he wouldn't tattoo his name beside the names of his four sloops. He would be ashamed of him.

Guma doesn't look at the moon. He'd broken the law of the waterfront. It isn't fear of Rufino that he has. If he hadn't been his friend it wouldn't have made any difference. He's ashamed, ashamed of himself and for Lívia. He'd like to kill Esmeralda and then die, sailing the *Valiant* onto some shoals. She tempted him, he didn't even think of his friend Rufino, of Lívia sick in the next room. And her aunt had looked at him suspiciously, he'd never been able to look her in the eye again. Maybe she hadn't suspected anything at all, she'd even thanked Esmeralda a lot for having taken such good care of Lívia. And the worst is that now Lívia was very thankful to Esmeralda, had ordered a present for her, the mulatto girl had taken advantage of it to spend all her time there, on the lookout for Guma. He would go out, go to the Beacon of the Stars, drink so much that they were even commenting about it on the waterfront. And she pursued him, every time she was able to talk to him she wanted to know where they could meet, said that she knew deserted places on the sand. Guma knew too. He'd taken lots of mulattoes, lots of black girls to the beach on full-moon nights. But he didn't want to take Esmeralda, he didn't want to see her anymore, what he wanted was to kill her and kill himself after. But he couldn't leave Lívia with a child in her belly. It had been without thinking, desire sees nothing. At that moment he hadn't seen anyone, not Rufino, not Lívia, not anyone. He'd only seen Esmeralda's dark body, her protruding breasts, her dazzling green eyes. And now to suffer. He'll have to run into Rufino sooner or later, have to chat with him, laugh with him, give him a hug the way you hug a friend who's done favors for you. And behind Rufino's back Esmeralda will signal him, make dates, smile.

What about Lívia, who suffers so much when he goes away, Lívia who's so afraid for him? Lívia doesn't deserve that either, Lívia was sick because of him, she had a child of his in her belly. From the living room he'd heard Lívia's rapid breathing and still he hadn't thought about any of that. Esmeralda had lain down in the hammock, he'd only seen the mulatto's body, her lustful eyes. Then he'd tried to kill her. He would have strangled her if the aunt and uncle hadn't arrived.

The night in Santo Amaro is clear. On the river banks the cane fields stretch out, green in the moonlight. Beetle shines in the sky, he was a brave man, it was never said that Beetle had had a friend's woman. He was a man who respected his responsibilities, a friend of his friends. Guma had abandoned everything, now all that was left for him was to journey under the waters. What would his life be like otherwise? He would run into Esmeralda every day, someday he would have to be with her, lie down with her, moan with love with the mulatto woman. On those days he would see Lívia too, working in the house, weeping for him, thinking that he would die in the water someday. He would see Rufino with his loud laugh, putting his arm around his shoulder, saying "my buddy, my old buddy." He would see all those he had betrayed, because he'd betrayed Esmeralda too, he no longer wanted her, didn't have any more desire for her voluptuous body. He'd betrayed them all, he'd betrayed his son, too, by making him be born, he wasn't leaving him a tradition on the waterfront. No one would point at him, saying with pride:

. "There goes the son of Guma, a tough cookie who used to be in these parts..."

No. He was a traitor, he'd done the same thing as the person who'd stabbed Beetle in the back. That fellow had called himself a friend of the bandit, one day he put a knife in his back, called the others to cut the knife out of him. He became a police corporal, but today they only mention him by spitting so his name won't stain the mouth of the person saying it. That's what Guma's like. He stretches out on the sloop, puts his hand in the cold water. On the waterfront nobody knows yet. It's just that they're surprised that he drinks so much now, he'd never done things like that. But they don't know why, they think it's the happiness of having a son about to be born.

Lívia is probably thinking about him at that moment; suffering for his being on the water. Old Francisco's wife had died of joy the day he came back. That's how Lívia waits for him too on his return trip. It was certain that she'd like him to give up the sloop, go up to the city, work at something else. But she never spoke about that, because she knew quite well that men who live off the sea never stay on land to work in some other profession. Even those people who come to the sea, like Dona Dulce, don't ever go back. The enchantment of Iemanjá is very strong. But he could go away. He would go with Lívia to someplace far away from there, somebody had already told him that a man can make a lot of money in Ilhéus. He'd go work at some other trade, run away from that place.

He looks at the *Valiant*. It had belonged to old Francisco, it had been the fifth one that the old man had owned. It wasn't new anymore, it had been plying those waters for many years. It had cut across the bay and gone up the river countless times, it had gone with Guma to save the *Canavieiras,* a few times it had been on the point of foundering, one day it had got a leak in its hull. It had already gone through any number of sails, it was a sloop with tradition. And now Guma is prepared to end its career. Sell it to some skipper and go away: that's the best solution. It's the punishment he deserves: leave the waterfront, abandon the sea, go to other places. One day he'd thought about traveling, sailing the seas on a big ship like Chico Tristeza. Then he'd met Lívia, abandoned his ideas of traveling, stayed with her, brought her to the sad life of the waterfront, for the suffering of expecting certain death for him every day. And then he'd betrayed even her, betrayed Rufino, his friend. If he hadn't been a sailor he would have wept like a child or a woman.

Now all that's left for him is to wait for an adventure that will carry him off and carry the *Valiant* off too, because he'd rather not turn it over to someone else. Because fleeing the docks, going to other lands is impossible for him to do. Only those who live on the sea know how impossible it is to abandon it. Even for those who can look a friend in the face or stare at the bright moon in the sky.

If he hadn't been a sailor, Guma would have wept like a child, like a woman, like a prisoner in a gloomy dungeon.

He met Rufino in the middle of the bay, and it was better that way. Rufino's canoe was taking on water, he'd left port without noticing. Guma helped him bail. Part of the cargo was lost, the black man was carrying sugar. The sacks on the bottom were wet and the sugar was dissolving. Guma transferred them to the *Valiant* and laid them out in the sun. He tried not to look at Rufino, who was worried about the damage:

"The freight money is lost at least, to pay for the damage."

"Maybe not. The sacks will dry out, we'll see how much has been lost. I don't think too much."

"I don't know how it happened. I'm always careful about things like that. But Colonel Tinoco sent his men to load the sugar, I was with them without doing anything. I went off to have a shot of painkiller because it was raining out there, and when I got back everything was ready. I left, I only noticed something halfway across. The canoe was so heavy I couldn't handle it. I went to see what it was, shipping water..."

"You shouldn't pay anything and still collect for the hole in the canoe. It was made by his men."

"But I can't be sure of that. When I left I scraped the shoals at the mouth of the river. That was what did it."

They went along chatting a bit. But soon the sloop went ahead. Rufino was rowing in the stern to help the canoe along. Until he disappeared. Guma couldn't see him anymore. He didn't even know how he could talk to him, how he could bear his look, laugh when he laughed. What he should have done was to tell him, let Rufino hit him over the head with his oar. The sloop races over the water, the wind blows.

Lívia is waiting on the dock. Esmeralda is with her, and asks with an innocent air:

"Did you see my black man out there?"

"He's coming in his canoe. I even brought some sacks of sugar for him. His canoe was taking on water..."

Lívia is interested:

"Did anything happen?"

Esmeralda stares at Guma:

"Did anybody do anything to him?" He can see that she's afraid there'd been a fight between the two of them.

"It looks like it was in coming back, he hit a shoal... He'll be tying up over there soon. He's all upset about the damage."

He moored the sloop, was heading home with Lívia. Esmeralda told them:

"I'm going over to the Pôrto da Lenha to wait for him."

"Tell him the sacks are here."

"O.K."

She stood looking at the couple going up. Guma was running away from her. Afraid of Rufino, afraid of Lívia, or didn't he like her lovemaking? A lot of men on the waterfront were wild about her. They were afraid of Rufino, but even so they found ways of paying compliments, making propositions, sending presents. Only Guma ran away from her. Guma, whom she wanted because he was light, had long dark hair almost down to his neck, red lips like a baby's. Her breasts stood out, her eyes went with the man going up the beach. Why was he running away? She didn't think it could be remorse. She'd write a letter to Janaína, she'd find out. She was going along by the Pôrto da Lenha. The canoemen greeted her, a sailor who was painting the hull of a freighter stopped work, whistled with admiration. Only Guma ran away from her. To get him once she'd had to do any number of things, even throw herself at him, offer herself like a streetwalker, then he'd even tried to kill her. Esmeralda's hips were worth their weight in gold, they said on the docks. Guma didn't pay any attention to them, Guma was running away from her. He was running away from her body, from her eyes. He only had eyes for Lívia, skinny and teary. Esmeralda heard the sailor's thin whistle. She looked and smiled. He signaled with his fingers that he was off at six o'clock, pointed to the sand. She smiled. Why was Guma running away from her? It was fear of Rufino most likely, fear of the black man's vengeance, of his muscular arms, strong from rowing in a canoe all day long. Esmeralda didn't think about remorse. Maybe she didn't know the word. A cold wind was blowing along the waterfront. In the distance she spotted Rufino's canoe cutting the water.

Night fell cold, the wind curled the sand on the beach and the water on the sea. A few sloops were going out. That wind rarely brought on a storm. The fine sand flew over the waterfront, it was heading toward the streets of the city. There was a festival at the church of Conceição da Praia, women passed wrapped in shawls, men were coming down the slope. The wind passed through them. Bells tolled. Businesses had closed, the lower city was becoming deserted.

After dinner old Francisco went out. He was going over by the church to chat, to tell and listen to stories. Guma lighted his pipe, thought of going to the docks later on to see if they'd unloaded the sloop, see if he could dig up a trip for the following day. Lívia was washing the dishes, her belly stuck out in front of her, she'd lost a little color, she was dull now, a little pale. She was carrying a child in her belly, she

went to see Dr. Rodrigo every day, she had nausea. Guma
spied on her. She was coming and going, washing the tin
plates, the thick mugs. The dog, a small black pooch, was
gnawing on bones on the earthen kitchen floor. The empty
demitasse cup was resting on the edge of the table. Guma
heard Rufino get up in the living room of the house next
door. He had just eaten, no doubt. He was talking to Esmeralda, it was as if they were talking in Guma's parlor, he
heard everything:

"I'm going over to talk to Colonel Tinoco about that
bunch of sacks that got wet. It's going to be a good argument."

Esmeralda was speaking in a loud voice:

"Are you going to let me go look in on the festival at
Conceição? The church is all prettied up and she's one of my
favorite saints."

"Go ahead, but come back early, I'm tired. I want to turn
in early."

Esmeralda had spoken in a loud voice. Naturally, it had
been for him to hear, Guma thinks. But he won't go to
Conceição da Praia. From the window he can see the
church all lighted up like a passenger ship. And if he goes
it will be with Lívia, who no doubt will want to say a
prayer for their child. The bells are tolling an invitation.
The wind comes in through the window. Guma studies
the grayish sky. The afternoon had been so beautiful!
Night wasn't forecasting anything good, however. The
moon is waning, a thin yellow thing in the sky. Rufino's
voice comes through the wall:

"You there, buddy?"

"I am."

"I'm going over to lock horns with old Tinoco."

"It wasn't your fault."

"But he's a tough old snapping turtle, you cut off his head
and he still hangs on wanting to stay alive."

"Explain it to him."

"I'll holler at him a couple of times..."

Esmeralda was taking her leave on the other side:

"I won't stay long."

Rufino's voice came, muffled:

"Let me just nuzzle you, girl."

Guma felt bad. He didn't want to have anything to do with her, not even see her, but it worked on him as if Rufino had stolen something from him. He was really the one who'd stolen something from Rufino, betrayed him. Esmeralda's steps went off. Rufino spoke loudly:

"She's off to church. . ."

And he shouted at her, reminding her:

"Hell, aren't you going to ask Lívia?"

"She told me she's going with Guma," and the steps were lost on the hill.

Rufino was walking around the room now. Guma looked at the sky again. The wind was getting stronger all the time, a few rare stars appeared among the clouds. "There's going to be a storm," he thought. Lívia had finished washing the dishes, he asked:

"Do you want to go to the festival?"

She was pale, very pale. Her belly stuck out under her dress, it might look ridiculous. But Guma didn't notice any of that. He only knew that she was carrying his son, she was sick because of it and he'd betrayed her. He heard Rufino go off. Lívia was standing, waiting for an answer:

"Go change your dress."

She went into the bedroom but came out again because there was a knock on the door:

"Who is it?"

"A friend of the house."

The voice was unfamiliar, however, they didn't remember ever having heard it. Lívia looked at Guma and her eyes were frightened. He got up:

"Are you afraid?"

"Who is it?"

The knocks on the door were repeated:

"Isn't anybody home? Is this a cemetery or a sunken ship of a house?"

It was a sailor no doubt. Guma opened the door. In the darkness of the street a pipe was glowing and a shape appeared behind it, wrapped in a large cape:

"Where's Francisco? Where's that son of a bitch? He's not dead, I know that, he's such a rotten piece that even the devil doesn't want him..."

"He went out."

Lívia was peeping from behind Guma. The shape moved, seemed to be coming into the vestibule. And that's just what it did. The head came forward, looked inside. It seemed that only at that moment did he spot Guma:

"And who might you be?"

"Guma."

"Who the hell is Guma? Do you think that means anything to me?"

Guma was getting annoyed:

"And who are you?"

The answer from the shape was to come forward and through the door. But Guma put out his arm, barring the way:

"What do you want?"

The old man shoved Guma's arm aside, held the sloop master against the wall, and Guma couldn't move at all. The shape had the strength of twenty men. Lívia came forward:

"What is it you want, sir?"

The man let go of Guma, went into the room lighted by the candle. Now Guma could see that it was an old man with a white mustache, tall, almost a giant. The cape opened slightly and Lívia noticed the dagger that appeared. The old man was looking around the house, the red light from the candle making the shadows larger:

"So this is where that fool Francisco lives, eh? And you, who are you?" he pointed to Lívia.

She was going to answer, Guma crossed in front:

"First tell me who you are?"

"Are you Francisco's son? I never heard that he had a son."

"I'm Frederico's son. I'm his nephew." He was sorry he'd answered.

The old man looked at him with surprise:

"Frederico's?"

He looked at Lívia, looked at Guma again:

"Is she your wife?"

Guma nodded yes. The old man spotted Lívia's belly, turned to Guma again:

"Your father never got married..."

He had white hair and seemed to be cold, even with his cape on. In spite of everything he'd said, Guma didn't feel insulted.

"He died some time ago, didn't he?"

"A long time ago, yes."

"But Francisco didn't die, did he?"

He looked at the candle, turned to Guma:

"Don't you know who I am? Francisco never told you?"

"No."

The old man asked Lívia:

"Have you got any liquor here? Let's have a drink to celebrate the return of a relative."

Lívia went out but almost at the same instant she heard the roar from Francisco who had arrived and was peeking through the window to see who the visitor was:

"Leôncio!"

He came quickly into the living room. Lívia came back with the bottle of cane liquor, stood watching. Francisco still couldn't believe it:

"I'd given you up for dead. It was so long ago..."

Guma said: "Who is he, then?"

Old Francisco spoke almost in a whisper, he looked like a man who was tired from a long race:

"It's your uncle. My brother."

He turned to the newcomer, pointed to Guma:

"He's Frederico's boy."

Lívia served the drinks, the old man drank his down in one swallow, put the glass on the floor. Francisco sat down:

"Aren't you in a hurry?"

"You're in a hurry to get rid of me, right?" The old man held in a laugh. His white mustache quivered.

"You've got nothing to do here. Everybody thinks you're dead, no one knows you anymore."

"Everybody thinks I'm dead, eh?"

"Yes, everybody thinks you're dead. Why did you want to come back? There's nothing for you here, nothing at all…"

Guma and Lívia were startled, she was clutching the bottle of liquor. Old Francisco had a look of weariness, of a man near death, he seemed much older, he was facing a story he'd never told. Leôncio looked at the waterfront through the window. A woman passed by the house, it was Judith. She was dressed in black, carrying a child in her arms. Her house was far off, her mother was with her now, had come to help her, they both washed clothes, the child was thin and they said he wouldn't last long. Leôncio asked:

"A widow?"

"She's a widow, what's it to you? I've already told you that you've got no business here, none at all. Why did you come? You were dead, why did you come?"

"Why did you come…" the old man repeated, and it was as if he were weeping. But he laughed. "You're not glad to see me. You haven't even given your brother a hug."

"Go away. You've got no business here."

Once more the old man's eyes sought the docks, the cloudy sky. It was as if he were trying to recognize all that, an old sailor who had come back to his port.

It was as if he were trying to recognize all that. He was staring at the sky for a long time, the waterfront lost in the mist. The night was getting cold on the sea. The old man turned to Francisco:

"There's going to be a storm tonight… Did you notice?"

"Go away. Your place isn't here."

He made an enormous effort, went on:

"This isn't your port..."

The old man had lost his aggressiveness, lowered his head, and his voice became pleading, as if he had come from far off:

"Let me stay for just a couple of nights. It's been so long."

Lívia held back old Francisco's refusal:

"Stay, this is your house."

Francisco looked at her with sorrow.

"I'm tired, I've come from a long way off."

"Stay as long as you want," Lívia repeated.

"Just two nights..." He turned to Francisco. "Don't be afraid."

He looked at the sky, the sea, the docks. There was the joy of an arrival in his whole being. An old seadog who had come back to his waterfront. Francisco closed his eyes in the chair, the wrinkles in his face opened. Leôncio only turned to ask:

"Do you happen to have a picture of my father?"

As if he didn't have an answer, he was silent for a long time. Then he said to Guma:

"Do you go to bed early?"

"Why?"

"I'm going to the harbor, leave the door open. When I come in I'll lock up."

"All right."

He buttoned up his cape, pulled his hat over his head, and went toward the door. But he turned and, coming close to Lívia, put his hand to his enormous chest, took out a medal, gave it to her:

"This is for you."

Old Francisco, after he had left, was still saying:

"Why did he come? You're not going to let him stay here, are you, Lívia?"

"Tell me about it, uncle," Guma asked.

"It's no good stirring up the dead. Everybody thinks he's dead."

He went out again and they saw that he was heading for

the Beacon of the Stars. No ship had dropped anchor that
day, how had Leôncio arrived? Nor had any ship gone out
that night, and yet he hadn't returned that night or any other.
The medal he'd given Lívia was gold and seemed to have
come from a faraway country, from a time long past. He,
too, seemed to have come from far away and to have belonged to a different time.

They still went to the church of Conceição da Feira. Lívia
had asked Guma if he knew anything about that story. He
didn't know anything, old Francisco had never spoken about
that brother. He didn't see Esmeralda in the church. Naturally, she'd grown tired of waiting and had gone away.
Guma felt relieved. He wouldn't have been able to have
taken her signaling. Could it have been because of a tale like
that that Leôncio couldn't appear on the waterfront, had lost
his port? A sailor only loses his port, his waterfront, when
he does something miserable. Esmeralda wasn't in the
church that smelled of incense. There were booths outside,
"Doctor" Filadélfio was earning a few nickels at his table
where he put poems and letters together. A black man was
singing to a group:

> "On the day I wake up in the morning
> Damned to my very bones,
> I turn scones into bananas,
> I turn bananas to scones."

They returned home. From the other side of the wall Rufino's voice asked:

"Is that you, buddy?"

"It's us, yes. We just got in."

"Is the festival all over?"

"The one in the church is. But there's a fair on the
square."

"Did you see Esmeralda there, Lívia?"

"I didn't see her, no. But there wasn't much to do there."

Rufino muttered a threat. Guma asked:

"How did it go with the colonel?"

"Oh! we're going to split the damage…"

A few minutes later he spoke:

"It's a nasty night. It looks like we're going to have a bad one."

Guma and Lívia went into the bedroom. She looked at the medal Leôncio had given her. Guma examined it too: "It's pretty." They could hear Rufino walking about in the other house. Esmeralda was capable of lying in the sand with someone else, anywhere. Rufino was going to suspect, she was capable of telling him that Guma was her lover too. And then it would really be a bad one, worse than any storm. He wouldn't lift a hand against Rufino, wouldn't fight with him. He'd let himself be killed because he was his friend. But what about Lívia, and their child, and old Francisco? He'd be a sailor without a port, even after he was dead. He was left with that anxiety until he heard Esmeralda's steps as she went in and her words for Rufino:

"I got held up, love. But I was looking at everything. I thought you'd put in an appearance."

"You bitch, where were you hanging out? Nobody saw you there."

"Come on, in that crowd of people. I even saw Lívia…"

Then they heard the slaps. He must have been hitting her:

"If I catch you cheating on me I'll send you straight to hell."

"Cheating on you? I deny that. Don't you hit me…"

Then there weren't any more slaps, there was no more fighting. The mulatto woman had green eyes and round hips. The noise wasn't of fighting, slaps anymore. She had her pointed breasts and Rufino was crazy about her.

The storm broke at midnight. Normally that wind didn't bring on a storm, but when it did it was terrible. It fell in the middle of the night, caught a lot of ships at sea. Guma was awakened by old Francisco, who was coming back from the Beacon of the Stars. He woke up Rufino too:

"It seems that three boats had already turned over. They're asking for help. Some boats are going out, they want you people to go too. Some of the boats had families on board, everything went over."

"Where?"

"Close by. At the harbor mouth."

They ran out. Guma cast off the sloop, Rufino went with him. The breakers were hitting the edge of the docks. Other sloops were already ahead of them, Guma soon caught up with them. They saw a sail from one of the shipwrecked sloops in the black night. The *Sailor Without a Port* was going a little ahead, cutting the sea. The shape of Master Manuel appeared in the light of the lantern. Guma called:

"Ahoy, Manuel!"

"Is that you, Guma?"

Rufino was sitting down. Suddenly he asked Guma:

"Have you heard them talking about Esmeralda on the waterfront?"

"What kind of talk?" Guma asked with an effort.

The waves were hitting the sloop. In front the *Sailor Without a Port* seemed to disappear with every wave.

"Talk that she's loose. They wouldn't say it to me..."

"I never heard anything, no."

"You know I've been off on trips. I want you to do something for me: When you find out something, let me know... I don't want to be a sucker. I'm talking to you like this because you're my friend. I'm worried about that mulatto."

Guma didn't even know which way the sloop was heading. Rufino went on:

"The worst of it is that I love her."

"I never heard any talk..."

They reached the harbor mouth. Pieces of three sloops were floating. The storm was trying to wreck the ones who'd come to rescue them. People were hanging onto pieces of boards, hulls of the sloops. And they were shouting, crying, except for Paulo, who was skipper of one of the wrecked sloops and was holding a child in his arms. The sharks had already got two people and had taken off the leg of a third. Master Manuel began to pull people into his sloop. Others were doing the same, but it wasn't always easy, the sloops were moving about, some people in the water let go of the planks they were holding on to, didn't have time to reach the sloop, and disappeared under the water. Paulo handed the child to Manuel. When he got into the sloop he said:

"There were five. Only that one is left..."

They'd saved the child's mother, too, who was staring like a madwoman with the child clutched to her breast. The man whose leg had been eaten by a shark was lying in Guma's sloop crying out. An old man had also got into his sloop. Rufino jumped into the water to save somebody who hadn't caught the sloop in time. But he didn't see him, he only saw the shark that was chasing him, that was swimming around him. Guma looked, let go of the *Valiant*'s tiller, dove in with a knife in his teeth. He swam under the fish, Rufino came up unhurt. At the moment of death the shark was still swinging his tail and almost knocked Guma out.

Rufino told him:

"If it hadn't been for you..."

"It wasn't anything."

Now they were looking for the bodies. A piece of arm floated by, it was that of a young woman, and the rest of her was with the sharks. Pieces of clothing, bodies. Seven people had died. Four children, two men, and a woman. The ones saved came in with the corpses. The mother who was holding the child against her breast was looking at the other one with curly hair lying in the sloop. There were five, there were five children that the father was waiting for on the docks. They were coming from an outing to Cachoeira, the storm caught them. The two men who had died were skippers of two of the wrecked sloops.

Only Paulo was saved and only in order to save the child. Otherwise he too would have died with his passengers, would have gone to the bottom with his ship. There were five children, and now the mother was hugging to her breast the only one left alive. The body of another was traveling in the sloop. The other three had stayed with the sharks, the mother wouldn't even see their bodies again. The one on the *Valiant* is that of a little boy with curly hair. The mother doesn't weep, she just clings to the only child she has left. The sea rises up in great waves. The sloops return. The hull of one of the wrecks slowly disappears. There were five children.

# CALM WATERS

Since the return and new disappearance of Leôncio, old Francisco didn't spend much time at home. He lived on the docks, talking, drinking at the Beacon of the Stars, coming home drunk in the wee small hours. He hadn't wanted to tell Leôncio's tale, and he asked Guma never to bring it up in his presence. Guma was concerned about old Francisco's drinking bouts. Dr. Rodrigo had already told him that the old man wouldn't last very long that way. He called his uncle's attention to it but got a discouraging answer:

"You live your own life..."

Rufino had changed too. At first Guma thought he might have suspected something, but even Esmeralda had put him completely aside for a long time. It looked as if she'd found someone else. Guma was more relaxed, calmer. All he thought about was her death, that was certainly what he thought about most: Esmeralda dead and he free of the whole burden. He had the feeling that if the mulatto woman died, all reason for sadness and remorse would disappear. He thought so much about it that he even came to see her body laid out in the parlor, her green eyes closed, the mouth that had been thirsty for kisses locked in death. He saw Rufino soon consoling himself with someone else. Lívia would weep beside the coffin, the men on the waterfront would come to take one last look at her. She'd been a pretty mulatto.

The worst, however, was that she wasn't dead, she's alive and is most certainly cheating on Rufino with someone else. Guma felt jealous in spite of himself. The talk on the waterfront was that it was a sailor. A freighter had put in for repairs over eight days ago. A sailor had taken a look at Esmeralda's hips, tasted her kisses, possessed her flesh. Rufino was suspicious, he spied on the mulatto woman.

One afternoon Guma had just returned from a trip. Rufino sought him out, then he spoke right up:

"She put horns on me!"

"What?"

"She cheated on me, she's making a sucker out of me."

And he explained:

"I already had a bee in my bonnet. I took a good look and I ended up learning about the whole dirty affair. I found one of his letters today."

"Who was it?"

"A sailor on the *Miranda*. The ship sailed today, that's why he didn't swallow a piece of steel."

"What are you going to do?"

"I'm going to teach her a lesson. She played around with my love. I liked that mulatto a lot, buddy."

"What are you going to do? You're not going to get yourself in trouble because of her, are you?"

"I've known all along she wasn't worth nothing. She was a cheating woman right from the start. When I picked her up she'd already had a lot of men, she had a rotten reputation. But when people fall for somebody they don't see nothing."

He was looking at something on the horizon line. His voice was low and flat. He didn't seem to be the same Rufino who sang *emboladas*.

"I was thinking it would be like other times. I'd make it with her and take off. But she got to me, it was too late. And everybody's laughing at me on the waterfront."

He lowered his voice even more:

"And you knew and didn't ever tell me anything."

"I didn't know anything. I'm just learning it from your mouth now. What are you going to do?"

"All I feel like doing is breaking her in two and sinking the guy."

"Don't get yourself in trouble because of her."

"I'll tell you something: I'm not sure what I'm going to do, but if anything bad happens, I want you to do one thing for me."

"Stop thinking about doing anything foolish. Just kick her out…"

"Every month I've been sending twenty *milreis* to my mother, she's an old lady. She lives over in Lapa, she can't work anymore. If I get in trouble you sell my canoe and send her the money."

He left suddenly, without giving Guma time to hold him back. He was running toward the docks. In the house next door Esmeralda was singing in a loud voice. Guma ran after Rufino but he couldn't catch him.

The moon, the full moon that's white in the sky, hears Rufino's song. "I miss her, a woman who was false and tricked my heart." The song was popular on the waterfront, and Esmeralda was riding along in the canoe without suspecting anything. She was wearing her green dress because he'd said they were going to the festival in Santo Amaro. And since the green dress was his favorite she'd put it on to please her man. She didn't like him, that's true. But when the black man sang there was no one who could resist that hot voice. Esmeralda was moving closer to him. The oars were cutting the water, helping the wind that was pushing the sail. The river is deserted, opening up its great breadth and reflecting the stars like a mirror. Rufino continues singing his song. But since the time has come, he stows his oars, his voice falls silent. Esmeralda leans against him:

"That was pretty…"

"Did you like it?"

He looked at her. Green eyes that tempted, a mouth that opened for a kiss. Rufino looked away, maybe he wouldn't be able to resist. At that moment a sailor on board the *Miranda* was laughing at him.

"Do you know what I'm going to do?"

"What?"

"I'm going to kill you."

"Stop kidding..."

The canoe was moving slowly, the breeze was blowing softly. It was a night for love. Rufino was speaking with sadness in his voice, there was no hate there:

"You cheated on me with a sailor off the *Miranda.*"

"Who squealed to you?"

"Everybody knows, everybody was laughing at me. If you didn't love me why didn't you leave? But you wanted everybody to laugh at me. That's why I'm going to kill you."

"It was Guma who told you, wasn't it?" (She knew that death was certain, she wanted to torture him as much as possible.) "And you're going to kill me? Then you'll do time in jail. It'd be better if you didn't kill me. Let me go away, I'll never show my face on this waterfront again."

"You're going to see Janaína. Get ready."

"It was Guma who told you, wasn't it? He was jealous, I'd already spotted it. Did he think I only belonged to him? But I only did it with Guma a few times. The one I liked was the sailor."

"Don't try to turn me against Guma. He pulled me out of the shark's mouth, you're trying to turn me against him."

"Am I?"

She told him everything, down to the smallest detail. She told him how Guma had had her the night Lívia wasn't feeling well. And she laughed.

"Now you're going to kill me. There are a lot of people on the waterfront to laugh when you go by, there's Floriano, there's Guma."

Rufino knew that she'd been telling the truth. His heart was sad, he was wishing for death. He didn't feel capable of killing Guma, who'd saved his life once. And, besides, there was Lívia, who wasn't to blame. But his heart was asking for death and it could no longer be Guma's, it would be his. The great sea moon was shining in the sky. Esmeralda was still laughing. And she was laughing like that when she died, when the oar split her head open. Rufino kept watching the body as it sank. The sharks were coming at the call of the blood that was floating in the waters of the river. He watched, it was a most beloved body that was sinking. A good body, sexy, with green eyes and pointed breasts. A body that had warmed his on winter nights. Flesh that had been his. He didn't think about Guma for a single moment. It was as if his friend had died a long time ago. He ran his hand slowly over the hull of the canoe, he looked at the distant lights of his port for the last time, and the waters opened up for his body. And at the moment when he came up for the last time (he no longer noticed the canoe without a canoeman that was going along ungoverned), before his eyes paraded all those the black man had loved: He saw his father, a giant, and smiled; he saw his mother, bent over and shuffling; he saw Lívia at whose wedding he had stood up, and Lívia appeared in the bridal procession; he saw Dona Dulce; he saw old Francisco, Dr. Rodrigo, Master Manuel, sloopmen and canoemen. And he also saw Guma, but Guma was laughing at him, laughing behind his back. His almost lifeless eyes saw Guma laughing at him. He died without joy.

# THE *VALIANT*

Chico Tristeza is back! One day a ship brought him back, just as a ship had taken him away many years ago. He'd returned a black Hercules. He spent two days in port, the time that his ship, a Scandinavian freighter, stayed. Then he went out to sea again. But the night he spent on shore was a night of celebration. Those who knew him came to see him, those who didn't know him came to meet him. He knew strange languages, he'd traveled to lands almost as distant as those of Aiocá.

Guma shook his hand, old Francisco asked him what was new. Chico Tristeza laughed; he'd brought a silk shawl for his old mother, who sold coconut cakes. At night he came to the front of the Market, the men gathered around him, he told stories about those lands. Stories of docks, sailors, ships, stories that were sometimes comical, sometimes melancholy. Almost always sad, however. The men listened to him, puffing their long pipes, looking at the sloops. The hulk of the Market in the background hung over them. Chico Tristeza was saying:

"There in the lands of Africa where I was, my people, the life of a black man is worse than that of a dog. I was in black men's lands that belong to the French now. There a black isn't worth nothing, a black man is nothing but the white man's slave, takes a whipping. And it used to be their land..."

"Damned right it was..."

Chico Tristeza looked at the one who had interrupted:

"In their own land, not worth nothing. Only the white

man is worth anything, the white man is everything, he can do whatever he likes. Black men work on the docks, load, unload ships. They work fast, just a minute on board carrying a sack on their back. If they don't work fast the white man calls for the whip, which is a real beauty.''

The others were listening in silence. One black was trembling with rage. Chico Tristeza went on:

''It was in that land where the story I'm telling happened, my people. It was when I was there on a Lloyd Brasileiro ship. The black men were loading the ship, the white man's whip was in the air. He was just waiting for a black man not to hurry so he could let him have it on the back. There was a black man who was a stoker on the ship—by the name of Bagé—he was coming on board, he'd gone to visit a native girl. He was coming on board, a black man from that land stumbled as he went up the plank, they go on board across a plank. The black man stopped for just a minute, the white man's whip fell onto his back, he fell onto the ground. Bagé had never seen the white man's whip at work, it was the first time he'd ever been in that place. When he saw the black man twisting with pain, Bagé grabbed the whip from the Frenchman, gave him a right to the jaw, and the Frenchman's prow hit the ground. The Frenchman tried to get up, but Bagé socked him again, he ended up smashing his face in. Then the blacks from that place came out of the hold and sang a samba, because they'd never seen anything like that.''

The others were listening. One black man couldn't stand it any longer, muttered:

''I like that Bagé...''

But Chico Tristeza went away. His ship only stayed two days, on the second afternoon it weighed anchor and went off into the ocean sea, which was Chico Tristeza's destiny.

Guma said goodbye to him with feelings of longing. The story of black Bagé had remained inside him. And that was how Dona Dulce's miracle would soon come to pass.

Guma had thought about going off too when he was younger. He would have gone to faraway places, avenged humiliated black men, learned the things that Chico Tristeza knew. But he would remain on shore because of Lívia. He would remain only because of her and yet he had betrayed her, betrayed Rufino, betrayed the laws of the waterfront. Now neither Rufino nor Esmeralda was alive anymore, only pieces of their bodies had been found, the sharks at the harbor mouth had devoured the rest. Other neighbors had moved into the house next door, he never saw Esmeralda's breasts again protruding out the window in a challenge to men passing by. He never saw her swaying hips again, her sexy look. Sexy as she was with her sea-green eyes, it all stayed behind with the sharks, masters of that stretch of water where the sea ends and the river begins: the harbor mouth. Every so often he thought he could still hear Rufino's voice saying: "Buddy, my buddy," or then, feeling sorry for himself: "But I loved that mulatto woman, I was crazy about her." On the waterfront everything begins and ends suddenly, like a storm. Except for Lívia's fear, which is there every day, which is suffering without end.

Lívia is more and more afraid. She hasn't grown used to the life of eternal waiting on the waterfront. On the contrary, every day her worry increases, every day Guma's life seems more in danger to her. She waits for him daily, on stormy days her heart beats rapidly. During those months she'd already seen many come back in the arms of fishermen. She saw the pieces of Rufino and Esmeralda arrive, both dead, nobody knows how. The canoe had remained adrift on the water, without any direction, out of control, that was why they went out to search for the bodies. All they found were pieces of arms and legs, Esmeralda's head, her green eyes open in fright. Lívia had also seen the bodies of Jacques and Raimundo arrive. They were father and son, they'd died in a storm. Jacques left Judith a widow, their son had just been born, she was living an awful life, living almost on charity. She'd seen Risoleta turn to prostitution, going with one and another, she who had belonged to only one man for more than ten years. But her man had died in the sinking of the

*Flower of the Seas,* a sloop that had run onto a reef. She'd seen many other cases like that. Few sloop masters die on dry land, in a house on the waterfront. It's rare to die in bed without seeing the starry sky, the blue sea in one's last moments. Lívia is afraid. If she could only get used to it—like Maria Clara, who is a daughter of the sea—everything would be fine. Maria Clara has no anguish in her heart, because she knows it has to be that way, that it's always been that way. She was born on the sea, all of her people are in the ocean. Only Master Manuel still crosses the waters, and yet she'd had a large family, parents, brothers and sisters, lots of relatives. Only her man still resists, but his day will come. Then Maria Clara will look for a factory that will want to hire her hands, will sing her songs of the sea in a low voice beside the looms or the cigarette-making machines. She will return to the sea when she is close to the day of her death, because she was born there, her port is there, that's where she must die. That's what Maria Clara thinks. Lívia, however, comes from the land, she wasn't born on the sea, nobody in her family stayed behind in the waters, nobody had gone with Iemanjá to the Lands of the Endless Way. Guma will go. The fate of the waterfront, he can't escape. Maria Clara says that she has a foreboding about him, that he will indeed die like that. But so great is the certainty she has that every time she sees him come back it's as if she saw him resurrected.

Sad with waiting and fear are Lívia's days. The waterfront is beautiful, the sea comes to break on its rocks, there's no prettier sky. There's music on all the sloops, laughter in the mouths of the men. But for Lívia the days are sad and made of suffering.

One day Rodolfo showed up. He was troubled, looking for Guma. Lívia didn't ask where he was coming from. He dined with her, waited for Guma to arrive. His sloop was expected around nine o'clock. Rodolfo kept on smoking, he was quite impatient, walking back and forth. He said to Lívia who was looking at him:

"I didn't come to your wedding. It wasn't because I didn't want to, no. I got hung up. But I can see that things are going fine, I'm going to have a nephew…"

"How long are you going to live that aimless life, Rodolfo? You could stay, find something proper to do… That life is no good, you're going to end up bad, other people will be sorry…"

"No one feels sorry for me, Lívia. I'm just useless trash, nobody likes me."

He saw that he was being unfair and that Lívia was sad.

"I've given thought lots of time to getting out of this life ever since I found you. But I didn't have it in me, I get a job, I blow all my money, I'm back to being a bum again. After I met you I got away from it all at least three times. I worked for ten, fifteen days at a job, then I'd quit. I can't take it. Only three months ago I was in a gambling casino. I was working there, I even bet some money. I was earning a good piece of change…"

"What did you do there?"

"I was a shill."

Seeing that she didn't understand, he explained:

"I was the one who brought the suckers in. I gambled and I always won. Guys came over, they saw my good luck, they threw everything into the pot. They kept betting and losing," he laughed.

Lívia didn't say anything. He started pacing again:

"But I didn't last long. It was a drag. I quit. I don't know what it is, I really don't know. It's something inside me. I can only take on something complicated, something risky."

"You've got to reset your life. I might need you someday."

"You've got a good husband. Guma's a straight guy."

"But he might die." She covered her mouth with her hand, taking back her words. "Then there'd only be you to help me…" She lowered her head and murmured, "And the little one."

Rodolfo turned. His back was to her, only his face was turned toward her:

"I'm going to tell you. Do you know why I didn't come to your wedding? I wanted to, but I had to get some money. It was to buy you a present. But I got screwed up. I ran into a rich guy who looked half-asleep. I tried to cheat him."

He was silent for a moment. He seemed to be excusing himself:

"It was to buy you a watch. I'd spotted a pretty one in a shop window. When I came to, the man had me by the hand, the cop was next to me. I was given a few months... That's why..."

"I didn't want any present, I just wanted you to come."

"Even empty-handed? You're good, you're even a saint. But something happens to me, I just can't make it. But if you need me someday..."

She cradled her brother's head. He was weary and restless. Guma wasn't coming. Now she was afraid for both her brother and her husband. Rodolfo had come for some reason she didn't know about and he didn't want to tell her. He'd doubtless come to ask for money, he must have been broke, just out of jail. He stretched out on the mat on the floor. His hair well-combed, slicked down with cheap pomade. He rested it on Lívia's lap. She stroked his head, a head weary with adventures, with dangerous robberies, and sang a lullaby. Just as she would cradle her child, she was cradling her brother now. He was a thief. He was a swindler, he sold property that didn't exist, he took part in floating crap games, he hung out in the worst places, he even stuck a knife in men to steal their wallets. He'd been to prison, he had a cut under his lip, a knife scar on his hand. But now he was sleeping like a child, he was blameless, like the child that Lívia was carrying in her womb. He was a child that she was cradling, a newborn baby who was sleeping.

It was after eleven when Guma arrived. Lívia laid her brother's head gently on the mat and ran to her husband. He explained his being late, a delay in loading at Mar Grande. Hearing his brother-in-law's voice, Rodolfo woke up.

They embraced, Guma went to get the cane liquor so they

could have a drink. To celebrate Rodolfo's appearance, he explained, and also because he was wet from head to toe:

"I'm soaked to the skin."

Lívia brought Guma his dinner. Rodolfo sat facing his glass of cane liquor. Guma ate his fish rapidly. He smiled at his wife, then at his brother-in-law, indicating Lívia's belly with his lips. Rodolfo stared. He kept staring for a long time. He shook his head, smoothed his hair, finished his drink:

"Well, I'll be on my way."

"Are you leaving so early?"

"I just came by to see you people..."

"But didn't you say you wanted to talk to Guma?" Lívia asked.

"I really just wanted to see him, it's been a long time since I've seen him."

"Now that you know the way..."

Rodolfo laughed. He put his hat on carefully so as not to muss his hair, looked at himself in a mirror he took from his pocket, said goodbye, went out whistling.

Lívia murmured:

"He did have something he wanted to talk to you about. I think he needed money."

Guma pushed the plate away, called from the window:

"Rodolfo! Rodolfo!"

The other one was at the end of the street, came back. He stopped under the window. Guma asked him in a low voice:

"Are you broke? Is that what you wanted to talk about? I can dig up a five-spot."

Rodolfo rested his hand on his brother-in-law's shoulder, examined a tattoo Guma had on his arm:

"It wasn't anything like that..." He pulled some money out of his pocket, showed it. "I'm loaded."

"What was it, then?"

"It wasn't anything, guy. I just came by to see you people. I mean it."

He went back down the street. He was whistling but his mind wasn't on the music. He was thinking that he'd come there to propose one of his deals to Guma. Something that might be easy money for the both of them. It could mean jail too. He bit his well-trimmed mustache, whistled louder. Lívia was like a saint. And he, Rodolfo, was going to have a nephew. He smiled, imagining what the child's face would be like, crying as it was being born. He kicked a stone out of the way, he'd muffed a good deal. But he soon forgot that, even forgot that he'd muffed a good deal just so as not to get Guma mixed up in some risky business, because of his sister and his nephew. Now he was following the wake of a girl who was also going down the street.

The aunt and uncle came to see her, they were more prosperous now, the store was getting bigger, the old man wore a vest, the old woman brought some vegetables for Lívia. When they came in, old Francisco left, he didn't like the way they looked at the poverty of the house. The uncle twisted his nose, told Lívia that "there's no future in this sloop business." Why doesn't she convince Guma to move up to the city, leave the sea for good? With what he got from the sale of the sloop he could become a partner in the store. They'd enlarge it, even set up a warehouse, and they might even get rich and guarantee the future of the child who's going to be born. It was the best thing he could do, getting away from that risky waterfront life, from trips upriver, moving in next door to them. The aunt added that nothing else should be expected from Guma if he really loved Lívia the way he said he did. Lívia listened in silence. Deep down she was for it, she would like it to happen.

She would give anything to get Guma to leave the sea. She knew quite well that it was hard for a sailor to abandon his sloop, that they almost never take up another life, leaving the water behind. Someone born on the sea dies on the sea. That's why she didn't bring the subject up with him. But it would have been a solution for their lives. It would put an end to that fear that gave her no rest. And besides, their son wouldn't be born on the sea, wouldn't feel tied to it. Guma was already making plans to take the child on his trips at an early age in order to teach him how to sail a ship. After so much suffering because of her husband, Lívia would have to suffer more nights of waiting for her son.

And, when the aunt and uncle had left, she would think about talking to Guma. He had to be convinced. He'd sell the *Valiant* (with great sorrow, no doubt—even she would be sorry), set himself up with the aunt and uncle. She wouldn't be afraid anymore. She planned to speak to him, but when Guma arrived, all wet from the sea, still impregnated with his trip, the crossing, she lost heart, she thought that it was impossible to take him away from the docks. She would have the same lot as the others. She would be left without a man on some stormy night. And her son would soon be familiar with sails, with the keels of boats, with songs of the sea and ships' whistles. And nothing could change the destiny of Sinbad the Sailor.

It didn't rain. No clouds gathered in the sky that night. December meant a night for festivities in the city and on the docks. But the moon didn't appear, the ashen color of the sky didn't stay blue with the arrival of night. The wind darkened everything. It took the place of the rain, the lightning, the thunder, it played the role of all of them, that night belonged to it alone. No one heard the song that Jeremias was singing, the wind scattered it. The old sailors watched the sails coming in. They were coming too fast, you had to be a good sloop master to know how to dock a boat on a night like that. And several of them were still far out to sea, others were sailing toward the harbor mouth, coming from the river.

The wind is the most terrible master on the waterfront. It curls the water, likes to play with the sloops, make them tip over at sea, tearing at the wrists of the people at the tiller. That night belonged to it. It began by putting out lanterns, leaving the sea without its lights. Only the beacon was blinking in the background, pointing the way. But the wind carried them off on the wrong path, turned them from their course, dragged them out to sea where the waves were too strong for a sloop.

No one hears the song that the old soldier is singing in the abandoned fort.

No one sees the light of the lantern that he placed on the parapet of the pier that goes out into the sea. The wind puts out everything, destroys everything: lanterns, songs.

The sloops come along out of control, come along at the whim of the wind, come along spinning like toys. The sharks wait ravenously at the harbor mouth. On nights like that their prey is assured. The sloops come spinning in.

Lívia covered herself with a shawl (her belly was so big that she'd already sent for her aunt) and went down the slope. By the door of the Beacon of the Stars old Francisco was studying the wind. He went with her. Others were drinking inside there, but their eyes were turned outward toward the threatening night.

Groups were chatting on the docks. On the piers by the ocean liners the cranes were moving back and forth.

Lívia was also at the whim of the winds. Old Francisco went to find out the news from a group. Lívia heard snatches of the conversation:

"... it takes a real man..."

"... this little wind is worse than any storm..."

She waited a long time. Although it couldn't even have been half an hour. But it was a long time for her. The sail of the sloop that appeared in the distance wasn't that of the *Valiant*. It looked like Master Manuel's ship. It was coming along at a mad speed, the sloopman bent over the tiller, getting prepared for a maneuver that would bring the boat to a halt. Maria Clara was traveling bent over something stretched out on the deck of the boat. Her hair was flying in the wind. Lívia adjusted the shawl that covered her shoulders, watched the men going into the waterfront mud and went over to the wall. The sloop tied up, Maria Clara was leaning over a body. And even before she heard Manuel say: "The *Valiant* went down," she knew that it was Guma lying there on the planks of the *Sailor Without a Port*. Maria Clara was bent over him. Lívia walked like a drunken woman and then she was lying there in the mud between her and the sloop.

# THE SON

They sent for Dr. Rodrigo. Guma had a cut on his head, it was from running onto a reef. But when the doctor arrived he attended first to Lívia, who had advanced the birth of her child a few days with her scare. And the boy was crying when Guma was able to get up with his head bandaged and his arm in a sling. He stood looking at his son. Maria Clara found that he looked like his father.

"There's no getting around it. He's the image of Guma."

Lívia was smiling wearily. Dr. Rodrigo ordered them to leave so she could get some rest. Master Manuel went home, but Maria Clara stayed with Lívia until her aunt came. Old Francisco had gone to fetch her and to tell their friends. When she was alone with Lívia, Maria Clara said:

"You got both a son and a husband today."

"Tell me about it."

"Not now, you need rest. You'll find out how it happened later. The wind was impossible too…"

Guma was walking about the parlor. Now his son had been born and he was left without a sloop. In order to earn a living he would have to hire himself out to a fleet as a canoeman. He wouldn't have a sloop to leave his son when he went off to the lands of Aiocá. Now he would have to hire out his arm, wouldn't have a sloop that was his own anymore, a ship to steer. That was punishment, he thought. Punishment because he'd betrayed Rufino, betrayed Lívia. That was punishment. The wind had come down on him, driven him onto the reef. If Manuel hadn't seen him in the water Guma wouldn't have seen his son.

Lívia's aunt and uncle came in. They embraced Guma, old Francisco had told them everything along the way, they went in to see Lívia. Maria Clara took her leave, she would come back later. She cautioned them that Lívia was sleeping, that they shouldn't wake her. The aunt stayed in the bedroom, but the storekeeper came right out and went over to chat with Guma:

"Did you really lose your sloop?"

"It sank. It was a good boat..."

"What are you going to do now?"

"Who knows... Find work on a canoe or on the docks."

He was sad, he had no more ship, his son would never own a sloop. Lívia's uncle then offered him the store. Guma could go there, take over the business, help out. He planned to expand.

"I've even talked to Lívia. You could have found a buyer for the sloop, come in as a partner. Now you don't have to come in with anything."

Guma didn't answer. It hurt him to leave the waterfront, give up. And he didn't want to accept any favors from Lívia's uncle. The old man had been waiting for her to make a good marriage so he could expand the business, open a warehouse. He'd been against her marriage to Guma. Later he'd made peace, had thought of him as a partner. Now all his dreams were going under, they had to stick with the store and with Guma, getting what they could out of it in order to eat. The old man was waiting for an answer.

Francisco came in. The fresh ink gleamed on his arm. He'd had them write the name of the *Valiant* beside those of his four other sloops, which were: *Thunder, Morning Star, Lagoon, Windstorm,* with *Valiant* beside them. He showed them his new tattoo proudly. He put down his pipe, asked Guma:

"What are you going to do now?"

"I'm going to be a shopkeeper."

"A shopkeeper?"

"He's going to be my partner," Lívia's uncle said forcefully. "He's going to get away from all this."

Old Francisco picked up his pipe again, put in some tobacco, and lighted it. Lívia's uncle went on:

"He's going to live up above. You can come along too,
sir..."

"I'm still man enough to earn my own living without
need of any handout."

The aunt appeared in the bedroom door, put her finger to
her lips:

"Speak low, so she can sleep." She pointed inside the
room.

"I didn't mean any offense," Lívia's uncle explained.

Guma was thinking about his uncle. What would become
of him, alone on the waterfront? Soon he wouldn't be able to
mend sails anymore, wouldn't have anything to live on. Old
Francisco sucked on his pipe, coughed:

"I'm going to tell Dr. Rodrigo that he won't have to
bother..."

"What about?"

"Kid João is selling the *Snorter*. He bought three canoes,
he doesn't want the sloop anymore. He's selling it cheap, all
you have to pay is half down. Dr. Rodrigo said he'd help...
But you're going to be a shopkeeper..."

"Dr. Rodrigo will put up half?"

"As a loan. You can pay him off as you go along. The
other half is on credit, you pay every month."

"It's a nice boat."

"There's none so good in all this port." Old Francisco
was getting enthusiastic. "I'd only make an exception for
the *Sailor Without a Port*. None of the others are as good.
And he's selling it dirt cheap."

He said how much it was. Guma agreed that it wasn't expensive. He was thinking about his son. That way he'd be
able to own a sloop.

"Is Kid João around?"

"He's on a trip. But when he gets back we can talk."

"Doesn't anybody want the boat?"

"Who doesn't want it? People are waiting in line, but I

fixed things up with him. I knew Kid João when he was a boy, eating dirt.''

Lívia's uncle went into the bedroom. Guma was looking at Francisco as at a savior. The old man was puffing on his pipe, his arm on the table to let the tattoo dry. He commented:

''That was the boat of mine that lasted the longest...''

''The *Valiant?*''

''Do you remember when I ran it onto the rocks?''

He laughed. Guma laughed too. He went to get the bottle of cane liquor:

''You should change the name of the *Snorter.*''

''What name would you give it?''

''I've got a great one: the *Flying Packet.*''

Friends came by. The bottle of liquor wasn't long in being emptied. A smell of lavender filled the house.

When he was able to talk to her alone he told her about the accident. She was listening with half-closed eyes. The son was sleeping beside her. When he finished, she said:

''Now that you haven't got any more sloop, let's look for a different life.''

''But I'm already making arrangements for another sloop...''

He told her about the deal he had in mind. With a sloop like the *Snorter* he'd make money for sure. A big fast ship.

''You know I couldn't go into your uncle's business just like that, with nothing. But when we get a little money together with the sloop, we'll be able to sell it and go in with them. That way I will—''

''Do you mean it?''

''I swear.''

''How long will it take?''

''I'll be paying it off over six months... With another year we'll already have a little money set aside, we can sell the boat. Put it all together with what the old man has, set up a warehouse...''

''Do you swear?''

"I swear."

Then she showed him his little son. And with his eyes he was saying it was because of him. Only because of him.

# TOUFICK THE ARAB

He had arrived third class on a lugger that had touched at twenty ports. He had come from lands across the world, carrying almost nothing in the leather case that he clutched against his chest, to begin the conquest of the Mountain's slope. He had arrived on a stormy night, the night Jacques' sloop had capsized in the harbor mouth. On that night, in third class, looking at the strange city before him, he had wept. He'd come from Araby, from a village in the desert, he'd crossed seas of sand to come earn his living on the other side of the world. Others had come before him, some had gone back and owned olive groves, beautiful homes, were rich. He'd come for that too. He'd come out of the mountains, crossed stretches of sand on camelback, gone aboard the third-class section of a ship, lived on the sea for many days.

He still didn't know the language but was already selling umbrellas, cheap silk, purses to the maids and servants of Bahia. In a short time he became familiar with the city, with the language, with the customs. He lived in the Arab quarter in the Ladeira do Pelourinho, which he left every morning with his vendor's case. Then life began to improve for him. It was when he met F. Murad, the richest Arab in the city. F. Murad's great house of silks took up almost a whole block on the Rua Chile. It was said that he had become rich by smuggling silk. Many other Arabs hated him, said that he didn't help his countrymen out. Actually, F. Murad kept a record of his compatriots who lived in Bahia. And when one of them revealed a trait that could be useful to him, he sent for him, there was always work in his many businesses. For some time he'd been interested in Toufick. He'd received a letter saying that he was coming and telling the real reason for his arrival. It wasn't just in search of wealth that Toufick had come. He'd abandoned his homeland because he wanted to be forgotten there, he'd left a trail of blood behind him. F. Murad kept him under observation for several months. He saw how quickly he was prospering. He was, above all, a man of courage, capable of any deal that would bring him money. F. Murad called him in and hired him in the most profitable of his many businesses. Now it was Toufick who dealt with cargo masters, with ships' captains, with pilots, with everybody having anything to do with the silk cargoes that weren't to pay any duty. He'd shown himself to be quite able, business had never run so smoothly.

In a few years Toufick would also be able to go back, then in his mountain land he would erase the trail of blood that he had left in the sand, planting a grove of olive trees on top of it.

He knew the waterfront like few others. The sloop masters were familiar to him, he knew the names of all the boats, even if he did pronounce them in a picturesque way. Xavier, the master of the *Black Owl*, worked for him. And if Xavier never put any money away, it was because he'd had a misfortune in his life and his money barely paid for what he drank at the Beacon of the Stars or was gambled away on the crooked wheels of chance on certain streets in the upper city. It was the *Black Owl* that went out to pick up bundles of silk from ships in the dead of night and carried them to little-known spots. And by making all those secret and dangerous trips, Toufick the Arab was almost a regular sloopmaster by now. At least he would already listen in rapture to the songs that Jeremias the soldier sang in the old fort deep in the night. And one foggy night, in his own language, he sang a song of the sea that he had heard from sailors of his country in the port where he had embarked. It was a strange melody in the foggy night. But songs of the sea, diverse as they may be in language and music, always speak of love and death at sea. For that reason all sailors understand them, even when they're sung by an Arab from the mountains who had heard them in a dirty Asian port.

# SMUGGLER

Now the son was beginning to walk, he played with a boat old Francisco made. Abandoned in a corner, without even a glance from the boy, were an iron train that Rodolfo had brought, the cheap teddy bear that Lívia had bought, the clown that was a present from Lívia's aunt and uncle. The boat, made from a piece of mast, that the old man had given him was worth more than all of them. In the tub where Lívia washed clothes it sailed under the enchanted eyes of the boy and the old man. It had no rudder, no pilot, that's why it never reached port, stood motionless in the middle of the water, went along with no direction. The boy spoke his own language, which reminded one of that of Toufick the Arab:

"Grampa, makey funda."

Old Francisco knew that he wanted a storm to break over the basin. Like Iemanjá, who made the wind fall onto the sea, old Francisco puffed up his cheeks and unleashed the nor'easter over the tub. The poor boat rolled over, quickly went to the leeward, the boy clapped his dirty little hands. Old Francisco puffed up his cheeks more, made the wind stronger. He was whistling, imitating the nor'easter's song of death. The water in the tub, calm as that of a lake, became agitated, waves swept the boat, which ended up filling with water and slowly sinking. The boy clapped his hands, old Francisco always watched the boat go to the bottom with sadness. In spite of its being a miniature, made by his own hands, in some way it was a sloop that was sinking. The waves in the basin grew calm. Everything became as in a lake. The sloop at the bottom, on its side. The boy put his hand into the basin and drew out the boat. The game began again, and that was how the child and old man spent the afternoon, hunched over a miniature sea, over a miniature sloop, over the true destiny of men of the sea and ships.

Lívia looked with fear at the abandoned bear, the clown, the train. The boy never made the train run through the hallway of the house. He never made the bear kill the clown. Land destinies didn't interest him. His lively eyes followed the sloop in its struggle against the storm that was coming from old Francisco's cheeks. The bear, the clown, the train abandoned. Once a hope filled Lívia's heart. It was the day when Frederico (his name was Frederico) turned away from the basin in the midst of the most furious storm and went to get the clown. When he found him he picked him up carefully. Lívia watched attentively. Could he have grown tired of storms and shipwrecks? Could he only have been interested in the destiny of the boat as long as it was a novelty? Would he return now, bored, to the other forgotten toys? No. He took the clown to the boat. He wanted to make him a sloop master, a rather strange sloop master, of course, with those blue-and-yellow knickers. But so many sailors appear in strange costumes that nobody is startled at one in knickers. And from that day forward every time the sloop sank, the clown (he had struggled against the storm until the last moment) drowned, dying like a sloop master. At the bottom of the basin his cloth body puffed up as if it were full of crabs. The boy clapped his hands, laughed to his grandfather. Francisco laughed too, the game started all over again.

The ship sank so many times, its skipper drowned so much, that the cloth began to rot and one day he lost a leg. But a man of the sea doesn't ask for charity. And the strange sailor in knickers continued fighting against the storm with only one leg, leaning against the mast of his boat. The boy said to old Francisco:

``Sark ettem.''

The shark had eaten his leg, old Francisco understood. Then he ate the head that became detached from the body in the midst of a fierce storm. And even without a head (he was the strangest sailor on the seven seas) he stayed at the tiller of his sloop, going through storms with it. The boy laughed, the old man laughed. For them the sea is a friend, is a sweet friend.

Only Lívia didn't laugh. She was looking at the abandoned bear, the train. For her the sea is an enemy, the most terrible of enemies. And the men who live on the sea are like that clown in blue-and-yellow knickers whom fate had turned into a sailor: Even without a leg, even crippled, he fought against the fury of the sea without a show of hate.

The boy and the old man laughed. The storm blew furiously over the tub, the boat at the mercy of the wind, the sailor without a head or a leg was trying to steer his sloop.

The *Snorter* had been changed to the *Flying Packet* and given a new coat of paint. The necessary new sails had also been made, and the ship became one of the swiftest on the Bahia waterfront. Dr. Rodrigo had put up half, for Guma to pay off when he'd finished paying off the other half to Kid João. That part had been divided into ten monthly payments. The money they had at home he put into repairs for the boat. And he resolutely went to sea. The year's time that he had given Lívia to get enough money to go partners with her uncle he extended to two years. At the end of the first year, however, he still owed almost everything to Kid João, and he hadn't even begun to pay Dr. Rodrigo's share. Life had become much harder for canoemen and sloop masters. With very few cargoes, things were at a standstill, the rates were very low because of the gasoline launches that carried faster and quicker. There was little money to be made, and never had so much cursing been heard on the waterfront.

Lívia had already lost hope of getting Guma to abandon the life of the sea that year. He was working now to be able to pay what he owed, to be able to own his sloop free and clear. Kid João was hounding him, the payments were in arrears, Kid João wasn't doing well with the canoes he had bought either. Dr. Rodrigo didn't complain, but Kid João was hounding them, he almost never left Guma's doorstep, would go there to wait for him when he came back from his trips. But there weren't many trips now. Sloop masters and canoemen spent a great part of their time in front of the Market wharf, talking about about how hard life was, about the standstill at year's end. When they didn't, they went to drown their sorrows at the Beacon of the Stars, where Mr. Babau still served cane liquor on credit, jotting down the debts in an old notebook with a greenish cover. Guma was accepting all trips, even when there was only cargo to carry, he even took on short hauls to Itaparica, but not even in that way did he have any money left over at the end of the month to give Kid João. Lívia helped old Francisco repairing sails. She spent a large part of the day bent over the thick sailcloth torn by the storm, the needle in her hand. But almost all that work was on credit, because things were bad for everybody on the waterfront. They were so bad that the stevedores were even talking about going on strike. Guma spent all his time looking for work, he made his trips as fast as he could in order to keep the customer. Several sloop masters had sold their boats and taken up other work in the ports: on the docks, on long-distance ships, carrying passengers' luggage.

And since they had little to do, they sang and drank.

"Mr. Kid João was here…"

Guma tossed his trip jacket onto the bed. He looked at his son playing with Francisco. It was the end of the month and he'd promised to pay Kid João something. But there wasn't anything left over, that last trip had brought in a pittance, it was a trip to Itaparica. The boy was playing beside the tub of water. Guma didn't want any supper, he went right out. Not five minutes had passed when Kid João knocked at the door:

"Did Guma get in, Miss Lívia?"

"He got in but he went right out again, Mr. João."

Kid João looked inside, a bit mistrustful:

"Do you know which way he went?"

"I don't know, Mr. João. I was inside."

"Good night, then."

"Good night, Mr. João."

Kid João went down the street tugging at his mustache. Candles in the houses illuminated drab living rooms. A man was entering one drunkenly and Kid João heard a woman saying:

"So that's the way you come home, eh?... As if there wasn't enough trouble already..."

On the docks groups were chatting. Kid João asked for Guma. They hadn't seen him. In front of the Market, however, somebody told him that Guma was in the Beacon of the Stars.

"He's forgetting his troubles..."

Another asked:

"How are your canoes doing, Joãozinho?"

"How do you think they're doing? Who is there who's doing fine? Just enough to cover expenses..."

He continued on his way. He ran into Dr. Rodrigo, who was coming along smoking.

"Good evening."

"Good evening, doctor. I'd like to have a couple of words with you..."

"What is it, João?"

"It has to do with that sickness of the missus. You came by a lot of times, you got her back on her feet. As God is my witness, it was you who saved her. And I still haven't been able to pay you."

"That's all right, João. I know things aren't going too well..."

"They're real bad, doctor. But you should be getting something, sir. You can't live on air. As soon as things get better..."

"Don't worry about it. I'll get by."

"Thank you, doctor."

Rodrigo went off with his cigarette. Kid João thought about Guma. He wanted to go back (times were really bad...), he even went so far as to turn around, but he made a decision and headed for the Beacon of the Stars.

He immediately saw Guma at a table with a glass of cane

liquor. Master Manuel was with him. From behind his bar Mr. Babau was looking sadly at his customers with a sleepy face. Kid João saw Master Manuel shrug his shoulders in a gesture of discouragement. He almost didn't have the heart to go in. He looked at Guma with pity. His long, dark sloop master's hair fell over his forehead and his eyes looked frightened. He's afraid, Kid João thought—and he tried to withdraw again. But he had to pay his canoemen and he went forward. A few customers in the Beacon of the Stars greeted him. He answered with a wave, dropped into a chair beside Manuel. The latter asked:

"How goes it?" He seemed to have had trouble getting the greeting out.

"Mr. João..." Guma said.

Kid João tugged on his mustache, ordered a drink. Master Manuel seemed quite spiritless, he was silent, looking into his empty glass. And the three of them remained in silence for a time. They heard a customer shout in a corner:

"Hey, is that drink coming or not?..."

And Mr. Babau jotting down names in his notebook. Suddenly Guma raised his body and ran his hand over his head, pushing his hair back, and spoke:

"Nothing still, Mr. João. Things are so bad."

Master Manuel repeated, like an echo:

"So bad..."

And he asked in a louder voice:

"How long is this going to last?"

Mr. Babau looked over, held his hand over the notebook with the pencil suspended in the air. Kid João began to hear the *modinha* that the blind man was singing by the door. It was sad, no doubt about it. The *modinha* came in slowly and was taking over Kid João. Master Manuel answered his own question:

"I don't think it will ever end. And people are starving..."

Mr. Babau lowered his pencil. He shook his head and smiled, not knowing at what. He closed the notebook and stopped taking count of the expenditures. Now he laid his head on his arm and seemed to be sleeping:

"He furled his sails," someone commented.

"So bad..." Kid João said, referring to the months past.

The blind man's *modinha* was dragging along outside. There was no sound of any coin dropping into his tin cup. But he kept on singing. And Kid João had to listen to that *modinha*, even if he didn't want to. Guma spoke again.

"I was going to give you some money this month, but I'm cleaned out. I haven't had nothing, nothing at all, Mr. João."

A woman came in. It was Madalena. She looked at the tables. No one invited her over. She laughed, shouted with her full voice:

"Where's the funeral?"

They almost all looked at her. Master Manuel reached out his hand, they'd been lovers once. But it was because of Kid João that she came to the table:

"Buy me a drink, João."

The boy brought the cane liquor.

The blind man's *modinha* (he was talking about his poverty, asking for charity) went on and on outside. Guma continued:

"Mr. João, you've got to be patient. Let things get better..."

Master Manuel was doubtful:

"You think they'll get better someday?"

Madalena looked at them. Then she shouted to Mr. Babau:

"Aren't you playing the phonograph today, Babau?"

Babau raised his head from his arm, looked around, went over to crank the ancient phonograph. A samba began to fill the room. Even so, it was the blind man's *modinha* that Kid João heard.

"The only thing, Guma, is that I'm hung up too, Guma. Hung up like hell. I've got three canoemen to pay. The canoes haven't been bringing in anything, just expenses." He stared at Master Manuel, then Madalena, waved his hands:

"Just expenses..."

"I know, Mr. João. I've been wanting to pay, but how?"

"There's no way I can turn, Guma. Either I get some money or I'll have to sell off a canoe at a loss to pay my debts..."

The blind man's *modinha* was coming in despite the samba. Guma lowered his head. Mr. Babau had gone back to sleep on top of his notebook. Madalena was following the conversation with interest.

"I've been thinking..." Mr. Kid João didn't continue.

"What?"

"If you sold the boat you'd get your share, I'd settle for the rest. If you wanted we could make an arrangement, you could come work in my canoes."

"Sell the *Packet?*"

The blind man's *modinha* was completely dominated by the samba. The latter was louder, stronger, but even so they could only hear the blind man singing:

> *"Have pity on a person*
> *Who's lost the light of his eyes."*

Master Manuel didn't understand either:

"Sell the *Flying Packet?*"

Madalena pounded the table:

"It's such a nice ship..."

"If not, how are you going to arrange things?" Kid João asked.

He repeated:

"How?"

"Mr. João, wait another month, I'll find some money. Even if I have to go without eating for that month..."

"It's not for me, Guma. I've got payments to make too." He was afraid they'd think he was a loan shark. The blind man's music was torturing him.

"You know damned well I wouldn't be one to take ad-

vantage of bad times to screw a comrade. But things are
black, I don't see any other way..."

"Just one month..."

"If I don't pay the men tomorrow they won't go out in the
canoes."

Master Manuel asked:

"Can't you find a way?"

"How?"

"Arrange a loan?"

They sat thinking about who could loan the money. Manuel thought of Dr. Rodrigo. Both Guma and Kid João owed
him. He was laid aside. Kid João continued with apologies:

"Just ask old Francisco if I'm that kind of a man. He's
known me for a long time..." (He felt like asking the blind
man to stop.)

Madalena thought of Mr. Babau:

"Maybe he could loan something."

"That's right..." Manuel said.

Guma looked at them timidly, as if asking them to save
him. And Kid João kept on with his apologies, he felt like
making Guma a present of the sloop and then jumping into
the water, because he didn't have the courage to look at the
canoemen who were behind in getting paid. Master Manuel
got up, went to the bar, slowly tugged at Mr. Babau's arm.
And he brought him over to the table. Mr. Babau sat down:

"What is it?"

Guma shook his head. Kid João was completely taken
over by the blind man's *modinha*. It was Master Manuel
who spoke:

"How are you fixed for money?"

"When I get paid everything I'm owed for drinks I'll be
rich..." Mr. Babau laughed.

"But have you got some you could lend?"

"How much do you want?"

"It's not me. It's Mr. João and Guma here." He turned
toward Kid João. "How much do you need right away?"

Kid João kept on hearing the blind man's moaning. He
explained:

"It's to pay my canoemen. I've got some money coming from Guma, you know how bad things are..."

Guma added:

"I owe him, I'll pay just as soon as I get a little money in. Everything's so rough."

Mr. Babau asked:

"But how much is it?"

"With a hundred and fifty I'll get by..."

"I haven't even got half of that. I can open the safe and show you..."

He reflected:

"If it was a matter of only fifty *milreis*..."

"Can't you get by with fifty?" Manuel looked at Kid João.

"Fifty would only pay for one. The hundred and fifty will only just be paying part of it."

"How much were you supposed to pay, Guma?"

"A hundred a month... But I'm behind in my payments."

Mr. Babau got up, disappeared into the back room of the tavern. Madalena declared:

"If I had some..."

The phonograph had stopped. They remained in silence listening to the blind man. Mr. Babau came back with fifty *milreis* in notes of five and ten. He gave them to Guma:

"You'll pay me after your first trip, right?"

Guma gave the money to Kid João. Master Manuel laid his hand on Madalena's shoulder:

"Find a sugar daddy who can lend us a thousand."

She smiled:

"If I can get a five-spot today I'll be happy..."

Guma said to Kid João:

"Wait a few more days. I'm going to see if I can get it all paid off."

Kid João made a gesture of acceptance. Madalena sighed with fatigue and began to talk a lot:

"Do you people know Joana Doca? You know her, don't

you, Manuel? Well, today she was in her window when she
saw a guy who kept on looking. She went and—''

But Guma interrupted:

''You all know I haven't got anything except that boat,
that really isn't mine either, I owe almost all of it. I owe it to
you and to Dr. Rodrigo. If I'm left without the boat what
will I be able to leave my son? People don't live too long,
one fine day a storm comes and they go off. Even someone
who's got no wife or son...''

''A rotten life,'' Manuel put in. ''That's why I don't want
any son. The missus is the one who does...''

''She's a pretty woman, yours is,'' Madalena said to
Guma.

''Do you know her?''

''I've seen her walking with you.''

The blind man's music continued by the door. More
drinks arrived. Kid João spoke:

''If I could get a hold of ten more I'd give each man
twenty... Maybe they'd calm down.''

''I can get a hold of ten the day after tomorrow,'' Manuel
answered. ''The missus must have some.''

''It would seem that way, with the woman living at her
place now,'' Madalena put in.

''Have you got a new heifer at home now?''

''If you can call her a heifer... God save us.''

''Who is it?''

''An old dame. She says she was Xavier's woman.''

''Xavier? The master of the *Black Owl?*''

''The same.''

''He used to tell stories about her,'' Guma said.

''I was there,'' Master Manuel nodded.

''He liked her an awful lot. She ran out on him, he even
put the name on his ship... She used to call him Black
Owl.''

''Yeah, he was a strange one.'' Madalena twisted her
mouth. ''I never knew anyone like him. He was all kind
of—''

"You were a good friend of Rufino's, weren't you?" Kid João turned to Guma.

"Why do you ask?" He could hear the blind man's song clearly now.

"They say he killed his woman, that she was cheating on him with a sailor off a ship."

"I heard tell," Madalena agreed.

"This is the first I heard of it. And if he did, it was right. He was a straight black man."

"There wasn't another canoeman like him on the whole waterfront," Manuél said.

Guma could hear Rufino saying: "Buddy, my buddy." But he consoled himself with the thought that Rufino had died without knowing he had betrayed him too. Kid João closed the conversation:

"If it had been me I'd have killed the guy too."

Maneca One-Hand came in. He joined the group, but spoke to the whole room:

"Do you know what's happened?"

They were all waiting. Maneca One-Hand spoke:

"Xavier sold his boat to Pedroca for crap, signed on that Greek ship that was looking for a hand."

"What are you saying?"

"Just what I said. He didn't say a word to anyone. He left about half an hour ago..."

"It was the woman," Madalena muttered.

"They say the mess on Greek ships is miserable," a black man commented.

They left. The blind man was singing by the door. He held out the half cheese can and Kid João dropped in a two-cent piece. He wouldn't buy any pipe tobacco that night.

Toufick the Arab got a great shock from Xavier's flight. A ship was due within five days with a big load of contra-band silk. How could he get it off the ship without a sloop, without a skipper he could trust? He explained it to F. Murad:

"It was a binge, that's what it was. A guy who drinks is no good. Now I'm going to have to get a man who's sober."

"Try to get him soon. We have to unload the cargo."

Toufick went to the waterfront. He tried to get a line on the finances of different sloop masters from Mr. Babau. He found out about the case of the night before, the loan made to Guma, about the near sale of the *Flying Packet*. He asked:

"Is he a straight guy?"

"Guma?"

"Yes."

"There's nobody straighter on the whole waterfront."

He went right to Guma's house. It was Lívia who answered the door:

"Guma went out, but he'll be back soon, Mr. Toufick. Would you like to wait?"

He said he would. He sat in the parlor, rolling his hat in his hands, looking at the child who was getting all dirty in a puddle behind the house. And Toufick remembered what Rodolfo had told him a certain time (Toufick had looked him up, Rodolfo owed him for some clothes, to see if Guma wanted to get involved in the smuggling business): "My brother-in-law's not the man you're looking for, Turk." He'd said that Guma wasn't the kind of man who would get mixed up in something like that. And Toufick was wondering if it was worth the trouble waiting there. It was urgent for them to get a replacement for Xavier. Guma was the indicated person: He was looked up to, he was one of the best sloop masters on the waterfront, he had a good fast ship. But would he have the courage to get mixed up in that business? Toufick wasn't thinking about scruples. He got up, peered out the window. Guma appeared on the street. When he saw the Arab he picked up his pace:

"What can I do for you, Mr. Toufick?"

"I'd like to talk to you."

"Whatever you say..."

Lívia had come to peek from inside. Guma asked:

"Would you like a drink, Mr. Toufick?"

"Just a little, a small one."

"Bring a drink for Mr. Toufick, Lívia."

Toufick pointed to the child in the yard:

"Your son?"

"Yes, he is."

Lívia came with the cane liquor. Toufick drank. When Lívia disappeared inside he came over to the stuffed chair beside Guma's chest:

"Please excuse me, Mr. Guma, but how are you fixed for money?"

"Not good at all, Mr. Toufick. The slowdown is wicked. Why?"

"I knew it. Times are bad, very bad. But even so, a man of decision can still earn a lot of money."

"It would be hard..."

"You haven't paid off your new sloop."

"I'm behind. How can a person earn any money?"

"Did you know that Xavier has gone away?"

"I heard. It was his woman who showed up."

"What woman?"

"His. He was married."

"So that's what it was. Because he worked for me, did you know that, sir?"

"I'd heard tell."

"Well, he left Toufick holding the bag, as you people say. And his work brought in a lot of money."

"He picked up contraband."

"Some orders that were on board and—"

"You don't have to talk fancy with me, Mr. Toufick. Everybody on the waterfront knows all about it. And now you want to make a deal with me?"

"You'll be able to pay off your sloop in two or three months. It's work that pays well. You can earn up to five hundred *milreis* at one time."

"But if the police take a good look, the guy's ship-wrecked."

"The way we do it it's never found out. Have they ever found anything out?"

He looked at Guma hesitatingly.

"On Wednesday a German ship is coming in. It's bringing a big cargo. It's a business that pays—" He cut off the sentence. "What do you still owe on your sloop? A lot of money?"

"Around eight hundred *milreis,* more or less."

"Well, it's something that will pay around five hundred *milreis* in one shot. A good deal for three trips in a sloop. In less than one night you can have all that money in your hand."

Now he was speaking with his head very close to Guma's, speaking secretly, like one conspirator to another. Guma was thinking that he could do that job one or two times, just enough to pay off the ship, then he would cut out on Toufick. But the Arab seemed to be guessing that:

"With two or three trips you can pay for your boat and then quit if you want. I'm stuck because I haven't got anybody. You'll get rid of your debts. And besides, it's only one or two loads a month. The rest of the month you can make your trips, as if nothing had happened."

Toufick was waiting for an answer. Guma was thinking he would do it one or two times. He'd pay for the boat and quit. Toufick himself had said so. He wasn't afraid. He even liked risky deals. But he was afraid of Lívia's upset if he were arrested. She'd already gone through so much with her brother... He heard Toufick's voice.

"Do you need money?"

He saw Kid João, unable to pay his canoemen, wanting him to sell the sloop:

"Could you advance me a hundred *milreis?* I'll take the offer."

The Arab put his hand into his pants pocket, took out a wad of papers. There were letters, receipts, IOU's. And money mixed in with all that dirty paper.

"Do you know where Xavier unloaded the silk?"

"Where was it?"

"At the port of Santo Antônio."

"Near the harbor beacon?"

"That's right."

"Fine."

He took the hundred *milreis*. Old Francisco was coming in. Toufick took his leave, said in a low voice to Guma:

"Ten o'clock Wednesday. Have your sloop ready."

Old Francisco greeted him as he passed:

"Good morning, Mr. Toufick."

Lívia came to find out:

"What did he want?"

"To find out something about Xavier, who took off. It seems Xavier owed him something."

Old Francisco looked at him, not believing. Lívia still went on:

"I thought he'd never leave."

The son was crying in the yard. Guma went to get him.

The night was low over the land. But on the sea a cool breeze that gave an urge to bodies was blowing. There was an enormous yellow moon in the starry sky. The sea was calm and only the songs that came from everywhere cut the silence. A short distance away from the *Flying Packet* was the *Sailor Without a Port,* and Guma could hear the moans of love from Maria Clara. Master Manuel made love right on his sloop, moored at the dock on moonlit nights. The silvery sea spread out below them. Guma thought about Lívia, who must have been worrying at home at that time. She'd never been able to adjust to his life. Especially after the wreck of the *Valiant* she had been living a continuous agony, expecting to see Guma arrive dead at the end of every trip. If she had only known then that he was involved in the smuggling of silk, from now on she never would have had another moment of rest, because along with the fear of death at sea there would be the worry of imprisonment. Guma swears he will give up the business as soon as he pays off the sloop. Tonight will be the first time, and afterward he'll get five hundred *milreis*. It will go to pay everything he owes Kid João, he'll say that he got a loan. Then only Dr. Rodrigo will be left, and he hasn't been pressing him. With two more trips he will have paid for the ship. Then he'll earn a little more money, sell the *Flying Packet*, and go into partnership in a small warehouse with Lívia's uncle. Will he really sell the *Flying Packet*? After so many sacrifices to get it, it would be a shame to sell it just in order to be partner in a small warehouse. Leave the sea, the sloop, his port. That's something that pains a sailor, especially when the night is beautiful like this, full of stars and with such a pretty moon. It's after ten o'clock and Toufick still hasn't shown up.

Guma saw the German freighter when it came in. It was three o'clock in the afternoon, he was in the sloop. The freighter didn't dock, it was too big for the pier, it stayed out there, giving off puffs of smoke. From on board the *Flying Packet* Guma could make out the lights of the ship. Lívia thinks Guma has left already, is cutting the waters of the river now, carrying a load to Mar Grande. She'll be waiting for him at daybreak. She'll be anxious, full of fear, and when he arrives she'll ask when he's going to leave the sea. A warehouse... Selling his ship, leaving his port. He'd thought of that when he betrayed Rufino, when he lost the *Valiant*. But now he doesn't want to. You die on land just as much as you do at sea, that's Lívia's foolishness. But now they're singing that old *modinha* that says "unfortunate the fate of sailors' wives." Guma pats the hull of the *Flying Packet*. Faster than anything. The only one that can match it in the port is the *Sailor Without a Port*. Only because it has a skipper like Manuel. The *Valiant* was a good sloop too. Not as good as the *Flying Packet*, however. Even old Francisco, with his long experience on sloops and boats, said that he'd never seen another like that. And now he was going to sell it...

He hears Toufick's jump. Another Arab is with him. This one has a scarf around his neck in spite of the heat. Toufick introduces them.

"Mr. Haddad."

"Master Guma."

The Arab touches his head in a kind of salute. Guma says:

"Good evening."

Toufick examines the sloop:

"It's big, isn't it?"

"There isn't a bigger one in port."

"I think we can get everything in two trips."

Haddad nodded agreement. Guma asked:

"Shall we cast off now?"

"We'll wait. It's still early."

The two Arabs sat on the rail of the sloop and began to gab. Guma was smoking in silence, listening to the song that was coming from the old fort:

> *"He stayed behind in the waves,*
> *He went on his way to drown."*

The Arabs continued their conversation. Guma thought of Lívia. She was thinking of him taking a trip, crossing the harbor mouth at this time. Suddenly Toufick turned and said:

"Pretty music, isn't it?"

"Yes."

"Very nice."

The other Arab was silent. He buttoned his jacket, said something in Arabic, Toufick laughed. Guma was looking at them. The voice turned off in the old fort and they could hearing the bouncing of bodies on Master Manuel's sloop perfectly.

Around midnight Toufick said:

"We can leave now."

He weighed anchor on the sloop (Haddad kept looking at his tattoos), unfurled the sails. The boat picked up speed after the maneuver. The lights of the ship appeared. The tune from the old fort started up again. Jeremias was naturally singing to the moon on that night with so many stars. They went along in silence on the sloop. They were already quite close to the ship when Toufick said:

"Stop."

The *Flying Packet* stopped. On an order from Toufick, Guma furled the sails. The hull of the sloop rocked slowly. Haddad whistled in a special way. He got no answer. He tried again. The third time he heard an answering whistle.

"We can go," Haddad said.

Guma took two oars and kept the sails furled. The sloop went around the ship, came alongside its hull on the side facing Itapagipe. A head appeared. It chatted with Haddad in a tongue that was also strange to Guma. Then it disappeared. Then another one came. Another chat. Haddad ordered the sloop to go forward a little. They came alongside a wide opening. And two men began to lower bales of silk, which Guma and Toufick stowed in the hold of the sloop. They weren't worried.

He moved away from the ship. At a certain distance, after passing the breakwater, he hoisted his sails and ran with his lantern out. The wind helped him, he soon reached the port of Santo Antônio. Except that the waves were quite higher and the sea less calm. But the *Flying Packet* was a large sloop and stood up to it well. Toufick commented:

"We got here fast."

Men were already waiting for the sloop. One of them, well-dressed, came forward:

"Everything all right?"

"How many more trips?"

"With that sloop, only one more."

The well-dressed man was watching Guma, who was helping unload. The silks were going into a house that had its back to the port:

"Is that the boy?"

"That's him, Mr. Murad."

Guma looked at the moneybags. He was a fat guy, clean-shaven, dressed in black. He put his hand on Guma's shoulder:

"Boy, you can make a lot of money with me. It's just a matter of playing straight."

He took another look at the work, said to Toufick:

"See that everything goes O.K. I have to leave now, Antônio is sick."

Antônio was his son, a law student. He had a great love for that literate and wild son. He overlooked everything in him. He liked to see his son's name in the paper as the author of articles. That's why Haddad asked:

"Is Antônio sick? Then go see him."

F. Murad, before leaving, touched Guma on the shoulder again:

"Play straight with me and you won't be sorry."

"You can count on me."

The car was waiting for him two blocks away.

When the unloading was finished, the sloop went back. Again the hold was filled with bales of silk. Guma had already lost track of how many bales had been taken off. Toufick gave a wad of money to one of the men, who counted it by flashlight:

"It's O.K.," the one who was in the rear said with a terrible accent.

The sloop left, they picked up the wind again, opened the sails, and reached the port of Santo Antônio without incident. This time Toufick offered him a swig of cane liquor. The sloop was unloaded. Haddad had disappeared inside the house. Guma lighted his pipe. Toufick came over to him:

"I'll tell you later when we'll need you again."

He took the two two-hundred notes out, gave them to him.

"You never saw this house, understand?"

"You're talking to a sailor."

Toufick smiled:

"That was a pretty song, wasn't it?"

He buttoned up his jacket, went inside the house. Guma squeezed the two bills in his hand. He maneuvered the sloop, left in the dawn that was breaking. And only in the middle of the crossing did he feel the fatigue in his arms and legs. He stretched out on the sloop, murmured:

"It's beginning to look like I was scared the whole time."

The breakwater beacon was blinking in the dawn.

Kid João told him:

"You're a man of your word."

"I got a loan from my wife's uncle. Now I'll be paying

him. The store has been doing all right, it looks as though he's going to set up a warehouse. He's even asked me to be partners."

"I saw him at your house once."

"A good man."

"I can see that."


Rodolfo appeared some ten days later. Guma had come in the night before from a trip to Cachoeira, he was still asleep. Old Francisco had gone out to do some shopping. Rodolfo was playing with his nephew, talking to Lívia:

"Are you still so scared?"

"Someday I'll get used to it…"

"That day's a long time coming."

He looked at his nephew, who was pulling him to see the toy sloop in the tub of water. He spoke to his sister:

"Didn't you want him to go into the old folks' store?"

"I wanted him to, yes."

"It's about time, then…"

"What are you trying to say?" she asked anxiously.

He squinted at her. If she knew, she'd suffer even more.

"There's a reason. It's for the boy. He'll start liking it here."

She was still mistrustful, but she calmed down a little:

"I thought it was something else."

Suddenly she asked:

"Where did you get hold of the money you loaned Guma?"

"Me?" But he understood right away. "I put some things together. I just would have spent it…"

She came over and stroked his head:

"You're so good."

Guma was getting up. While Lívia was making coffee, Rodolfo spoke:

"You're mixed up in smuggling, aren't you?"

"How'd you get to know?"

"I know all about it. Once I was even sent here by Toufick, but I didn't say anything because of Lívia."

"During her time?"

"Yes."

"But I won't be at it for long. Just enough time to pay off the sloop. And there's not much left to go."

"Be careful. If that business blows up it will be a royal scandal. Nothing will happen to Murad, he's worth over a million, he can fix things. But it'll be hard on poor people like you. Be careful."

"I won't be in this business long. I don't want Lívia—"

"But one of these days she's bound to find out. What money did you get from me?"

Guma laughed:

"Did you give it away?"

"I almost tripped. Be careful. It's a dangerous business."

Lívia was coming in with the coffee and a portion of couscous. She was suspicious of that low-keyed conversation:

"What secrets are these?"

"No secrets. We were talking about the kid."

"Rodolfo also thinks you ought to go in with uncle."

"Because of the boy," Rodolfo put in.

"Let me finish paying off the *Packet*, girl. I'll pick up some change, we'll close the deal. It's so close now."

He grabbed his wife around the waist. She sat on his lap:

"I'm so afraid..."

Rodolfo lowered his head.

The second time it was a small cargo of French stockings and perfume. Guma got a hundred *milreis*. Everything went well. This time F. Murad went on the sloop and had a long talk with a gentleman on the ship. Then he paid a large amount of money. When they got back F. Murad told him, putting on a serious face:

"You never saw me on board any ship."

"You don't have to tell me."

"I've been learning some things about you. They tell me you're a brave lad. How much do you still owe on your sloop?"

"After paying this hundred I'll still owe three hundred and fifty."

"With only a few more trips you'll have your sloop free and clear. Are you going to leave us then?"

"Stop working for you, sir? I think I will, yes."

"You will?"

"That's what Mr. Toufick told me. I got into this, but I could get out whenever I wanted to. I only got in in order to pay off my boat."

"No one's stopping you from leaving."

"Don't be afraid of my opening my mouth to tell anything."

"I'm not afraid of that. I know you're a straight boy. But I think that if you stayed with us you could make a lot of money."

He put his hand on Guma's shoulder:

"Do you find the work too dangerous?"

"I've got a wife and child. If the police should grab me tomorrow,"—he remembered Rodolfo's words—"nothing will happen to you. You're filthy rich. The whole thing will fall on me."

F. Murad lowered his voice more:

"You think that nobody knows I'm smuggling? I've got people in the police bought off. It's going to be hard getting a boy like you."

They continued the trip in silence. When they were getting in, F. Murad advised him once more:

"If you want to keep on you'll make a lot of money."

"I'll think about it. If I decide..."

Toufick told him that a month from then a big load was coming in. He might earn two hundred *milreis* or more.

The next day he took the hundred *milreis* to Dr. Rodrigo. He'd made it on that trip, he told him. He'd been gambling in Cachoeira. He'd bet five *milreis* on a wheel of fortune and had come out with a hundred and twenty. And since he'd already paid Kid João his part, he'd come to pay the doctor's. Rodrigo didn't want to take it at first. He said that Guma might be needing it. But Guma insisted. The sooner he paid off the sloop, the better.

He left there to arrange a trip to Santo Amaro. He was going to pick up a load of cane liquor. He was living off his trips, the smuggling money was to pay off the sloop. After everything was paid he could stay in the business a little longer until he had five hundred *milreis*. Then he could satisfy Lívia's wishes. He would go up to the city, open the warehouse with her aunt and uncle. He might not even have to sell the *Flying Packet*. He could turn it over as a partner to Master Manuel or Maneca One-Hand. Either of them would be happy to have two sloops. Maneca One-Hand, besides, only had a canoe. He'd be quite glad if he could take over the *Flying Packet*, he'd make a lot more money. And Guma wouldn't have to leave the waterfront completely. He would come down from time to time, take his trips too. He would continue to be a sailor, have interests on the sea, sail. He would satisfy Lívia and be satisfied himself too, he wouldn't change completely. That was a good plan. But in order to carry it out he had to stay in the smuggling business a while longer so as to make the money needed to go into partnership with Lívia's uncle. A few more months, a few more trips, and he'd have what he needed. That business paid well. Too bad it had the danger of coming to a sudden end with all of their asses in jail. If the whole thing were discovered, it would be a horrible scandal. F. Murad had ten million, his ass was tough, nothing would happen to him. But Guma, who only had a sloop...

He wasn't afraid. If he thought about the dangers of smuggling it was because of Lívia and their son. He saw the son playing by the tub of water. He was playing at sloop master. He liked things of the sea, he was a real son of the waterfront. When he grows up he'll steer the *Flying Packet* too, sail over those waters. He'll say that his father was one of the best sloop masters around till then, and even when he moved up to the city he didn't sell his sloop, sometimes he would come down to make trips too. Guma runs his hand lovingly across the hull of the *Flying Packet*.

He went to check the hold. He saw the piece of silk. He'd completely forgotten about it. The night before, F. Murad had given him that piece of silk:

"For you, to give to your wife."

With the hurry he was in to get home he'd completely forgotten the silk. Lívia would be happy. She had few dresses and they were shabby. Now she would have a good dress, a stylish lady's dress.

He tied up the sloop and headed for home. He would go out after lunch. Lívia was waiting for him at the window with their son beside her. He showed her the silk right away:

"I'd forgotten it on the sloop."

"What is it?"

"Look..."

He went in. She came away from the window, put the boy on the floor. She examined the silk:

"But this is expensive silk." And there was a question in her eyes.

"I won it at a fair in Cachoeira."

"You're lying. Why don't you tell me?"

"Tell you what? I won it at the fair, I did."

She folded up the silk. She was silent for a minute, suddenly she spoke:

"Why do you let me find things out from other people's mouths?"

"What?"

"It's the worst."

"You're teasing..."

"You think I don't know already? People always find out something bad right away. You're mixed up in smuggling, aren't you?"

"Was it Rodolfo who told you?"

"I haven't laid eyes on him for a long time. But everybody on the waterfront knows that you've taken Xavier's place..."

"That's a lie."

But it was impossible to deny it. It was better to tell everything:

"Can't you see that there was no other way for us to get out from under? Kid João was already wanting me to sell the *Flying Packet,* we were broke. I would have had to hire out as a canoeman, I never would have been able to leave the waterfront the way you wanted…"

Lívia was listening in silence. The boy came running inside and grabbed her skirts. Guma went on:

"You see… I only made three trips for them, I've already almost paid off the sloop. With another month I'll have enough money to go in with your uncle."

He burst out strongly:

"If I'm mixed up in this it's because of you and the child."

"I'm afraid, Guma. It's not well-earned money. Someday it'll come out, you'll be in the place I don't want to mention by name. I've already been enough afraid, but now…"

"But it won't be for long. Nobody will find out, who's going to find out? Do you really think the police don't know? Everybody knows they're gobbling up Mr. Murad's money."

"Maybe only a couple of them know, someday things will change, it will really be serious, everything will be all over."

"By then I won't be in it anymore. I won't stay for more than three or four months. If it comes to that. It's time to make a little money…"

"Even now there's no way out," she said listlessly. "But will you promise to get out as soon as you can? Then you'll move to the upper city with me, won't you?"

"I guarantee it."

Then she unfolded the roll of silk. It was a nice piece. She tried it over her body, smiled:

"I'll only make something when you get out of that business."

"It won't be long."

And Guma began to count his smuggling days.

* * *

The new work didn't bring Guma what Toufick had promised. The quantities they'd been expecting hadn't come, the fellow on the ship explained in that language unknown to Guma during an endless conversation, Guma got only a hundred and fifty *milreis*, Toufick told him they were expecting still another cargo that week. But that was when the stevedores went on strike. The sloop masters and a great many canoemen made common cause with the men on the piers. The stevedores won, cargo rates for sloops and canoes also rose. But there were persecutions, and a stevedore by the name of Armando had to flee, and it was on Guma's sloop that he left that night along with a cargo carried under the new rates. And in the starry night the stevedore told him many things. It was no longer night for Guma, it was a dawn that was breaking.

Dr. Rodrigo gave a lot of help to the stevedores. After it was all over he wrote a poem where he ended up saying that the miracle that Dona Dulce had been waiting for so long had begun to take place. She agreed, smiling. She was more and more stooped, but she threw out her chest as she listened to the poem. And she smiled happily. She'd learned a new word to pass on in the poor houses along the waterfront. Now they could call her good and a friend. She knew how to thank them. She had faith again. Only this time it was different.

In the sky over Santo Antônio, Beetle's star had disappeared. It was with the stevedores.

Guma made several trips for Toufick. He paid off the sloop. And he became friends with the Arab, who was always very pleasant. Haddad was the one who remained silent, the scarf around his neck. Murad rarely appeared, only when he had important dealings with men on board the ship. Guma had two hundred fifty *milreis* at home now and was free of debts. Lívia was already talking about the day when they would move to the upper city as close at hand. When he had earned a thousand, he could go in with her uncle in the warehouse. And the old man, who was no longer up to the work, could take a rest. The sloop would stay with Maneca One-Hand, who would pay old Francisco a certain amount every month. Lívia had almost no more fear, she waited more calmly, her agony was greatly reduced. Everything had been going well lately. Even the rates had gone up, life on the waterfront had returned to normal, they'd managed to get through the crisis.

And she liked to go out on the sloop on the nights their son spent at her aunt and uncle's. She would lie down beside Guma, listening to the songs from the docks, watching the yellow moon, the countless stars, feeling the presence of Iemanjá, who was spreading her hair over the water. She thought that the sea is a friend, a sweet friend. And she felt sorry for Guma, who was going to leave the waterfront, leave his lot behind. But he wouldn't sell the sloop. Every so often, when the sea would be calm like that, they would have to come and take a ride on the water, look at the stars and the sea moon, hear those sad songs from the docks. Then they would make love again on board the sloop. The waves would bathe their bodies, love would be even better. Their flesh would have the taste of salt water, their ears would hear the murmuring of the wind, the moaning of black men with their guitars and accordions, the voice of Jeremias singing in the old fort. But they wouldn't hear the voice of Rufino because he had killed himself over a faithless mulatto girl. They would watch the sharks cutting through the water, see the beauty of the hair of Iemanjá, mistress of seas and sloops. They would feel nostalgia, nostalgia for everything. Guma would stroke the faithful hull of the *Flying Packet*. They would remember the *Valiant*. But the thought of their son's growing up on the streets of the city, growing up for a better lot, would console their hearts for the sacrifice they had made. But even then they would feel nostalgia, an immense nostalgia, the kind one feels for a beloved being. Because no one can be born or can die on the sea without loving it as a lover or friend. The ocean can be loved with bitterness. That love can be fear or hatred. But it's a love that never betrays, that never abandons. Because the sea is a friend, a sweet friend. And perhaps the sea itself is the land of Aiocá, which is the homeland of sailors.

# LANDS OF AIOCÁ

Rosa Palmeirão no longer carries a razor beneath her skirt or a dagger by her breast. Guma's message caught up with her in northern places, in a boardinghouse of the lowest order where she didn't pay because the landlord was afraid of her. When the sailor found her and said: "Guma wanted you to know that your grandson has been born," she threw away the razor from beneath her skirt, the dagger from her breast. First, however, she made use of them one more time to arrange for her return passage.

Lívia received her like a long-lost friend:

"Make yourself at home."

Rosa lowered her head, gave a strong hug to the child, who had run away from her at first, then tried to smile:

"Guma was a lucky bugger."

The kid asked if she was Francisco's wife, since she was his grandmother now. She would cry then, she no longer had the razor beneath her skirt, the dagger by her breast. She wore modest clothes, sat by the door of the house with the child clinging to her neck. There were nights when she could hear them singing her ABC ballad on the docks and she listened to it with confusion, as if it were somebody else's ABC. Only the sea gives its children presents like that.

For the first time Guma was going to catch a storm in his smuggling trips. But he saw that Lívia wasn't worried (she was calm, everything was going to be all over so soon) and he left satisfied. Toufick was waiting on the sloop, and this

time, in addition to Haddad, there was another young Arab.
It was Antônio, F. Murad's son, student and literary light,
who'd been curious to see how the smuggling was done.

The clouds were gathering in the sky, the wind was blowing furiously. The ship in the distance could be vaguely
glimpsed from on board the sloop. Toufick asked:

"Do you think there's going to be a storm?"

"A good one..."

The Arab turned to F. Murad's son:

"It would be better if you went home, Mr. Antônio."

"Knock it off. It'll be all the more fun that way. Just
right."

He turned to Guma:

"Do you think it'll be serious, skipper?"

"It's always dangerous."

"So much the better."

The sloop left, but it hadn't even reached the breakwater
when the rains came. Even so, Guma managed to furl the
sails and wait for the ship to signal. They had difficulty approaching, using the oars. Toufick was nervous, Haddad
was clutching the scarf about his neck. Antônio was whistling, showing a lack of concern that wasn't really true. The
sloop drew alongside the ship, the bales of silk began to appear. But the work became difficult because there were a lot
of waves, it was raining hard, and the sloop was bobbing up
and down, moving away from the ship. Finally the job was
finished. Guma maneuvered, passed by the breakwater,
made for the port of Santo Antônio.

But the furious wind was dragging them. There wasn't a
vessel on the sea, only a canoe that had put in by the old fort,
without the courage to continue its trip. The wind was driving the *Flying Packet* off its course. The sloop was heavily
laden, difficult to handle. Guma was gripping the tiller, the
waves swept over the boat. Haddad murmured:

"The silk will be ruined by the time we get it there."

He looked for some planks to cover the hold. He didn't
see the storm, didn't see death, only saw the silk getting
wet. Guma looked at him with wonder. Toufick was ner-

vous, he was afraid for the boss's son. The latter was pale
and had gone over by the mast. At one point he asked Guma:

"Do you think we're going to die?"

"People escape sometimes. It's all a matter of luck."

They went on in silence. They were right on course but
too far out toward the high seas, toward a sea that wasn't
meant for sloops. Guma was moving toward the sea of big
ships, it was as if he were realizing his dream of traveling to
distant lands like Chico Tristeza. They saw the light at the
mouth of the bay shining like a salvation. But they were still
very much out to sea, an unknown sea, that ocean sea of the
stories of great adventures told on the docks.

Straight ahead is the port of Santo Antônio. But they're
too far out to sea. Guma maneuvers to head into the port. A
little in front are the reefs covered with water. He is lucky in
his maneuvers, but the waters rise up in colossal waves,
throwing the sloop onto the reef. It was overloaded. It turns
over like a toy in the hand of the sea. The sharks came from
somewhere, they're always nearby when there's a shipwreck.

Guma saw Toufick struggling. He grabbed the Arab by
the arm, threw him over his back. And he swam toward the
docks. A weak light was shining at the port of Santo Antônio. But a glimmer was coming from the bay beacon and
lighted the way for Guma. Looking back, he saw the sharks
around the sloop. And arms waving.

He laid Toufick on the beach and as soon as he stood up
he heard F. Murad's voice:

"What about my son? My Antônio? He was with you,
wasn't he?"

"He was."

"Go save him. Go. I'll give you anything you want."

Guma could barely stand. Murad pleaded with clasped
hands:

"You've got a son too. Go, for the love of your son."

Guma remembered Godofredo on the day of the *Canavieiras*. Everybody who has a son pleads like that. He has a
son too. And he dives back into the water.

He swims with difficulty. He was already weary from the difficult crossing in the storm. Then he'd swum with Toufick on his back, had swum against the waves and the wind. Now his strength is failing him at every moment. But he goes on. And he arrives in time to see Antônio still hanging onto the hull of the capsized sloop that looks like the body of a whale. He grabs the boy by the hair and begins the crossing. The sea hinders him. The sharks, who had already devoured Haddad, are on his trail. Guma carries his knife in his mouth, holding Antônio by the hair. In front of him he sees Lívia, an almost calm Lívia, Lívia waiting for everything to change for the better. Lívia who has a son of his, Lívia the prettiest woman on the waterfront. And the sharks are coming behind, getting close, he's running out of strength. He doesn't even see Lívia anymore. He only knows that he has to swim because he's pulling a son by the hair, F. Murad's son or his son, he no longer distinguishes. Lívia, Lívia is going on before him. The waters of the sea are strong, the wind whistles. But he swims, he cuts through the waves. He's carrying a son, can it be his son?

Near the dirty sands of the port of Santo Antônio, his strength gives out. He lets go of the boy. But they're so close now that the water carries Antônio into the arms of F. Murad, who exclaims: "My son." And says:

"A doctor, quick..."

Guma tries to come too. But the swarm of sharks makes him turn, knife in hand. And he can still fight, still wound one, the blood spreading through the turbulent waters. The sharks carry him out alongside the overturned hull of the *Flying Packet*.

Some time afterward the storm abated. The moon appeared and Iemanjá spread her hair out over the place where Guma had disappeared. And she carries him off on the mysterious voyages of the lands of Aiocá, to where the bravest go, the bravest men on the waterfront.

The wind had tossed the *Flying Packet* onto the sands of the port.

# DEAD SEA

# THE SEA IS A SWEET FRIEND

It was here that Guma's body had disappeared. Master Manuel stops the sloop, lowers the sails. On the *Sailor Without a Port* are Dr. Rodrigo, Manuel, old Francisco, Maneca One-Hand, Maria Clara, and tearless Lívia.

They'd come in the morning, seen the *Flying Packet*. There was a hole in the hull, but it was small, a carpenter fixed it in a few hours. Master Manuel brought the sloop to the docks. He went to get Lívia at home after lunch. Rosa Palmeirão and Lívia's aunt stayed with the child. Maneca One-Hand came with them.

It was right there that Guma's body had disappeared. Now the waters are calm and blue. Yesterday they were stormy and green. But to Lívia's eyes the waters are motionless and are leaden. It's as if the sea had died along with Guma.

They're silent. Old Francisco lights the candle. He lets a few drops of wax fall onto the saucer, sticks the candle onto it. And he places it carefully in the sea. All eyes are fixed on it. Dr. Rodrigo doesn't believe that a candle can locate the body of a drowned man. But he doesn't say anything.

The candle moves slowly away. It goes slowly over the waves. It rises and falls, looking like a tiny ghost ship. Their eyes are fixed on it, their mouths don't speak. Dr. Rodrigo sees Guma again, bringing in wounded Traíra in the sloop, saving the *Canavieiras*, saving people in storms, smuggling in goods to pay his debts. Now old Francisco sees his nephew on board his ship, cutting the water. Manuel makes out the figure of Guma in the Beacon of the Stars, chatting in his quiet voice, tossing back his long, dark hair. Maria Clara thinks of him racing for a bet to the sound of her voice. Maneca One-Hand remembers the fights they'd had, they were good friends in spite of that. Only Lívia doesn't see Guma, only she doesn't catch sight of him or remember him. Only she still hopes to find him.

The candle floats around in the water. Leaden water for Lívia, water of a dead sea. Water without waves, water without life. The candle stops. Old Francisco says in a soft voice:

"He's there."

They all look. Master Manuel takes off his shirt, leaps into the water. Maneca One-Hand too. They both dive, return to the surface, dive again. But the candle goes off, continues its search. The swimmers return to the sloop.

Tomorrow old Francisco will have Guma's name tattooed on his arm. The names of five sloops are already on his arm. And also that of a brother. Guma's father. Now it will be his nephew's turn. The only name he will never tattoo on his arm is that of his brother Leôncio, a man who has no port on earth. Perhaps he will yet have inscribed on that left arm the name of Guma's son, the new Frederico. There will be two with that name then: grandfather and grandson. But Lívia, surely, will take him away from the waterfront, she'll go to the upper city to live with her aunt and uncle. So the name of Guma's son won't figure on Francisco's left arm alongside so many others. The candle goes slowly forward.

"She isn't completely alone," Dr. Rodrigo thinks. She still has her aunt and uncle. She'll live with them, help out in the warehouse. There are others more unfortunate, all they have is prostitution. Lívia deserved a different lot. She loved her husband very much, she'd rejected a better marriage out of love for him. Now she had a son, a useless sloop, she was looking for the body of her husband with a candle. The sunlight brightened the sea.

The candle doesn't seem to want to stop at all. Master Manuel looks. Guma was a good sloop master, the only one capable of beating Manuel in a race. He mutters to Maria Clara:

"He was a good boy. He never flinched..."

They all hear. He was a good boy, he died too young. The only one capable of beating Master Manuel in a race. Maria Clara remembers:

"He beat you once..."

"But the first time he lost. We're tied."

Lívia looks at the water. Her eyes are dry and tearless. She wept so much at first, when she found out. But her tears dried up, she's not thinking about anything, doesn't see anything, hear anything. It's as if they were speaking a long way off from her, about something that wasn't very interesting. She looks at the candle as it goes through the waves. She's stupefied, she can scarcely remember what happened. What she wants is to see Guma for the last time, see his body, look at his eyes, kiss his lips. It doesn't matter that by this time he will be all swollen, shapeless, with crabs inside him eating his flesh. It doesn't matter, he's her husband, he's her man. And suddenly the awareness of all that has happened comes back to her. They'll never make love again on the deck of the *Flying Packet*. She won't see him puffing his pipe anymore, chatting in his slow voice. Only his story will be left, among the many that old Francisco knows. Nothing will be left of him. Not even his son, because he'll go on to a different lot, will go to the upper city, forget waterfront, sloops, the sea his father loved so much. Nothing will be left of Guma. Only a story that old Francisco will bequeath to the men of the waterfront when he goes off with Janaína.

The candle stops. Maneca One-Hand jumped into the water. He swam, dove, found nothing. The candle remained halted, however. Maneca's head appears on the surface of the water:

"I can't find anything."

Master Manuel also dove. Again he didn't find anything. Maneca One-Hand got into the sloop. The candle was halted, didn't move from its place. Manuel was swimming, diving, searching in the depths of the waters. They couldn't find Guma's body, it had disappeared completely. Old Francisco said with conviction:

"It must be here."

Now Maneca and Manuel both dived. And since they didn't find anything, they swam around. Old Francisco took off his shirt and jumped into the water. He was certain.

But he didn't find anything either. With the waves that appeared in the water, the candle began to move again. The swimmers came aboard. Old Francisco didn't lose hope:

"He was here, but he's gone."

Lívia lowered her arms. She knew that she had to find Guma's body. That was all she knew. She had to see him for the last time, to say goodbye to him. Then she'll go away, turn her back on the waterfront forever.

The candle goes far off. The sloop goes with it. Dr. Rodrigo is becoming impatient over the race with the candle. He doesn't believe, he laughs at it, but the men's trust is such that he ends up following the candle. And it's he who almost shouts:

"It's stopped."

"He's there." Francisco points.

More useless dives. The candle doesn't linger long, it continues on its way. And they follow, the sloop goes along very slowly.

They'll never make love again lying on the deck of the *Flying Packet*. They'll never again hear those songs of the sea together. They have to find Guma's body so they can sail together on a sloop for the last time. He died saving two people, he had the most heroic death on the waterfront, the death of Iemanjá's favored children. He left a good reputation, he was a sloop master like few others. But Lívia doesn't care if he's remembered. Her eyes are fixed on the candle that moves along, that searches uselessly. The son at home is probably calling for her and for his father. Rosa Palmeirão probably has her eyes all swollen with tears, she loved Guma like a son. Lívia rested her head on her arm.

Dr. Rodrigo lays his hand on her and silence reigns once more.

Master Manuel lights his pipe. Maria Clara hugs Lívia, tries to console her: "It's our lot."

But Maria Clara was born on the sea, had always lived there. For her it's a law of fate: One day the man stays behind at sea, dies with the capsized sloop. And the woman looks for his body and waits for the son to grow to see him die too. Lívia wasn't born on the waterfront, however. She came from the city, she came from a different lot. The wide path of the sea wasn't her path. She followed it out of love. That's why she can't conform. She doesn't accept that law as fate, the way Maria Clara accepts it. She fought, she was going to win. She was going to win... Everything had been so close. The sobs burst from Lívia's breast.

Old Francisco lowers his head. Maria Clara reaches out a hand to Manuel and seems to want to protect him, as if death had him surrounded. The waters of the sea are calm, for Lívia they're dead waters.

Once more the candle stops. The afternoon had ended, the sun is disappearing. Manuel dives, Maneca Qne-Hand and old Francisco also dive. They come out with their clothes clinging to their bodies. Night is falling. Maneca One-Hand says:

"Maybe he'll come back at night. They always come back at night..."

"He's sure to come back," old Francisco confirms.

Dr. Rodrigo gives Lívia an injection. She's coming back like a dead person too. On the docks they're singing that old song:

> "He went off to drown."

Lívia opens her eyes. Coming from the mystery of the recently fallen night is the sad voice of the music:

> "... My man has gone away now
> In the deep green waves of the sea."

Lívia listens. He's gone away now in the deep green waves of the sea. Maria Clara holds her. The *Flying Packet*, anchored by the docks, rocks softly. But its pilot, the one who steered it, has gone away now in the deep green waves of the sea. The music spreads over the docks, curves over the men who leap out of the sloop. Night has come.

# THE NIGHT IS FOR LOVE

Guma's mother is waiting for her. She arrived without notice. She tells Lívia that she'd only seen her son many years
ago. She's old and feeble, half blind.

"I'm living out there, almost on charity. Some people I
know help me."

She doesn't confess that she's a cleaning woman in a
whorehouse. Old Francisco notes how old she's got. It's
been almost twenty years since she came to the port once,
looking for her son. She'd wanted to take Guma away, he
wouldn't let her. If she'd taken him, maybe it would have
been for the better. Lívia certainly wouldn't be crying now,
a child wouldn't have been left without his father at such an
early age. But fate is something that doesn't change.

Rosa Palmeirão comes out of the bedroom and tells Lívia
that she should eat something. Guma's mother asks:

"They didn't find him, did they?"

"No."

"Then I'll come back tomorrow. I can't be late."

And she leaves. Almost blind, she feels her way along in
the darkness. The moon lights her way. Lívia holds her son
to her breast and stays like that for a long time. The aunt and
uncle look at her, the aunt weeps softly. Rosa Palmeirão
serves a useless dinner.

For the fourth time Toufick the Arab stops by at Lívia's
house. Rosa Palmeirão answers the door:

"She's back now, Mr. Toufick."

The Arab comes into the parlor. That's where he'd invited Guma into the smuggling business. That's where he'd

invited him to death. Lívia appears. Toufick gets up, doesn't know what to say. She remains waiting.

"He was a straight man."

She remains silent. Her eyes are lost, she doesn't seem to see anything, hear anything. He continues:

"He saved my life, he saved Antônio's life too. I don't know..."

It's all the more difficult for him because it isn't his language.

"Do you need anything, ma'am?"

"Nothing."

"I'm here on Mr. Murad's orders. He says that any time you need anything from him you've got a friend at your command."

He lays the money on the table. Grips his hat in his hands, doesn't have the courage to suggest that she not tell anyone about the smuggling business. Goes slowly backing off toward the door.

"Good evening."

He runs down the street, bumps into a man coming along, has a lump in his throat, a mad urge to weep.

In houses where the radio is tuned to a certain station in Bahia at dinnertime that night, the people hear the speaker saying:

"The ladies of the waterfront ask that you say an Our Father so the body of a sailor who drowned last night may be found."

A young girl at a certain table (she was engaged to a pilot) felt a shudder, got up, went to her room, prayed.

Rodolfo arrived just as they were about to go out. He'd found out a few minutes before, had been sleeping all day. He joined the group that was heading toward the sloop. This time two sloops were going out. Maneca One-Hand was taking the *Flying Packet*. With him went Rodolfo and old Francisco. The others go on board the *Sailor Without a Port*. They head for the port of Santo Antônio.

The candle is in the same place. The sloops remain side by side. In the night of a thousand stars a candle cuts through the sea seeking a body. And the eyes of all follow it anxiously. It goes along slowly, from one side to another, it doesn't stop. They strike the sails of the sloops. The moon beams down on them, spreads out its soft light. Nights on the waterfront, when they're like that, are meant for love. On those nights the women who fear for their husbands so much get plenty of love. How many nights just like that one—Lívia has her head lowered and remembers—had she spent beside Guma, his head resting in her lap, the light of the pipe he is puffing mingling with the light of the thousand stars? When he would come in from a stormy night, a night of great anguish for her, the two of them would go to the sloop and make love in the rain, in the flash of the lightning. It was a desire mixed with fear, with an inexpressible anxiety. It was that certainty that aroused her love. He would be drowned, she was certain. That's why she loved him every time as if it were the last. Stormy nights, nights made for death, were nights of love for them. Nights where the moans crossed over the ocean sea, shouts of defiance. They made love in the storm. On nights dark with clouds, nights bereft of stars, orphans of the moon, they came together, and love had a taste of separation, of finality. On those nights where the wind ruled, the nor'easter or the south wind blows violently, shaking the heart of women on the waterfront, on those nights they say goodbye as if they would never see each other again. It was that way the first time. They still hadn't been married and yet they made love as if she were going to be widowed immediately after. It was on the River Paraguaçu, alongside the spot where the enchanted horse used to appear.

Manuel dives, Maneca One-Hand jumps out of the *Flying Packet*. The candle has stopped. Rodolfo is taking off his jacket, he's going to jump in too. And the three bodies cut the water that's greenish at that time of night. Manuel is the first to come up:

"He still hasn't come back."

If he came back that night—Lívia thinks—they would make love softly because the night is beautiful, sprinkled with stars, the moon spreading out its yellow light. On nights like that he would sit up on deck puffing his pipe. She would stretch out on the boards, stay listening to a melody that was coming from who knows where. From another sloop, from the old fort perhaps, from a canoe. Then she would lean on him, rest her head on his broad chest. She would listen to the story of his last trips, listen to his plans, a faint desire would come over them. They would stay looking at the sea, feeling that it was a sweet friend and that the night was made for love. Their bodies would come together without violence, there would be no shouting, there would be slow moans. The music of a black man, sad and nostalgic, a song of the sea, spread out over them. That's how it was on nights like that. But he's not coming back, he's off on the last trip heroic sailors make in search of the lands of Aiocá. "He went off to drown," as the song says. The lot of sea people is all written down in their songs.

Dr. Rodrigo is smoking cigarette after cigarette. Old Francisco's pipe has gone out. He asks for a light:

"Would you give me a light, doctor?"

In the hold of the *Flying Packet* Master Manuel and Maneca One-Hand, wet all over, are talking to Rodolfo. The latter leaves the group, leaps onto the *Sailor Without a Port*. He goes over to be with Lívia, runs his hand over her face. His hand is wet from the sea.

"What's it going to be like now, Lívia?"

She stares at him without understanding. She hasn't been completely convinced that everything has changed.

"You'll go stay with your aunt and uncle, won't you? Look, Master Manuel and Maneca are quite willing to rent your sloop, even buy it if you let them do it on time. It's the best thing you could do."

She turns her head, looks at the *Flying Packet*. One of the best and fastest sloops on the waterfront. Few like it. With what pride Guma used to say that! She loved his sloop, he'd bought it for their son, he'd died in order to keep it. Now she was going to sell it, give to another man all that was left of Guma on the sea. It was as if she were handing over her body, as if she were letting herself be possessed by another.

"Let me think about it first."

But she remembers what Rosa Palmeirão had told her that afternoon. Nobody's fate changes. She asks her brother:

"Does Manuel have much cargo?"

"He doesn't travel empty…"

"Ask him later if he can arrange some for me."

"Who's going to handle the sloop?"

"I am."

"You?"

Rodolfo doesn't understand. Who could possibly understand her? Old Francisco understands. And he's angry at being so old, at not being able to hold the tiller of a boat anymore. Lívia looks at the *Flying Packet* and feels a great love for it. Selling it would be like selling her body. And they were Guma's things, she couldn't sell them.

The candle halted up ahead. Rodolfo dives, old Francisco goes right behind him, he wants to do something too. Dr. Rodrigo looks at Lívia, who doesn't take her eyes off the swimming men. There's still much that Dr. Rodrigo doesn't understand. But he sees that Lívia's decision not to prostitute herself, to give herself over to work on the sea, is also part of the miracle that Dona Dulce is waiting for. It's taking place.

It was at that moment that they heard the whistle of the ship. Manuel spoke:

"It's asking for help."

The night was beautiful and calm, however. They heard the whistles, calls of SOS from a lost ship. Lost like the body of Guma that men are looking for in the sea with the light of a candle. A ship that's not sure of its port, that got off its course. Eyes turn to the place from where the whistling seems to be coming. It's a plaintive whistle, a sad lament in the moonlit night.

Those searching for the body come aboard. The candle is

moving again. Dr. Rodrigo bites his cigarette. A tugboat passes in the distance, going to the aid of the ship. Rodolfo is chatting with Master Manuel, who is more and more fearful.

Maria Clara is lying in a corner. Everything is painful for her too. She remembers the night Jacques died. That time she wept, hugging Lívia, it was as if they were two sisters. When would their men's day come? When would they search for their bodies in the waters of a dead sea? The light of the tugboat disappears.

Rodolfo turns to Lívia:

"He's asking if you're up to a trip to Itaparica tomorrow. He's got a lot of cargo for there..."

"Of course."

The sloops rock on the water that has almost no waves.

In the middle of the night the candle went far off. The sloops went along with it. Master Manuel, old Francisco, and Rodolfo jumped into the water again. Maneca One-Hand was ready to leap if they found the body. And he kept thinking that Guma must be full of crabs, he'd be enormous, disfigured. He put his hand to his face, cutting off his sight. The waves are higher here. They hear the ship's whistle for the last time. But it's whistling in a different way now, it must certainly have noticed the tugboat by this time. The men come on board without having found anything. The candle moves, goes around the boat. Lívia rests her head in her hands. A desire for Guma, a desire for his flesh, for his voice, for its taste of sea come over her. She's completely possessed by that desire and then, only then, does she feel that she'll never have him again, the nights will never again be for love. Her sobbing becomes intense. And Maria Clara, who goes over to console her, weeps too in the certainty that one day she will suffer like that.

The candle twirls, a quick wave overturns it, the saucer capsizes, sinks. Old Francisco comments:

"It's no use anymore. He won't appear again. When the candle capsizes..."

They set the sails on the sloops. Lívia bows her head. The blowing breeze raises her hair. It mingles her tears with the sea, she belongs to it irremediably because Guma is there. In order to feel herself with Guma she will have to come to the sea. There she will always find him for nights of love. Through her tears she sees the oily waters of the sea. Rodolfo is all consolation. Dr. Rodrigo rubs his hands, he wants all that to end so that they can all stop suffering. But he thinks that Lívia will always suffer. He bites on his cigarette.

In the sea she will find Guma for nights of love. On the sloop she will remember other nights, her tears will be without despair.

# NIGHTTIME

Lívia with folded arms. Lívia silent. The cold was entering her body. But the music was coming like heat, like heat and happiness.

Her man was far away, dead in the sea. Lívia icy, Lívia perfect, wet hair running down her neck. She wouldn't see the corpse of Guma that the men had wearied of searching for with a candle on the sea of oil, halted, closed in tight, like Lívia's body.

Others courted by her door. Courted her body without an owner, her perfect body. Lívia, desired by all, folded her arms. No sob moved in her dark breast. The black man's warm music arrived:

*"It's sweet to die in the sea..."*

No sobbing. Only the cold that invaded and the vision of the dead sea of oil. Beneath it Guma's body would be traveling like a ship without a rudder. The fish would gather around. Iemanjá would be going with him and would cover him with her hair. Guma would go to other lands like a sailor on a big ship. He would go traveling through the most mysterious corners of the sea, accompanied by Iemanjá. He would follow his course, a sailor at sea seeking his port.

Lívia looks at the sea of leaden waters. A sea without waves, heavy, a sea of oil. Where are the ships, the sailors, and the castaways? Dead sea of sobs, where are the women who don't come to weep for their lost husbands? Where are the children who died on the night of the storm? Where is the

270

sail of the sloop that the sea swallowed? And Guma's body that floated with long dark hair in the water that was blue? In the leaden heavy water of the dead sea of oil the light of a candle in search of a drowned man runs like a specter. It's the sea that has died, it's the sea that is dead, turned to oil, come to a halt, without a single wave. A dead sea that doesn't reflect the stars on its heavy waters.

If the moon comes, if the moon comes with its yellow light, it will run across the dead sea and search like that candle for Guma's body, the one with long dark hair, the one that went off over the road of the sea to the path of the Lands of the Endless Way, of the coasts of Aiocá.

Lívia looks out her window at the dead sea without a moon. Dawn is breaking. The men who courted by her door, courted her body without an owner, had returned to their homes. Everything is a mystery now. The music has ended. In a short while things will become alive, the scenery will move, men will become merry. Dawn is breaking over the dead sea.

Only Lívia has a cold body and a cold heart. For Lívia the night goes on, the starless night of the dead sea.

# STAR

Dona Dulce looks out from the school. The night is still struggling with dawn. The sloops are going out. Lívia's son is at home with her aunt and uncle. Rosa Palmeirão has put the razor back beneath her skirt, the dagger by her breast again. She looks like a man on board the *Flying Packet*. But Lívia is very much a woman, a fragile woman.

The *Sailor Without a Port* breaks the waters first. Maria Clara is singing a waterfront song. It tells of love and longing. Master Manuel goes along opening the way, looks behind to see how Lívia is doing. Rosa Palmeirão is at the tiller, Lívia hoists the sails with her woman's hands. Her hair flies, she is standing. She catches up with the *Sailor Without a Port,* Master Manuel lets her take the lead, he will go along convoying the *Flying Packet*.

Sea birds fly about the sloop, pass close to Lívia's head. She goes along erect and thinks that on the next trip she'll bring her son, his destiny is the sea. Maria Clara's voice stops suddenly. Because in the breaking dawn a black man sings, dominating the mysterious sea:

*"All hail, oh morning star."*

Morning star. On the docks, old Francisco shakes his head. Once, when he did what no sloop master would do, he saw Iemanjá, the mistress of the sea. And isn't it she who now goes along standing on the *Flying Packet?* Isn't it she? It is, yes. It's Iemanjá who's going there. And old Francisco shouts to the others on the docks:

272

"Look! Look! It's Janaína."

They looked and they saw. Dona Dulce saw too as she looked from the window of the school. She saw a strong woman who was fighting on. The fight was her miracle. It was beginning to take place. On the waterfront the sailors saw Iemanjá, she of the five names. Old Francisco was shouting, it was the second time he had seen her.

That's what they tell by the edge of the docks.

*Rio de Janeiro, June 1936*

# AVON BARD DISTINGUISHED
# LATIN AMERICAN FICTION

**AUNT JULIA AND THE SCRIPTWRITER**    63727-8/$3.95
Mario Vargas Llosa

**CANEK: HISTORY AND LEGEND**    61937-7/$2.50
**OF A MAYA HERO**   Ermilio Abreu Gómes

**CELEBRATION**   Ivan Angelo    78808-X/$2.95

**DEAD GIRLS**   Jorge Ibargüengiotia    81612-1/$2.95

**DON CASMURRO**   Machado De Assis    49668-2/$2.95

**DORA, DORALINA**   Rachel de Queiroz    84822-8/$4.50

**EL CENTRAL**   Reinaldo Arenas    86934-9/$3.50

**EMPEROR OF THE AMAZON**    76240-4/$2.95
Marcio Souza

**EPITAPH OF A SMALL WINNER**    01712-1/$3.50
Machado De Assis

**THE EX-MAGICIAN AND OTHER STORIES**   69146-9/$2.95
Murilo Rubião

**EYE OF THE HEART**   Barbara Howes, Ed.    00163-2/$4.95

**FAMILY OF PASCUAL DUARTE**    01175-1/$2.95
Camilio Jose

**GIRL IN THE PHOTOGRAPH**    80176-0/$3.95
Lygia Fagundes Telles

**GREEN HOUSE**   Mario Vargas Llosa    01233-2/$4.95

**HOPSCOTCH**   Julio Cortazar    00372-4/$4.95

**LOST STEPS**   Alejo Carpentier    46177-3/$2.50

**MACHO CAMACHO'S BEAT**    58008-X/$3.50
Luis Rafael Sanchez

**MULATA**   Miguel Angel Asturias    58552-9/$3.50

**P'S THREE WOMEN**    86256-5/$3.50
Paulo Emilio Salleo Gomes

**PHILOSOPHER OR DOG?**    58982-6/$3.95
Machado De Assis

**SERGEANT GETULIO**    67082-8/$2.95
Joao Ubaldo Ribeiro

**SEVEN SERPENTS AND SEVEN MOONS**    54767-8/$3.50
Demetrio Aguilena-Malta

**ZERO**   Ignacio de Loyola Brandao    84533-5/$3.95

**62: A MODEL KIT**   Julio Cortazar    57562-0/$3.50

---

# AVON BARD DISTINGUISHED LATIN AMERICAN FICTION

## BY JORGE AMADO

| | |
|---|---|
| DONA FLOR AND HER TWO HUSBANDS | 54031-2/$3.95 |
| GABRIELA, CLOVE AND CINAMMON | 60525-2/$4.95 |
| HOME IS THE SAILOR | 45187-5/$2.75 |
| JUBIABÁ | 88567-X/$3.95 |
| SEA OF DEATH | 88559-X/$3.95 |
| SHEPHERDS OF THE NIGHT | 58768-8/$3.95 |
| TENT OF MIRACLES | 54916-6/$3.95 |
| TEREZA BATISTA: Home From the Wars | 34645-1/$2.95 |
| TIETA | 50815-X/$4.95 |
| THE VIOLENT LAND | 47696-7/$2.75 |

## BY GABRIEL GARCÍA MÁRQUEZ

| | |
|---|---|
| THE AUTUMN OF THE PATRIARCH | 64204-2/$3.50 |
| IN EVIL HOUR | 64188-7/$2.95 |
| ONE HUNDRED YEARS OF SOLITUDE | 62224-6/$3.95 |

AVON Paperbacks

Buy these books at your local bookstore or use this coupon for ordering:

Avon Books, Dept BP, Box 767, Rte 2, Dresden, TN 38225
Please send me the book(s) I have checked above. I am enclosing $________
(please add $1.00 to cover postage and handling for each book ordered to a maximum of three dollars). *Send check or money order*—no cash or C.O.D.'s please. Prices and numbers are subject to change without notice. Please allow six to eight weeks for delivery.

Name ____________________

Address ____________________

City __________ State/Zip __________

# NEW FROM AVON ✦ BARD
## DISTINGUISHED
## MODERN FICTION

**DR. RAT**           63990-4/$3.95
**William Kotzwinkle**
This chilling fable by the bestselling author of THE FAN MAN and FATA MORGANA is an unforgettable indictment of man's inhumanity to man, and to all living things. With macabre humor and bitter irony, Kotzwinkle uses Dr. Rat as mankind's apologist in an animal experimentation laboratory grotesquely similar to a Nazi concentration camp.

**ON THE WAY HOME**       63131-8/$3.50
**Robert Bausch**
This is the powerful, deeply personal story of a man who came home from Vietnam and what happened to his family.
"A strong, spare, sad and beautiful novel, exactly what Hemingway should write, I think, if he'd lived through the kind of war we make now."    John Gardner
"A brilliant psychological study of an intelligent, close family in which something has gone terribly and irretrievably wrong."   *San Francisco Chronicle*

**AGAINST THE STREAM**     63693-X/$4.95
**James Hanley**
"James Hanley is a most remarkable writer.... Beneath this book's calm flow there is such devastating emotion." *The New York Times Book Review*
This is the haunting, illuminating novel of a young child whose arrival at the isolated stone mansion of his mother's family unleashes their hidden emotions and forces him to make a devastating choice.

# NEW FROM BARD
# DISTINGUISHED MODERN FICTION

## TOAD OF TOAD HALL
A.A. Milne                                    58115-9/$2.95

This stage version of Kenneth Grahame's classic novel *THE WIND IN THE WILLOWS*, by the author of *WINNIE THE POOH* brings to life the comic, splendid world of the River Bank, and the misadventures of the unforgettable Mr Toad.

## STATUES IN A GARDEN
Isabel Colegate                               60368-3/$2.95

A novel of an upperclass Edwardian family and the tragedy that befalls them when a forbidden passion comes to fruition. "Beautifully graduated, skillfully developed... Isabel Colegate is a master." *The New York Times Book Review*

## THE MOUSE AND HIS CHILD
Russell Hoban                                 60459-0/$2.95

"Like the fantasies of Tolkein, Thurber, E.B. White, THE MOUSE AND HIS CHILD is filled with symbolism and satire, violence and vengeance, tears and laughter." *The New York Times*. By the author of the widely acclaimed novel RIDDLEY WALKER.

## REDISCOVERY
Betzy Dinesen, Editor                         60756-5/$3.50

A remarkable collection of 22 stories by and about women, written over a period of 300 years and structured to explore the life-cycle of a woman. These stories reveal the perceptions of women writers, past and present, showing how these women responded to the restrictions and exploited the opportunities—literary and social—of their age.

**Avon Paperbacks**